Praise for Amanda Prowse

'Prowse handles her explosive subject with delicate skill... Deeply moving and inspiring.' *Daily Mail*

'A deeply moving and eye-opening tale about a struggling mum.' *Heat*

'Uplifting and positive, but you may still need a box of tissues.' *Hello*

'A tragic story about a family torn apart by the death of their little girl from sepsis.' Fay Ripley, *Good Housekeeping*

'A book everyone needs to read.'
Shaz's Book Boudoir

'An incredibly emotional, powerful and heartfelt story about a family dealing with a tragedy; beautifully written and captivating.' *A Spoonful of Happy Endings*

'A powerful and emotional work of fiction.'
Piers Morgan

ALSO BY AMANDA PROWSE

Novels

Poppy Day

What Have I Done?

Clover's Child

A Little Love

Will You Remember Me?

Christmas For One

A Mother's Story

Perfect Daughter

Three-and-a-half Heartbeats

The Second Chance Café

Another Love

My Husband's Wife

The Food of Love

The Idea of You

The Art of Hiding

Anna

Theo

How to Fall in Love Again

Short Stories

Something Quite Beautiful

The Game

A Christmas Wish

Ten Pound Ticket

Imogen's Baby

Miss Potterton's Birthday Tea

Three-and-a-half Heartbeats

Amanda
Prowse

HEAD of ZEUS

First published in the UK in 2015 by Head of Zeus, Ltd

This paperback edition first published in 2018
by Head of Zeus Ltd

This is a work of fiction. All characters, organizations,
and events portrayed in this novel are either products of the author's
imagination or are used fictitiously.

9 7 5 3 1 2 4 6 8

A catalogue record for this book is available from
the British Library.

ISBN (PB): 9781788546973
ISBN (E): 9781784972479

Typeset by Adrian McLaughlin

MIX
rces
471

roup (UK) Ltd,
YY

td
reet
RG

S.COM

AMANDA PROWSE is the author of eighteen novels including the number 1 bestsellers *What Have I Done?*, *Perfect Daughter* and *My Husband's Wife*. Her books have sold millions of copies worldwide, and she is published in dozens of languages. Described by reviewers as 'the queen of family drama', Amanda's characters and stories are often inspired by real life issues.

Amanda lives in Bristol with her husband and two sons. As her many twitter followers know, she almost never switches off. But when she does, she can be found drinking tea in her favourite armchair, scribbling ideas for her next book.

www.amandaprowse.com

Prologue

Grace Penderford had, for as long as she could remember, yearned for a child. That yearning was a physical ache that sat in the base of her womb and pulsed at the sight or smell of a newborn. It was something she kept secret, knowing that her parents wanted her to do the smart thing and have a career. Her mum's sensible words of advice were etched on her brain. *'Get a good job under your belt, Grace, and then go for babies. That way, you'll always have your work to fall back on. They don't stay babies forever, you know! And when they're at school you can get back in the saddle. Security, that's everything.'* Grace had nodded, knowing this was indeed the smart thing. This knowledge, however, did little to quell her burning desire for a baby. As she strived to climb the career ladder at the agency, her dreams weren't of flash cars or designer clobber, although these were now within her reach. No, Grace dreamt of arriving at a high point in her career where she was comfortable, where she could look back at all her achievements while holding a tiny bundle wrapped in a white crocheted blanket from which would poke a minute fist, the fingers of which would coil around her finger.

It had taken thirty-six years, three months and six days, but finally that point had arrived. On the day her dream came true, Grace inhaled the gas and air and rubbed her tummy beneath the thin cotton gown as the baby shifted in tiny, getting-comfortable movements. Her hand patted the stretched skin as she cooed, 'It's okay. Don't be scared. You're nearly here and I'm waiting for you. Don't be scared, my little one. I'm right here.'

She felt excitement at knowing she was finally going to meet her child, but also a sense of loss that their time spent together in this unique, wonderful way was about to come to an end. It was as if Grace instinctively knew that this was the best possible place to keep her child, tucked away inside her, curled up and safe.

Chloe had looked at her. Every medical textbook and expert on the topic said this was not possible, that the newborn infant would have been far too busy taking her first breath, adjusting to her first time in the light. Grace listened to this sound medical opinion and nodded, but as a mother she knew differently. She knew that her daughter had looked her in the eye as she had been passed over Grace's head and in that split second had imprinted her mother's image on her brain. Chloe had seen her and committed her to memory as if communicating with Grace, sending a message.

As she took her baby into her arms, Grace noticed that Chloe had a particular smell, a bit like newly baked bread. Grace breathed in the scent of her, kissing her little face and crying as she studied the most incredible gift she had ever been given. A gift so precious, Grace knew that she would fight until her last heartbeat to keep her safe.

'Hello, Chloe! Well I never, a little girl!' It was a joy to say the name aloud. 'See, I told you it would all be okay. How was your journey? Not too bad? Good. Welcome to the world, little one. I'm Grace, I'm your mum and I love you.'

One

People suffering from sepsis might have slurred speech, just as people do when they have a stroke

Grace slipped out of her suede wedges, tucked them neatly with heels together into the space under her desk next to the wastepaper bin, and climbed into her trainer5s. As was her habit, she placed her foot on the edge of her desk, letting her skirt ride up and hoping no one was watching as she tied the laces in a double bow. Particularly Jason Jordan, the competitive, backstabbing prat, who she could imagine having a sneaky peek up her skirt. That would be right up his street. She was still smarting at him having hijacked a campaign of hers, claiming it was in the best interest of the client to bring his experience to the project. Grace knew he couldn't care less about the client and that it was all about giving him a chance to shine. And shine he had. For years the two had competed. Whenever they met in the foyer, she would note the way he eyed her footwear, wondering if he could race her to the top. It was like being at school with two kids jostling for the number one spot in a particular subject. Pathetic. She knew that if she thought about his recent antics she'd get angry all over again, but the fact remained, he was now her boss, heading up the department and reporting directly to the board. She felt her pulse race as once again she pictured him receiving congratulatory high-fives from anyone within reach, the bastard.

Her laces were a little too tight, but she figured that by the time she'd pounded the pavements at her very brisk pace, ducking and diving around groups of tourists and weaving between irritating lovers and amblers with all the time in the world, they would slacken off to be just so. Casting an eye in the direction of Jason's office, she was glad to see he had already left for the day. Not that she was taking part in the competition exactly, but where and when possible, she liked to arrive before and leave after him; she had a point to prove and was waiting for him to screw up, then she would pounce!

Grace stood, lifted the receiver, popped the phone in the space between her chin and shoulder and punched the three-digit speed-dial code that her finger performed automatically.

'Hey, you, just about to leave. What's she up to?' She spoke quickly, hoping her husband would match her pace; it was important to keep things moving. As she waited for his response, she gathered up the printed promotional sheets that required her approval, her chunky notepad and the mock-ups for the photographic shoot she needed to organise, and shoved them into her bag, along with a selection of her favourite pens, that morning's *Metro*, which she still hadn't had a chance to open, and half a banana, the fate of which she was undecided about. She might eat it on the train or lob it in the bin.

Tom drew breath. His unhurried response made her jaw muscles tense, just a little. 'She's had a great day. I've tried not to mention... y'know... our little upcoming adventure, but we did read her book about the tiger who had to go into hospital and her only question was, did the tiger's daddy stay with him while he was in hospital, so I guess that gives us a bit of a clue about what she's worrying about.'

No mention of the tiger's mummy? 'Okay, well, we can go through that. I'm literally leaving right now...'

'Bye!' she mouthed, waving her palm at Jayney, who was finished for the day. As with anyone who spends too much time at work, her shared PA straddled the line between colleague and friend.

Jayney rushed over to Grace's desk and placed a neon-pink Post-it on her bag before making her way from the office. As ever, she ignored the conversation being had; it was the same whether Grace was talking to a client or sorting supper at home, Jayney appeared wonderfully disinterested in the detail.

Grace read the message. *Have a great w/end. Tell Chloe good luck for Monday. See you Tues! x* She winked at her friend and confidante.

Tom had started discussing supper. She cut him short. 'I'll get something when I get in. Don't worry too much. I had a late lunch at my desk. Look, Tom, I've got to go or I'm going to miss my train. I'm cutting it fine as it is.' She glanced at the clock on the wall. 'See you in a bit. Love love.'

'Okay, love love, Grace, see you in a bit.'

Tucking her chestnut-coloured bob behind her ears, she dashed down the wide marble staircase, ignoring the corporate advice to walk slowly and grip the shiny handrail as she descended. Who had time for that? Certainly not her; she had a train to catch. With her rucksack on her back, her light mac belted tight and her yellow Radley bag lying flat against her stomach, she quickstepped across the palatial, marble reception area. Head down, she did her best to ignore the throng of staff that had streamed down from the sixteen floors of the Shultzheim Building, where advertisers, marketeers and the pretty people who worked in PR rented floors, smiled at each other in the communal gym and fought competitively from their individual offices. Grace eyed the revolving doors, waiting for the right moment to step in.

Having been cocooned inside her double-glazed, climate-controlled office since that morning, she found the noise of the city impossible to ignore. Cabbies beeped, bus engines wheezed and a thousand individual voices shouted into mobile phones. The cacophony fuelled the beginnings of a headache. She headed for the station as if she was on automatic pilot, her internal satnav set to N1C 4QP. She no longer paid attention to the London landmarks, grandiose architecture, red buses and telephone boxes that apparently screamed photo opportunity to those who crowded her path.

Grace remembered when there had been something exciting about being in London. Many streets held haunts she associated with fun times in the past. Sometimes she could actually glimpse herself, young and smiling, outside a particular pub. Wearing sassy clothes, too much lipstick and holding a glass of wine aloft as the younger carefree Grace laughed long and loud at nothing very much in particular. She had been high on life, fresh out of uni and with the man she loved; her career was set and nearly everything was hilarious! Yet now, as she knocked on the door of her forties, the big city, with its bright lights and frivolous distractions, had gone from being a place of fascination to an absolute chore. The airless Tubes frustrated, the crowds infuriated and the exorbitant cost of her daily coffee horrified her. The moment her foot stepped from the train onto the platform at St Pancras, she wanted to get back to the countryside and gulp down its exhilarating air. Her preferred destination on any day was home with Tom and Chloe, make-up-free, sofa-bound and in her comfies.

She knew part of her disillusionment could be attributed to age. Things that she wouldn't have paid heed to in her youth now struck her as totally unacceptable. Why did politeness have to come at a premium? *Oh my God*, she thought as she circled yet another loiterer, *I'm turning into my mother!* Grace smiled and pictured her mum, Olive. That wasn't necessarily a bad thing. Her mum managed to effortlessly pull off being all things to all people. A great mother, devoted wife and lovely friend, everyone loved her. Olive was honest, blunt, fiercely loyal and fun. Grace knew that if she morphed into half the character her mum had become, then she would be doing okay.

Grace was tired. Battling with Jason was wearying; it added an unwelcome layer of stress to an already demanding role. She felt the throb of a bone-deep ache. This was no normal fatigue; her body was firing warning shots across the bows. Its message? Slow down or fall prey to one of any number of bugs that will render you useless. That wouldn't do at all. She didn't have time for illness; if it wasn't scheduled on the kitchen calendar, it simply couldn't happen. Instead, she would do as she always did, medicate her headache, down mugs of industrial-strength coffee to try and kickstart her flagging system, and get on with it.

Her day had been exceptionally hectic. Mid morning had been worst, with Jayney standing in front of her holding up two mood boards, asking her to approve one, while she herself had been on the phone listening to another client explain in agonising detail why they simply couldn't stretch to the suggested budget; meanwhile Jason had stood in the hallway tapping the face of his watch, reminding her she was already late for their meeting. She had felt like running away, but then she felt like that most days at one point or another. And running away was not an option.

The rhythmic sway of the hot, sticky carriage encouraged her to doze. Grace cast a sleepy gaze over her fellow commuters. She considered the strange relationship they enjoyed, this cluster of strangers who made the same journey together year round. In the mornings they convened in the same carriage and at the end of the day they met at St Pancras and travelled home together. Anyone not present would have their absence noted with a cursory glance up the platform. Factoring in the inevitable waiting time at either end, she calculated that she spent two hours and forty minutes in the company of these strangers on a typical weekday – more than she did with Chloe. Yet, apart from the briefest of smiles or heads nodded in acknowledgement, there was no real interaction.

She, of course, had her own name and life story for each one of them. There was Mr Mumble, who tutted a lot, shook his head and spoke quietly from beneath his bushy, grey moustache, chatting to himself and clearly not always happy with things. His incomprehensible ramblings sometimes reached her ears along the platform. She was sure he lived with his mother and fifteen cats and was smarting because his mum had taken away his Xbox privileges. Maybe he had left his room in a mess, a wet towel on the floor, or a pizza box on the landing, something like that. He sulked despite the fact that he was fifty and a justice of the peace. Even thinking about that made her smile. Then there was Mr Stress, whose tie was permanently askew around his bloated neck and whose tone and demeanour both screamed heart attack. Though he was a rather portly chap, he always tried to squeeze himself into the tiniest of vacant seats, the sort you'd only really want occupied by a close relative. He would then spend the remainder of the journey awkward and consciously trying not to squash those sitting either side of him, meanwhile shouting into his mobile about various meetings and ideas he had. She imagined him running the training department of a medium-sized supermarket and thought that his stress levels might be due to the unrequited love he had for Marjorie in the fruit and veg aisle. Grace could tell by the tightening of his jaw and his fake laugh that he was anything but 'delighted' about Colin's promotion over his own more than capable head. She knew how that felt. Then there was her favourite, Miss I-Love-You, who spent large chunks of each journey cooing down the phone to her man. Grace had decided, however, that the man belonged to her cousin and that the two lovers were therefore forced to smile politely at family functions, clink glasses of Buck's

Fizz at Christmas over the kids' heads and feign indifference when their other halves announced they were buying a bigger house or new car. This would explain her barely concealed snivels into a tissue as they neared St Pancras. Grace wondered what story and name they had given her. Ms Prim, Ms Sour Puss, Ms Stuffy Professional? Quite likely. The idea made her smile. They didn't know her – very few people did, maybe two in the whole world, her sister, Alice, and Tom, her husband.

Grace laid her head against the window but couldn't drop off despite her tiredness; she was worried about Monday. Sending her little girl off to hospital, no matter how minor the procedure or how often she reminded herself of all the benefits, felt like a big deal.

Grace wondered what Chloe would be doing right now. Probably having her bath, or her bedtime story. She felt the familiar stab of resentment that she was away from home, working or travelling as usual. But what was the alternative? *You're just tired. Hot bath, good sleep, tomorrow is another day.*

The train began to draw up alongside the platform, shuddering to a halt. Grace gathered up her bag and briefcase but decided to leave the now well-thumbed *Metro* behind. She ditched her banana in the little bin between the seats and stepped over the outstretched legs of her fellow travellers who were continuing further along the line to Leagrave, Harlington and Flitwick.

The station was comparatively quiet at that time of night, save for a few nattily dressed teens with carefully structured quiffs, uber-tight jeans, and tweed jackets that made them look part pheasant beater, part chemistry teacher. It made her smile. When she and Tom were at university, he used to think he'd done well if he'd managed to put on a clean T-shirt; she had to remind him to brush his hair and couldn't imagine him or any of his mates going to this level of effort for a Friday night on the town. *You must be getting old, Grace.*

The single lamppost gave off a modest orange glow as she tried to locate her car keys. When it came to handbags, she fitted the female stereotype perfectly: the bigger the bag, the more junk she could fit in it. She sifted through bits of make-up and items of electronic wizardry that made her accessible no matter how remote she was from the office. Her fingers fumbled over wet wipes, and books and toys on hand to amuse Chloe at a moment's notice; chewing gum, notebooks, several pens and a box of cornflour. She had no idea how that had got in there, but could probably at a push name her prime suspect.

Finally she found the keys, running her finger over Chloe's photograph, which had been made into a key ring. It was a cheesy gift that her mum and dad had bought as a souvenir of their day at the seaside. Tasteless, yes, yet that two-inch square gave Grace pleasure on a daily basis. She thought again of Chloe, who had been to pre-school that morning, which probably meant another masterpiece for the kitchen wall. They would soon have to find another 'gallery' as the kitchen was already groaning under the weight of macaroni glued onto card, paper chains, coloured-in handprints, and bells and stars made of painted salt dough. Her art portfolio was growing weekly. Chloe, darling, sweet, chubby Chloe...

Grace approached the car and pressed the button. Popping the hatch, she threw her briefcase into the boot and slammed it shut. It was bloody cold. The large 4x4, with its leather seats and softly glowing interior light, looked invitingly warm and comfortable. She considered what music to listen to on the journey home, deciding on Ryan Adams, with whom she would duet.

It was a twenty-minute drive via a series of high-hedged lanes to Nettlecombe, where her family would be waiting. Despite losing herself in the lilting lyrics of 'Gimme Something Good', her mind whirred through her never-ending to-do list. It was this virtual catalogue that routinely kept her awake into the early hours, caused her to lose her thread of thought when in conversation, and was responsible for the random shouting of words as she remembered something urgent that she'd forgotten. *Must get milk out of freezer as we're running low. Shit, I didn't return Ruthie's call.* Her school friend had left her two messages asking about lunch. *What can I get Mum for her birthday? I could organise a bouquet, but that feels a little like I haven't bothered to put any thought in. I'll ask Alice if she's got any ideas. Must get Jayney to send the proofs off to Nell, if we're going to make the lead-time. Did I reply to Angharad about the final cost? Need to check that. Wonder if Tom has packed Chloe's bag for Monday. What will she need? Not much, I suppose. I'll have to check. God, I'm tired.*

Grace dipped the headlights and pulled up to the house in darkness. Their solid, red-brick, Edwardian home sat in the centre of the circular driveway, a later addition that allowed cars to turn and park. The evening had become still. No breeze ruffled the wintry shrubs, but the air was crisp. A large moon lit up the back of the house, their brick oasis, their haven, a place of peace and belonging. Their lovely home.

A light shone over the garden, casting a honey-coloured glow. It came from the kitchen, in the extension to the right of the property. Grace sat taking in the scene that greeted her. She felt quite remote, a casual observer. Chloe was at the table in her special chair. She was up late and in her pyjamas, suggesting that she had been put to bed once but had resurfaced, probably so that she could see her mummy. Her mouth was full of tomatoey pasta, her hands gesticulating wildly as the day's events were relayed to her daddy, who was carving a bloated loaf. She was a lively, energetic child, a chatterbox, thoroughly inquisitive and slightly naughty, all the things that Grace and Tom had hoped she would be and more.

Bread in hand, Tom now sat slouched at the head of the table, his crisp cotton shirt visible beneath his favourite dark green jersey. His fingers toyed with the stem of a wine glass. He swilled the red wine around the bowl before throwing it into his mouth and instantly reaching for a refill.

Grace watched, mesmerised, as Tom lunged forward quickly and jabbed two fingers in the direction of Chloe's ribs. He stopped just short of actual contact, at which point Chloe threw back her soft blonde curls and screamed, spraying the area with pasta. Scrambling out of her seat, she dropped herself into Tom's lap and nuzzled into his chest, smearing his jersey with her sauce-covered face. He kissed her forehead and tried in vain to smooth down her defiant curls, cuddling her tight.

The sight of her little girl caused Grace's stomach to twist with longing. Chloe still carried a wonderful layer of fat that meant to hug her was like folding a warm and comfortable cushion into your chest. Around each wrist was the fleshy bracelet that all small children have, as if she'd been constructed like a doll and there was a seam where her hand had been stuck on to her arm. Grace missed her. Even one day working away felt like too much.

The carefully positioned lamps sent arcs of warmth around the room, the checked cushions in the window seats were plumped just so and at the far end of the scrubbed pine table sat a shallow blue bowl full of snowdrops, no doubt the fruit of Chloe's labours. It was magazine perfect. Her perfect family in their perfect home. It was one of those images that would crystallise in her mind for her to look at whenever she wanted, like a favourite picture or landscape.

She watched her husband sip his wine and stretch his long legs under the table, crossing them at the ankle. Grace wondered not for the first time how he managed to run the house and look after Chloe while still giving the impression that life was one long party. It fascinated her that he seemed to always have time for a natter and a glass of plonk, whereas she could barely find the time to think straight.

Theirs was one of those relationships that people on the outside couldn't fathom; he was the life and soul, whereas Grace came across as sober, her every action and syllable considered. The select few that were close to the couple, however, knew that Grace had evolved this persona as a counterbalance to Tom's often reckless antics and sometimes irresponsible attitude. They had met during their final year at university, where he was reluctantly studying architecture and she was reading English literature, thinking it would be a good way to harness her love of words and help develop her creativity. They had grown into a single unit to which all the clichés really did apply – they genuinely were two halves of a whole, soulmates and all the rest. Trust, open and honest communication, extreme kindness and a strong friendship: these were the foundations on which their life together was built before Chloe came along. They had found their perfect formula.

It had been no surprise to any of their inner circle that, following the birth of Chloe, Tom had jumped at the chance to give up the daily grind of travelling into London to a job that bored him stupid. He had long ago decided he would never become the next Norman Foster and he was sick of daily swallowing the bile of disappointment as he sketched plans for remodelling projects in Holland Park and kitchen extensions on the better side of Wandsworth. It fascinated and exasperated him how many meetings were necessary to discuss minutiae such as the position of a mirror or the particular finish on a bathroom tap. He was fed up with dealing with women who had too much time on their hands and too much money with which to indulge their whims. It therefore made perfect sense for him to stay at home. Grace earned more than he did and if Chloe was with him, they would never have to worry about her well-being.

It had worked well on both counts: Grace's earnings were more than enough to cover their outgoings and Tom was a devoted and patient father. With Mrs Roper coming in twice a week to clean, and Grace's parents on speed dial for any minor emergency, he was free to be the perfect parent. He was now pushing for a second baby, confident that he could cope just as easily with two, once Grace had dispatched said infant and tootled off back to work. It was becoming a bone of contention, with Tom harassing her, pointing out cute pictures in magazines and going on about how much Chloe would love a sibling, how lonely it must be to be an only child, how his brother, Jack, had been the one thing that had kept him sane during his crazy childhood. Grace couldn't counter his arguments but found it hard to explain how difficult it was to leave one child behind every day; leaving two would be unbearable. That she sometimes felt deeply resentful as she jumped up to her alarm at 5 a.m. each morning, and begrudgingly watched as Chloe instinctively ran to Daddy for all her immediate needs, was rarely mentioned. She was lucky, really. She had it all.

Tom loved her deeply and with a certainty that sometimes bordered on complacency; he looked at their friends and knew that none of them shared what he and Grace had. They were perfectly matched intellectually and though their physical desire for each other was no longer all-consuming, it was still very present, just a little less passionate. It was as though they had a secret world that existed behind their bedroom door, known only to the two of them. No matter what kind of challenge the day presented, the promise and comfort their intimacy brought made everything okay.

Grace had never been physically confident and Tom's relationships, of which there had been many, had all been short-lived. When he met Grace, it was as if he could finally shake off the outer persona that impressed his peers. She was the first person in his life to love him unconditionally because of how he was and not who he was. In fact, the bullish antics and sarcastic humour that garnered the respect of his mates were the very aspects that Grace liked the least and it was with an almost perceptible relief that Tom allowed his softer, more human side to be exposed.

People would tell Tom he was lucky. He knew it wasn't luck but fate that had steered his soulmate into his path. He had been warned that things would 'change' when the baby arrived and he inferred from the long sighs, the sucking of teeth and consolatory pats on the back from his contemporaries who were already parents that those changes were not necessarily for the good. They had been wrong, all of them. The arrival of Chloe was not just a good thing, it was a wonderful thing, and it had been the making of them as a couple. She was the creeping vine that bound them even closer together, covering their ordinariness with something entirely beautiful.

From the moment of Chloe's conception he had loved her, or at least the idea of her, and the reality had proved even better. He relished every aspect of being a dad. He saw being a father as a gift and an opportunity to take all that he had learnt about parenting from his own childhood and do it differently. In return, Chloe adored her daddy. She knew that he would never let her down, never be too tired or otherwise occupied to give her the attention she wanted or to solve any problem she might have.

Grace felt torn as she stared fuzzy eyed at Chloe and Tom in the kitchen. At one level it hurt that she was often the outsider, yet she was also delighted and fascinated by the commitment and love that her husband demonstrated on a daily basis. She let the car roll closer, and Chloe spotted her immediately. Waving furiously with both hands, she hopped off her dad's lap, ran to the conservatory wall adjoining the kitchen and stuck her lips onto the windowpane, leaving a tomatoey print.

'Mummy! Mummy!' Chloe mouthed, jumping up and down on the spot, eager to regale Grace with the story of her day.

Grace jumped from the car and grabbed her bags, letting herself in via the kitchen door.

'Hello, little one!'

Chloe ran full tilt towards her mum with her hands outstretched.

'Whoa there! Tom, can you get some kitchen roll?' she called out to her husband as she held her daughter by the wrists. 'I love you, Chlo, but I don't want pasta sauce all over my skirt.'

'It's only tomatoes!' Tom tutted.

'Only 'matoes Mummy!' Chloe echoed as Grace wiped at her sticky fingers with the kitchen roll.

'I know it's only 'matoes, Miss Chloe May, but I can still do without a trip to the drycleaners!' she said as she bent down, scooping her little girl into her arms and inhaling the scent of her as she grazed the top of her baby's head with a kiss. She squeezed her a little too tightly so that Chloe wriggled to be free of her grip.

'Chloe has made you a present!'

'Oh, how lovely. I love presents.' Grace smiled, knowing a present could be anything from a work of art to a leaf glued into an empty yoghurt pot.

'It's this big!' Chloe spread her arms wide.

'Wow! That's as big as a whale!' Grace kissed her nose. 'Where is it? Can I have it now?'

'No. It's not a present for today, Mummy; it's for a special day.' She nodded. 'I going to the hostipal soon to have my noperation.' She opened her mouth wide and tilted her head back, hooking her index fingers into the sides of her mouth so Grace could see the cause of her pain.

'I know, darling!' Grace kissed her chin. 'It's quite exciting, going to hospital! You might see Dr Ranj.'

'I love him,' Chloe asserted, dreamy eyed.

'I know you do.' Grace kissed her face again, as Chloe arched backwards and slid down to the floor before waddling off to re-join her daddy. Grace wiped the tomato sauce from her cheek.

'Hey, you! All good?' Tom said.

'Yes, fine.' Grace nodded after their daughter. 'She seems on good form.'

'She is. Sod's law, isn't it; the days before she goes in to have her bloody tonsils removed, they're behaving perfectly.

Makes me wonder if we're doing the right thing.' Tom drained his glass.

'Oh God, Tom, just think of all those nights, up at silly o'clock, her crying, unable to swallow or eat, it's just not worth it. It's as we agreed, the right thing to do if we can stop her going through that in the future. And no more bloody antibiotics!'

Tom ran his fingers through his short, thick hair. 'I know, no more bloody antibiotics. Just don't like the idea of her having an anaesthetic and all that. You caught your train okay, then?'

'Yep, just made it, everywhere was packed. But I tell you what...' She yawned. 'It's been one of those days.'

'Gracie, it's always one of those days.' He sighed.

'True.' She smiled. Her phone beeped. 'Shit, sorry.' She slid the screen and fired off a text to Roseanne before returning her attention to her husband. 'I'm all yours!'

'Have you eaten?' He was, as ever, preoccupied with feeding her.

She washed her hands in the large square kitchen sink. Her husband padded up behind her and pulled her hair free of her collar. Grace tensed as his fingers touched her neck. *Just give me a little bit of space, I'm too tired...*

'I've cooked pasta, if you're hungry?' He jerked his head towards the stove, where a large pot sat on the hob.

Grace shook her head, knowing she was too exhausted to eat.

Tom continued, wanting to chat to his wife. 'You look shattered, babe.' His worry was genuine and touching, sending a spike of guilt through her.

'I am actually.' She felt him retreat and was guiltily grateful. 'Where's my lovely present from Chloe? That'd be a nice way to start my weekend.'

'Ah, it's a beauty!' Tom smiled.

'Yes, and it's as big as a whale, apparently.' Grace laughed.

'Hmmm, not sure about that, and I'm afraid you can't have it tonight. It's for your birthday, she was quite firm on that.'

Grace frowned. 'Guess I'll just have to wait.'

It was two hours later, after a catch-up on the news and a large glass of red in front of the telly while trying not to fall asleep, that Grace crept into Chloe's room. The little girl lay in the middle of her little bed with her arms raised above her head and her chubby legs forming an O-shape. Her eyelids fluttered in sleep. Grace reached out and moved a stray curl from her forehead. 'Goodnight, baby. I love you, Chloe. You have the whole wide world at your feet: dream it and make it happen, my beautiful girl.'

The little girl tipped her head back and so began the characteristic snoring that, post operation, Grace wouldn't miss.

Tom stole up behind her. 'What *does* she sound like!'

The two folded into supressed giggles against the wall as the sound resonated.

'She sounds like my grandad after a full lunch, having his afternoon snooze!'

'Can you imagine her at uni, pulling the captain of the rowing team and he wakes up in the middle of the night listening to that!' Tom pointed at his sleeping daughter. 'She's never going to get a second date!'

'Oi! She is not going to be pulling the captain of the rowing team. And if she does, she certainly won't sleep with him on the first date. She's going to be studious and smart and save herself for marriage.' Grace smiled.

'Oh, I'm sorry, I just assumed she'd take after her mum and put out for little more than a bottle of Budweiser and a bag of chips.' He hid his face behind his raised arms as if expecting a battering.

'I only put out for you because I knew I was going to marry you, clever clogs!' She thumped him playfully on the arm.

He caught her wrist and pulled her out onto the landing, shutting Chloe's door after them. 'Let's continue this fight under the duvet. Let's go make her baby brother or sister...' He waggled his eyebrows.

Grace let her head fall against her chest. 'Tom, pleeeease don't nag me! I can't think about that when I'm this tired, and you badgering just makes it awkward. I've told you it will happen when it happens, and you going on about it isn't fair.'

'Are we going to fight about it?' He stepped forward and kissed her nose.

'Tom, we don't fight, you know that. We just keep talking and sort through the muddle until we're in agreement.' That had always been their way.

'Shame, I was looking forward to a bit of a tussle.' He winked.

'What has got into you, Mr Penderford?' She tutted.

Tom grinned as he took her by the wrist and led her into the bedroom. He peeled off his socks and flung them in a heap by the wall before removing his jersey with one hand, tugging hard on the back of the neck until it slipped over his head, something she had never worked out how to do. She figured it was a bloke thing, guessing he'd be just as bad at shrugging off his bra without taking off his top, a neat trick she had learnt at school.

He placed his fingertips over his nipples. 'Don't look, I get shy.' He could make her laugh like no one else.

Grace let her shoulders sag and lolled her head onto one side. 'I can't do sexy stuff tonight, I'm too tired...' She closed her eyes and swayed as if to prove it.

'Oh, Grace, you don't have to do sexy stuff.' Tom pulled her towards him and held her close, resting with her head under his chin as they stood in the half light of their bedroom. 'In fact you don't even have to be awake. I'll be very quick.'

Grace thumped him lightly again and made her way to

the bathroom for a teeth clean and a trip to the loo. Finally, she slid under the duvet and placed her head on the pillow. Its familiar scent rose up to meet her.

'Stay awake, Grace! I'm just cleaning my teeth and I'll be right through.'

She heard his sigh of frustration as her lids closed in long languid blinks and she slipped into the deep, deep sleep that she had been longing for all evening.

Two

People suffering from sepsis can experience extreme shivering or muscle pain

Grace couldn't recall falling asleep, but evidently she had, because she was now waking. Daylight peeked beneath the hem of the Roman blind; no matter that it was early, she still considered it an absolute treat to wake naturally before the alarm clock or before Chloe's morning crowing. It was even better to know that she didn't have to rush and catch a train that would take her away from her family. Instinctively she rolled over and laid her head on Tom's chest. He placed his hand on her back and stroked her silky skin. Without speaking, he raised her mouth to his lips and kissed her gently. This was always their time: no Chloe, no noise, just the two of them and their desire for the other's touch.

'I'm not awake enough for sexy stuff,' she murmured into his skin.

'Blimey, too tired for sexy stuff, not awake enough, you going off me?' He yawned.

Grace pulled her body up and flipped over until she was on all fours, hovering over him. 'Going off you?' She bent low and bit his neck. 'I don't think so.'

He gathered her bobbed hair into his palm and pulled her mouth onto his. Kissing was still one of the best bits for them.

She pulled away. 'Remind me to get the leg of lamb out of the freezer for tomorrow.'

'Grace, we are mid passion! I don't want to talk about tomorrow's bloody lunch!'

'Sorry, sorry!' She waved a hand in front of her face. 'I was just thinking out loud.'

'Marvellous! Now I know what's running through your head, and it isn't sexy thoughts, it's frozen lamb!'

Grace sat back until she was resting on her husband. 'You're right.' She exhaled. 'Come on, Grace, think sexy thoughts.' She bent forward again and closed her eyes.

'You used to think about me and that was enough.' He smacked her bottom, slowly running his hand over her back, palming the outline of her shape.

Grace whispered into his ear, 'I am thinking about you.'

'Oh, well, that's a start, I guess.' He smiled as their passion built. They held each other tightly, locked together in another world.

She closed her eyes. 'I'm thinking about you and picturing

you reminding me to take the lamb out of the freezer.'

Tom laughed as her gripped his wife's hips, the two collapsing in a heap on their messy bed. 'How do you do that to me?'

'Do what?' she asked as her breathing slowed.

'Make me laugh, make me happy, make me feel like everything is bloody brilliant!' He thumped the mattress.

Grace propped her head on her elbow and looked at her handsome man. She rather liked the cluster of faint lines that had appeared at the corners of his eyes, liked the fact that they were ageing together, as if this gave them some sort of authenticity, proof that they had stayed the course, a pedigree that could only be earned by time. A proper couple.

'Everything *is* bloody brilliant, Tom, that's why. We're so lucky.' She slipped down and welcomed the feel of his arms about her shoulders. 'I know I get tired—'

'I hate how tired you get,' he interrupted.

'But we've got it all. Our lovely house, our beautiful girl, each other.' She ran her thumb along his ribs.

He kissed her scalp. 'I love you.'

'I love you too.' She beamed. 'Tom?'

'What?'

'I'm thinking sexy thoughts right now and they have nothing to do with frozen lamb.'

'Quick, quick, quick!' He manoeuvred his wife into the middle of their bed and was about to take thorough advantage of the situation when they heard the creak of their daughter's bedroom door.

Grace scrambled across the mattress to her side of the bed, pulled down her nightie and restored the bedclothes.

'We can never get that creak fixed,' Tom whispered.

'No. Never,' she agreed.

Their bedroom door opened and in rushed Chloe. Bounding up to their bed, she flung her little leg up onto the mattress and, gripping the duvet with both hands, hauled herself up, climbing until she was sitting in the middle of the bed, with her parents pushed to the edges.

'Here I am!' she announced with her palms splayed.

Grace and Tom laughed at their wild-haired, rosy-cheeked daughter. 'Yes, baby, here you are.'

'Did you have sweet dreams?' Grace asked, as she did every morning.

Chloe nodded. 'Can I have my brexbrus?' Her thoughts were, as ever, not very far from food.

'You bet!' Tom jumped from the bed, reaching for his sweatpants. 'What we having, Chlo? Scrambled eggs?'

'And toast and red dip-dip!' Chloe clambered off the bed, eager to get to the kitchen.

Tom scooped her up and rested her on his arm as he kissed her face. 'Of course, toast and red dip-dip!' He looked at his wife. 'You have your shower and I'll put the coffee on.'

Grace showered slowly, feeling ridiculously happy that she wasn't on a timer and that she would get to spend the day in her jeans, both an absolute luxury. She tried to imagine what it would be like to be one of those women who got to stay at home every day, who pottered in their kitchens and sauntered to the shops and could watch CBeebies with their babies. Bliss.

'Here's Mummy!' Tom declared as Grace took up her seat at the table.

The log burner was roaring away, emitting a warm glow that filled the room. Heart Breakfast supplied the soundtrack, with tunes they could nod and hum along to.

Grace smiled as her husband placed a mug of hot coffee in front of her and two slices of wholemeal toast with her favourite lime marmalade. 'This is the life!'

'Did I mention I'm meeting up with Paz this morning?' Tom spoke as he unloaded the dishwasher and placed the clean rustic pasta bowls into a pile on the shelf. His school friend's parents lived close by and the two never missed an opportunity for a catch-up.

Grace bit into her toast. 'Why is it that toast made by someone else is a million times nicer than when you make it yourself?'

'Don't know, as no one in this house ever makes me toast!' Tom threw a tea towel at his wife.

'I could make you toast if you wanted!' she mumbled through a mouthful of crumbs.

'Do you know how, Grace? Because I really doubt you do.'

'I do!' she yelled. 'It'll be nice to see Paz. Is Polly with him?'

'No, she's gone to Majorca. That friend of hers, Jessica, has that retreat out there. She's over there for a week, apparently, chanting around a candle and sunbathing during the day, and drinking sangria by night!'

'Ooh, half their luck.' Grace reached for her phone and checked her email.

'Polly would love to take you along, you know that, but to be honest I can't see you chanting around a candle, babe. You couldn't cope with the slow pace, admiring nature and all that, and being without your phone. And mid way through the yoga, you'd have to stop and rewrite your to-do list, then come up with ways you could rebrand the candle experience and ideas on how they could increase sales!'

'I can't help it. My brain doesn't turn off. Ever!' she scoffed, washing her toast down with hot coffee. 'What are you and Paz up to?'

'Man stuff!' Tom flexed his muscles.

'Man stuff? Like what?' Grace laughed.

Tom closed the dishwasher door. 'Like meeting in Costa and going for a large latte with a hazelnut shot.'

'A hazelnut shot!' Grace put her hand to her mouth. 'That's serious man stuff! Who's got their kids and that bonkers Border terrier?'

'Paz's mum and dad.'

'Well, give him my love. While you're gone, Chloe and I are going to do some cooking!'

'Hey, hear that, Chlo? You're going to have to teach Mummy how to do some cooking, because she's useless! What is she, Chloe?'

'She's looseless!' Chloe shrieked.

'I'm not that bad!' Grace protested.

'Yes, you are! You are absolutely looseless,' Tom said.

Grace balled the tea towel that had landed on the table and threw it back at her man. Chloe clapped her delight. She loved it when they were all together and it felt like a party.

An hour later, Chloe sat at the kitchen table in her special seat, a hideously expensive Scandinavian invention that Tom had had shipped over, having seen it in one of his fancy interior design magazines. She was raised high enough to see everything that was going on, at just the right level for conversing with the adults without having to look up. Wearing her shiny navy blue apron with its front patch pocket, she was kneading the cookie dough with her little fists, pulling it apart and sticking it back together into random shapes. She thumped and thumbed the mixture on the table in front of her until she had formed a structure not dissimilar to Mount Vesuvius, post eruption.

'You are making a great job of that, Chlo! It looks lovely.'

'I doing cooking!' She nodded confirmation.

'I can see that. You're very good at it. And whatever you do, Chloe, never forget all you can do is your very best.'

Chloe nodded. Lesson learnt.

It was a tactic that Grace employed regularly as a way of buying time. Engaging her daughter in an activity might mean as much as half an hour of work time while she was engrossed. Some days it was painting, on others she could be found sticking shells and small stones onto loo-roll tubes, but today it was baking. Grace didn't feel too guilty. It was a mutually beneficial arrangement; she got a small amount of work done, while Chloe had fun. She consoled herself with the fact that some mothers would shove their tot in front of the television for the same reason; at least Chloe's time was being eaten up constructively.

Grace recalled her own childhood, when her mother would not have dreamt of leaving her alone to perform any task with an arts and crafts slant. Instead, Olive would have been at the helm, getting stuck in with her sleeves rolled high, often quite literally elbow deep in paint and glue or mixing batter or dough.

Grace looked up from her screen and surveyed the culinary delight that her daughter was absorbed in. Her thoughts turned to the previous night and Tom again pushing for another baby.

'I heard that Olly has got a new little brother. That's exciting, isn't it? I bet he's teeny tiny and cute!'

Chloe ignored her. Concentrating on her task.

'Would you like a little brother or sister, Chloe?' she asked, keeping her tone casual.

'No.' Her answer was clear, definitive and instant.

'No?' Grace queried. 'I thought you'd like a little baby that you could dress up and play with and look after. Like a real dolly!'

'No.' Chloe again shook her head. 'I don't want a baby. I want a green bike with a basket.'

'Instead of a baby?' Grace pushed.

'Yes. 'Stead of a baby.' Chloe gave an exaggerated nod.

Grace laughed loudly. Well, that was easy then. Decision made. A quick trip to Halfords was a darn sight more attractive at that point in time than going through nine months of struggle and then a grotty labour. She smiled at her baby girl. 'And I must say, what a lovely cookie you've made, honey. Is it for you?'

'No! It's for my daddy.' She was adamant.

'Ooh, lucky Daddy.' Grace felt the familiar twinge of envy as Daddy was again declared the favourite. She tried to ignore it, silently reprimanding herself for harbouring such a thought.

'Can I put these in it?' Chloe asked.

Grace looked up again to see what her little girl was suggesting. In her tiny palm, sticky with wet dough, was a selection of the smallest Lego bricks and a green paperclip. *Well, so long as the cookie is for Daddy...*

'Of course you can, darling. That's a lovely idea.'

Chloe beamed with delight. Despite being only three, she had fully expected her suggestion to be rebuffed. It was Lego and a paperclip after all.

Grace watched as her daughter peppered the mixture with the little multi-coloured plastic bricks, pushing each one into position with her podgy fingers and using the paperclip to crown her glorious creation.

'I finished!' she announced as she dragged the remnants of the cookie mixture along the front of her apron.

Grace grabbed the greased baking tray. 'Come on, baby, help Mummy put your cookie on here and then we can bake it.'

Chloe's tongue popped out of the right side of her mouth, one of her many endearing habits that denoted extreme concentration. Grace had seen Tom do something similar when they were playing backgammon or when he was writing emails; she loved how nature asserted itself in the strangest of ways.

Many hands in this case did not make light work; instead it rather confused what should have been a straightforward task. As they wrestled with the dough and Grace tried to manoeuvre the metal tray, the slippery mixture somehow managed to end up in a squashed mess on the floor.

Tears at the injustice of this sprang instantly from Chloe's eyes. 'My cookie! Silly Mummy!' Chloe wailed. 'You silly Mummy!'

Grace pulled her little girl from her chair; she held her a

little too tightly and cooed into her sweet-scented scalp. 'I'm sorry, Chlo. Please don't cry. We can scoop it up and cook it anyway and no one will ever know. Okay?'

''Kay.' Chloe sniffed and wiped her eyes with her dough-covered fingers, sticking blobs of cookie mixture onto her long eyelashes. 'My eyes are sticky!' She rubbed them again and blinked furiously.

Grace reached for the kitchen roll, hoping she'd saved the email she'd been composing before she'd had to abandon her phone. As ever, she wondered how things had deteriorated so quickly into farce.

That afternoon, the three of them sat on the sofa with their legs stretched out on the large, square, padded stool that doubled as a table, watching Mr Bloom plant things.

'How was Paz?'

'Good. Happy.' Tom smiled as his daughter wriggled back into his arms and rested her head on him. 'Wow, now *this* is the life.' Tom winked at his wife.

Grace nodded, hoping for a sly snooze while Chloe was engrossed in the television. She looked at the utter contentment on her husband's face and it made her smile. His own childhood had been privileged but lacking in affection and he'd been very clear to Grace about wanting them to parent Chloe in a different, if not a better way.

Tom was the oldest son of Maxwell and Fiona Penderford and home had been a solid mansion on the edge of the

North Yorks Moors – not that he'd spent much time in it, as he and his younger brother Jack were sent away to school at the age of seven. Tom had once explained to Grace that he had always felt his visits home upset the delicate balance that was his parents' existence. His mother always appeared to be slightly flustered by his presence, as though she really didn't know what she was supposed to do with 'the boys' when they were home. It made Grace sad that Tom could recall no more than a couple of occasions when they'd sat down to dinner as a family; and when they had, there'd been stilted conversation and discomfort all round.

Maxwell Penderford had taken his family's land and cash and established one of the country's largest construction companies. He'd been delighted when Tom had announced his intention to be an architect; Maxwell assumed that it was a roundabout way of learning the family business. The fact that Tom then chose to carve his own way and, since the birth of Chloe, hadn't worked at all, had been met with thinly disguised disgust. This was the latest reason why Tom chose not to speak to his parents unless it was absolutely necessary.

Grace's upbringing could not have been more different. Her parents were wonderfully supportive. It had been no surprise for Tom to learn that Olive had not only baked three times a week for her family, but that Mac, despite being a bigwig in the Metropolitan Police, had been a school governor, making sure he was as fully involved as possible in the girls' education. Tom knew with certainty that his parents had never known what class he was in, much less the name of any of his tutors.

Holidays for Grace had been idyllic, epic camping trips to the remote Scottish wilderness. Her mum and dad would share tea from the plastic cup on the thermos flask and she and Alice would argue over the last warm, squashed, cheese and pickle sandwich that languished in the bottom of their dad's rucksack. Grace smiled at the memory of them bickering and paying no attention to the majesty of their surroundings while her parents tried to snooze hand in hand on a bed of heather. She knew her husband felt a physical twist in his stomach when he compared that with his own family's summer breaks, where he and Jack would be collected from school by an ever changing nanny/au pair/housekeeper and flown to their house in Barbados. The neighbours there were an eclectic mix of writers, screen stars and minor royalty and his parents worked hard to infiltrate the club, conscious that it was a pretty good outcome for a family of builders from Yorkshire.

It upset Grace to learn that the feelings Tom associated most with his childhood were nervousness and an anxious tummy, not dissimilar to being obliged to live among strangers. He and his brother were close because they shared their unique upbringing, yet there was also a coolness between them as neither wanted too much reminding of what life used to be like for them. Tom hoped that Jack would be fortunate enough to find the kind of happiness he had with Grace and that he too would build a family that would heal him, in the way that his had.

Tom never wanted Chloe to feel the way that he had felt, never wanted her to feel she couldn't be herself, speak her mind or ask for a hug if she needed it at the end of a tricky day. Her life would be very, very different. He would make sure of it.

'Eat your biscuit!' Chloe demanded, watching as her dad gingerly prodded the rather grey-looking pastry that was full of what looked like lumps of plastic and had a paperclip sticking from the top.

'It looks lovely, Chlo, but I don't want to spoil my tea, so I might save it and eat it later.'

Grace sat up straight and turned to her husband. 'Nonsense! Don't worry, Tom, your tea isn't for ages. You can eat all of your cookie up and still have plenty of room for tea later.'

Chloe nodded in agreement.

Tom grimaced at his wife and narrowed his eyes as he spoke through gritted teeth. 'Well, okay, thank you for that. But I insist that we share it, half each. Half for Mummy and half for me, that's fair, isn't it, Chloe?'

'No! It's all for you, Daddy!' Chloe shouted and pushed the biscuit towards her dad.

'You heard the girl.' Grace smiled and sank back against the cushions and folded her arms across her chest.

Tom rolled his eyes at his wife as he tentatively took a small bite from the edge of the cookie. Grace heard the crunch of grit between his teeth.

'Oh, Chloe, this is delicious!' he enthused.

'Eat it all up!' Chloe again pushed the plate towards her dad's face.

'Yes, Daddy, eat it all up!' Grace echoed.

'I certainly will. But I'm just going to make a nice cup of tea to drink with it.'

'Make sure you bring your cookie back in here so we can watch you eat it. That's the best bit!' Grace laughed.

Tom disappeared towards the kitchen and his voice drifted back along the hallway. 'I was going to get the lamb out of the freezer for you, but you can P-I-S-S-O-F-F.' Tom spelt out the endearing phrase to his wife; that was the benefit of having a small child who was too young to spell.

Grace laughed, which made Chloe laugh too. 'I love you, Chloe.'

'Loveoo, Mummy.'

Grace swallowed. Hearing those words uttered by her child still had the power to melt her heart.

Three

People suffering from sepsis sometimes pass no urine in a day

Grace, Chloe and Tom watched as the little car chugged into their driveway. Chloe was beside herself with excitement. She trotted alongside the green Austin A40 Cambridge and banged on the passenger window. In her hand she clutched the painting that she had made for her grandma, now slightly ripped where her fingers had pushed through the paper when it was sodden with wet paint, but her creation was no less beautiful for it.

Olive heaved herself out of the passenger seat in the rather ungainly manner typical of many women of her height and stature. She was as usual resplendent in many mismatched layers, topped today with a grey cashmere wool cardigan of indeterminate shape, which was fashionably draped over one shoulder and held in place with a large kilt pin. Three strings of green glass beads sat on her generous chest. Mac, her husband, elegantly unfurled his long legs and raised his arms over his head to crack his back after the rickety journey. The Austin certainly looked wonderful, but it lacked the modern upholstery and suspension that made long journeys comfortable. Mac was dressed as if he had just come from a cricket match, as usual paying no heed to the season or temperature, in cream slacks, straw panama hat and cricket jersey, with a striped tie loose at the open neck of his shirt. For him, whether it was November or indeed January was immaterial; in sartorial terms, it was permanently August.

'Hello! Hello, my little darling!' Olive beamed at her one and only grandchild as she scooped Chloe up into her arms and covered her freckly little face in kisses.

'Yuck, Grandma, stop! I don't like that! Have you got me some sweets?'

Olive roared with laughter at the unabashed frankness of her granddaughter. She reminded her so much of Alice at the same age. 'I might just have, my darling. Let's go and dig in my enormous bag...'

Chloe glanced back towards her grandpa. Though preoccupied with the promise of sweets, she called over her shoulder, 'Hello, my grandpa!' and waved her chubby hand in the air.

'Hello, my little one!' He smiled after her as she disappeared into the kitchen. It was what he had always called her, his little one, the littlest of his girls.

Mac walked forward and embraced his son-in-law and ruffled his hair, in the way that only an upright man in his eighties can do with true confidence.

'How's it going, son? Keeping chipper?'

'Kind of, Mac. Bit nervous about tomorrow, but trying not to be. Don't want Chlo to pick up on it, but I really don't like the idea of her having an anaesthetic.'

'So I gathered from your call. You're doing the right thing, Tom; it'll all be fine. The medics do this day in and day out and it'll be great for Chloe to come out the other side, no more rotten sore throats.'

'That's what I said,' Grace chipped in as she hugged her dad. The three of them followed Chloe and her grandma into the kitchen. 'And if they offer to fix me with a quick onceover, I won't say no! I'm knackered! The joys of parenthood, I guess. No chance of flopping on the sofa all weekend with Princess Pickle around.' Grace yawned.

'Ah, darling, that's the kind of exhaustion your sister would envy.' Mac sighed.

'Oh, Dad, I know. Poor Alice!' She wrinkled her nose with a mixture of guilt and empathy.

'What will be, will be, darling.' His words were as ever both soothing and authoritative.

Mac and Olive had made the journey from the coast to Bedfordshire in no time at all on this quiet Sunday in January. When Mac had retired, they'd swapped their house in the suburbs for a little haven in Brighton. They loved being close to the sea and yet were only a short train ride away from civilisation, as they now referred to the Big Smoke. Like many couples their age, they spent a great deal of time and energy thinking and talking about their children and grandchild. Grace and Alice knew with certainty that they only had to pick up the phone and their parents would be on their way or reaching for the chequebook, whichever was required, without comment, questions or conditions attached. It had always been that way.

'Cup of tea, Olive?' Tom asked as he filled the kettle.

'Lovely.' She nodded. Grace's mum had set up base camp at the kitchen table. Her vast handbag and its contents spilled over the surface and one of her many scarves was now draped over the chair on which she sat. Olive didn't merely arrive somewhere; she seemed to alter the environment, spreading her wares about her, as if she was running a market stall or holding court in a regal fashion with her favourite objects and courtiers in close proximity.

She was thoroughly engrossed in the painting with which she had been presented. 'Well I never, my darling! I didn't realise what a clever artist you were. This is a magnificent picture! Have you seen this, Grandpa?' She held it up for Mac's scrutiny.

'Well I never!' he gasped. 'It's very Jackson Pollock!'

'Is that rhyming slang?' Tom quipped.

'Don't be mean!' Grace whispered through her laughter. 'She's a very talented artist.'

Chloe wriggled about on her grandma's large lap, playing with her beads and trying to get comfortable.

'Did you do this by yourself, Chloe?' Olive marvelled.

'Yes, I did and Daddy only helped me a little bit.' Chloe pinched her thumb and forefinger together to emphasise her point.

Olive winked at Tom, who was busy making tea and artfully arranging homemade cookies on a plate.

Chloe continued. 'It's a picture of up my mouth and my tonsils.'

'Well of course it is, I can see that!' Olive feigned offence as she surveyed the grey-black blobs that were scattered over the page. She was mightily glad that she hadn't tried to guess at the subject; she'd been veering towards flowers or possibly a cat.

'I'm going to hostipal the day after today and they are coming out.' Chloe again opened her mouth wide and pointed down her throat.

'Yes, and you will feel so much better! Grandpa and I brought you a little something to take with you.'

Chloe clapped her hands with excitement as Olive reached into her bag and produced a tiny, black and white, bean-filled bear. 'He's a panda and he's a doctor and so we thought he could show you the hospital and you could show him what's going on.'

'I can!' Chloe beamed.

'What do you say, Chlo?' Grace prompted.

‘Thank you.’ Chloe threw her arms around her grandma’s neck and kissed her on the lips.

‘Are there spare kisses going? If so, I’m in the queue.’ Mac bent down as Chloe jumped from her gran’s lap and ran towards her grandpa, leaping into his arms with no regard for his age or frailty as she threw her arms around his neck.

Grace felt her eyes prick with tears at the wonderful exchange between her dad and her little girl, knowing she would never have been so demonstrative towards him; age and embarrassment held her back. It was lovely to see.

A car horn honked.

‘That’ll be Alice!’ Olive smiled, truly in her element when the whole family was together.

Chloe squirmed free from her grandad’s arms and ran towards the back door, where she pogoed up and down on the spot, waiting excitedly for her aunt. Alice was quite unlike her sister. She had always been shorter, plumper and more vivacious, very unselfish and in Grace’s eyes completely gorgeous. Where Grace would choose quiet sophistication and muted hues, Alice was gregarious; her colours of choice were red and orange. Grace’s boyish figure and dark, short hair were the envy of her sibling and similarly Grace jovially begrudged her sister’s confidence, which she was convinced came from having a more than ample bosom. She remembered trying on her younger sister’s bra as a teenager and marvelling at the empty pouches that mocked her reflection.

The two had a deep love for each other, and open and honest exchanges were commonplace. Olive was grateful for the relationship her girls had and believed it was their differences that allowed them to adore each other. Unlike with many siblings close in age, with Grace and Alice there had never been an element of competition; both had always been extremely happy about the other's successes and confident that they didn't have to fight for their parents' attention. The hierarchy had been established a long time ago: their parents first and foremost adored each other, and the love that was left over was divided equally between their cherished girls.

Alice thundered into the room and leant over the table to hug her sister tightly, too tightly, before planting several kisses on her face; it was her way. Mac continually remarked on the fact that their youngest daughter had been born without the embarrassment gene.

'Hi, everyone!' She waved as she dumped several bags behind the door. 'Gracie, you look hilarious, so grown up!' Alice pinched the neck of her sister's V-neck jersey.

Grace stared at her little sister's jeans, which harboured several pockets of no apparent use, except perhaps to hold the odd paintbrush or tool; the jeans were also at least five sizes too big. Her hair was a tumbling mass of uncontrolled corkscrew twists, some falling over her face, others secured by a turquoise hairband. Her shoulder was bare where the hand-knitted jersey of multi-coloured wool had slipped away and on her feet were floral Doc Martens. All her fingers bar two sported a large Indian silver ring.

'Yes, Alice, I know, it's me that looks hilarious.' She smiled at her sister.

'I don't mean it in a bad way – you just don't look like anyone else I know. You look so professional, so serious and very capable! Like a proper grown-up. I love it!' She clapped her hands in delight, reminding Grace of Chloe, whose natural exuberance she had inherited from her non-conformist aunt. God forbid she should ever confide the fact to Tom, who would be less than impressed that his daughter contained even a trace element of her whacky aunt and her alternative views.

'Where's my girl?' Alice yelled.

'Here I am!' Chloe bounded up with her hand in the air.

Alice lifted her niece into her arms and swung her round, smothering her face with kisses.

'Grandma got me a Dr Panda!' Chloe held the toy millimetres from her aunt's face, forcing her to pull her head back on her shoulders to see it properly.

'Oh, he's lovely! What's he called?'

'Dr Panda.'

'Of course he is!' Alice kissed her again.

'And he's coming to the hostipal with me.' Chloe nodded.

'Well, that's a very good idea!' Alice said. 'I'm afraid I only bought sweets. Sorry.'

'I love sweets!' Chloe shouted.

'No sweets until after lunch, Chlo.' Grace smiled at her little girl.

'Who fancies a walk in the garden?' Mac's voice cut through the cacophony.

'Me! Me!' Chloe ran towards her grandpa, gripping his hand as she dragged him towards the back door.

Alice sipped from the large glass of plonk that her brother-in-law had presented her with. 'She seems quite unfazed about tomorrow.'

'I think it's because she doesn't know what to expect,' Tom said. 'And it's not as if she'll be on her own at any point. We'll stay with her until they put her under and then we'll be there the second she wakes up.'

'I think we're more worried than she is,' Grace admitted.

Olive sighed. 'I remember you going into hospital when you were little, Grace, when you broke your arm. I was beside myself. But you took it in your stride, calmly. Daddy and I were absolute wrecks.'

'Well, that's Grace all over – Miss Calm Under Pressure 2015,' Alice teased.

'Bit like yourself then, Alice!' Tom winked.

Olive and Grace both laughed loudly.

'God, Tom, I wish,' said Olive. 'We've had two calls this month alone because of end-of-the-world events. One turned out to be a power cut and she'd run out of matches. I had to point out we were over an hour away and it would be far quicker for her to go to the shop! And the other was when she called me to ask if the ham in her fridge was off. I pointed out that yes, I do have a very keen sense of smell, but asking me to detect mouldy ham when I was fifty miles away was a bit of a stretch!'

'I am here, you know, Mum!' Alice shouted, delighted by the ribbing.

Grace pulled the lamb from the oven while Tom began to clear the table.

'I'll give you a hand, Tom.' Olive began packing items away into her oversized handbag.

Grace set the meat to rest and reached for the gravy granules. 'Cheating, I know, but who cares?' She laughed and looked up at Alice, who was sipping her wine as she rested against the work surface. Grace was aghast to see the big fat tears that rolled down her sister's face; she was making a sad little whimpering noise. It had to be said that her sister, for all her gorgeous sex appeal, was an ugly crier. Grace felt this was because, unlike most people, who generally disguised their emotional state in some way, either by covering their face, closing their eyes or hiding their distress in a tissue, Alice would simply let herself cry, childlike and unabashed, runny nose, funny noises and all.

'Oh God, darling! Whatever's the matter? We were only teasing! You know that. We love that you are dramatic and scatty. You're our Alice! And we wouldn't change a single thing about you.' Grace pulled her sister towards her and gave her a big hug.

Alice pushed her away, shaking her head and swallowing her tears. 'It's not that.' She sniffed.

'What is it?' Grace persisted, ripping off a couple of squares of kitchen roll and putting them into her sister's hand. Placing her arm around her back, she could feel the bony knobs at the top of her spine through her jersey.

'I'm sorry, Gracie. I promised myself I wouldn't do this, it's just all so bloody hopeless.'

'Nothing is that hopeless. Tell me what's wrong and we will fix it. That's what big sisters do.'

She kissed the top of Alice's head, inhaling her scent of coffee, patchouli and something akin to warm cookies. 'Come on, let's go to the lounge. Mum? Tom? Can you keep an eye here? We're just going for a gossip.'

'Oh, Alice darling!' Olive saw her younger daughter's tears. Her tone was resigned, telling Grace that whatever the issue was, their mum was already fully informed.

The two made their way onto the long, comfy sofa.

'I need you to let go of me, Gracie. If you're hugging me, I'll just keep on crying.'

Grace loved her sister's openness and simple logic: remove the safety blanket and she would toughen up, pronto.

'Righto. I can hold your hand though, right? That won't set you off?' She was only half joking.

'You can hold my hand, yes, that's fine.' Alice sniffed one last time.

Grace took her sister's little hand and decided not to comment on the huge Indian silver rings that looked like they weighed down her arm, resplendent with skulls and what appeared to be snaking vines. 'So, come on, spill.'

'I just can't get pregnant.' Alice raised her hands and let them fall into her lap as her tears came again.

'Oh, honey, you just have to keep trying. You know the score, relax, but keep trying.'

'How can I relax when every time I'm at my most fertile I'm jumping on Patrick like he's a bloody stud horse and hoping for the best. I had to call him back from the garden centre the other day and he actually huffed and said, "Just give me a minute, I'm looking for compost," as if that was preferable!'

Grace bit her lip to stifle an inappropriate giggle.

'You can laugh.' Alice smiled. 'It's as funny as it is ridiculous. There's him in the B&Q garden centre, lumping sacks of horse manure to the car as fast as he can because it's my optimum time, and there's me at home with a thermometer and my legs up the wall. Where's the romance? The passion? It's all become a bit medical. A bit mechanical.'

'Oh, honey!' Grace rubbed her sister's hand.

'And we've tried so many times and it's so disappointing. Every time is worse than the last. You just keep thinking, maybe this time, maybe it's our turn, in fact it must be our turn because of all our previous failures, like we're owed success. But we're not owed anything and it never is our turn and it never will be. That's it. As Patrick said, there comes a point when you have to admit defeat.'

'I don't want to give you clichés, but you do have a lot, Alice. What you and Patrick have is so rare and so special. Who knows, maybe he's your compensation for not having children. Maybe you just don't get everything in life and things have a funny way of levelling out. I do believe that.'

Alice swiped at her eyes. 'That does sound clichéd, and the only people who say it to me are the ones that go home and get called Mummy.'

Grace felt suitably admonished. 'I'm sorry, honey. You're right; I don't know what it feels like. I'm just trying to make you feel better.' She squeezed her sister's hand, feeling all the little bones roll under her fingers.

'It's so bloody unfair, Gracie. I don't want a football team, just one! I just want one little baby of our own. It would have been perfect. I have this image of Patrick holding a small bundle.'

Grace felt her sister's pain and started to run a mental checklist. What could be done? How would they fix this? She was already rushing headlong into solution mode. 'I'm so sorry for you, for you both, but let's think, Alice, there must be other options.'

Alice exhaled as though she needed to clear her head before continuing. 'There are other options, but I don't want to think about them, not yet. I feel like I'm in mourning, if that makes any sense, and until I get my head around the fact that I'm never going to have my own baby, I can't think about anything else.'

'It does make sense and I can't begin to imagine how it must be for you.'

'Patrick and I have been over and over it and even though we can talk it through and agree that we do have a lot to be thankful for, I still have this gaping baby-shaped gap in my life that nothing else can fill. It's like a bad hunger pain that no amount of food can sort.'

Grace listened intently. It was unusual for Alice to discuss her pain so openly, odd to see her without her smiley mask in place.

'When I read in the papers or hear on the news about a child that's been hurt or neglected by its parents, it makes me howl. How can someone do that to something so precious and how is that fair, when I would give anything, anything to be a mum? How can people waste that opportunity, spoil it?'

'I don't know, honey.' It was the best she could offer.

'I know time is running out for me, Grace, and I need to consider other options—'

'Like adoption?' Grace interrupted. 'I think you're right, Alice. There are hundreds of kids that need homes; not necessarily babies, but older children maybe? You and Patrick would make excellent parents, that's never been in doubt. Mum is always saying that since you were a little girl you've been a mum-in-waiting.'

'Gracie, I know it doesn't make me a very nice person,

but I don't want an older child, I want a little baby and I really want our little baby, one that is half Patrick and half me. Can you imagine how amazing that would be?'

Grace pictured Chloe. Yes, she could imagine exactly how amazing that would be.

Grace wanted what was best for her sister. She decided to change tack. 'Of course, there are lots of advantages to *not* having a baby. You get to have spontaneity in your life, you can lie in bed at the weekend, make love where and when you want to, you keep your figure, and you're not permanently exhausted...'

Alice smiled at her sister's transparency. 'You've always been a crap liar. We both know that you wouldn't swap Chloe for all the lie-ins in the world.'

Grace thought for a second and exhaled slowly. 'No, honey. No, I wouldn't.' She felt embarrassed at having tried to humour her smart little sister. 'I guess all you can do, Alice, is not give up. And when the time is right, it'll happen.'

'Or not,' Alice said.

'Or not,' Grace conceded. 'But if that's the case, we can deal with it then.' She leant forward and kissed her sister.

'All okay?' Tom asked from the doorway.

'Yep.' Grace nodded.

'Lunch is nearly ready.' He smiled.

It was a lovely family gathering. Grace was a little quieter than usual; tiredness, Alice's words, and the prospect of taking Chloe into hospital tomorrow were all taking their toll.

'You look tired, love. Why don't you go and grab forty winks? Alice and I can take Chloe for a play in the garden,' Olive suggested.

'Actually, I wouldn't mind.' Grace kissed her little girl and made her way upstairs, noting that Mac had already bagged the best sofa seat for dozing.

'I'll wake you up with a cuppa in a bit,' Tom said as he headed for the sink.

Minutes later, Chloe, Olive and Alice were in front of the kitchen window, bundled up like snowmen in scarves and hats and boots representing every colour of the rainbow – and that was just Alice's ensemble. Olive lifted Chloe up to the window and the little girl planted a sticky kiss on the pane. Tom reached forward over the sink and met her lips with his own through the cold glass.

Chloe found this hilarious. 'Bye, Daddy!'

'Bye, darling!' Tom felt the familiar tightening in his throat as she said the magic word 'Daddy'. He knew that whether she was three or thirty-three, hearing her little voice use that term would always constitute his greatest joy. He watched as her little pink raincoat and matching wellington boots disappeared around the garden hedge.

The day was crisp, unusually cold and still, the sky a beautiful winter blue. Not a breath of wind moved the wispy clouds. Grace opened the bedroom window and waved down at the three generations that trundled the path, breathing the cold air through scarves and with their fingers warm inside gloves. Chloe was holding the hand of her grandma on one side and her aunty on the other, jumping and swinging so that they were forced to take her weight when her feet lifted from the ground. They stopped every few steps so that Chloe could forage for the chocolate buttons that Alice had snuck into her pocket.

'I need to get one for Dr Panda.' Chloe placed the slither of chocolate at her panda's mouth before quickly transferring it to her own.

'Can I have one please, Chloe? They're my favourite!' Grace called down, enquiring not because she wanted the sugar, but to test her daughter's sharing skills.

Chloe beamed up at her mum, waving, happy to see her. 'No, Mummy, you can't have one because you didn't eat all your lunch!'

The trio roared with laughter.

Olive shook her head as she gripped the pink plastic arm of Chloe's raincoat and swung her high. 'Miss Chloe May Penderford, you are incorrigible!'

'You are too, Granma!' Chloe replied. 'You are porridgeable!'

Grace smiled as she retreated beneath the soft, warm duvet, trying not to dwell on her sister's sadness, which threatened to keep her awake. Forty winks was just what the doctor ordered.

Four

People suffering from sepsis can have severe breathlessness and may sometimes gasp

Her cry ricocheted off the ceiling and pierced Grace's skull, where a headache still lurked.

'But I want my... my brexbrus!' Chloe rubbed her eyes and stammered through her tears. Her nose was running and she began to wail.

Tom hitched her up onto his lap and smoothed her hair. 'Oh my darling, I know, I know. But you can't have breakfast, Chlo, because the medicine they give you before you have your operation might make you sick if you eat something now.'

'I don't... I don't mind,' she managed.

'Oh, darling.' He wiped her nose.

Grace watched as he cradled her to him.

'I don't want to go to hostipal any more. I want to stay here and have something to... to eat.'

Tom's voice was soft, steady, reassuring. 'I promise you we'll be back here before you know it. And Mummy and I will get you lots of goodies, like ice cream, ice lollies, whatever you fancy. And tonight, if you feel up to it, you can have some lovely things to eat on the sofa, snuggled up under a blanket, and we can watch *Frozen*. How does that sound?'

Chloe nodded, despite her continuing tears. 'G... good,' she hiccupped.

'Tell you what, Chlo...' Grace assumed a positive and assertive tone, all part of her plan to distract. 'I just need to make a quick phone call to Jayney, then I'll read you *The Gruffalo* while Daddy has his shower. How about that?'

Chloe nodded against her dad's T-shirt, gripping Dr Panda in her little fist and holding him up to her face. Grace crept out to the patio and blew smoky breath into cold morning air.

'Blimey, one day off – can't you resist calling?' was how Jayney answered the phone.

'I know, I know, but there are just a couple of things that *have* to happen today or we will really be pushing it time-wise,' Grace said.

'And you told me about them on Friday. Let me guess: Nell needs the final proofs and Angharad has to okay the figures. I'm on it! Please don't worry; things are not going to fall apart in one day. I have your very, very detailed notes to go from as well as your verbal instructions and, believe it or not, a tongue in my head, so if I am unsure about anything, I can call you!'

'Oh God, Jayney, am I that bad?'

'Worse. It's not even half seven and you're calling me! Good job I love you, isn't it?'

'It is,' Grace admitted. 'Good weekend?'

'Ah, the usual. Met Mr Right, who turned out to be Mr Just About Bearable by the time the Sambuca had left my system.'

'I won't bother dusting off my fancy hat and matching bag just yet then.' Grace laughed.

'No, not just yet. How's Chloe doing?'

'She's fine. You know, bit tearful cos she can feel we're tense and she can't have breakfast, which is a big deal for Chlo.'

'Big deal for all of us, mate!' Jayney laughed.

'Good point. I tell you what, I might hop into a bed myself at the hospital, I feel like shite!'

'Oh, not good. What's up?'

'Don't know, just a bit blurgh. Tired and headachy. I suppose if I had the time, I would have the flu.'

'But you haven't got the time. You've got deadlines!' Jayney reminded her.

'Exactly, which is why I'll be back in tomorrow. But seriously, please promise you'll call me if you need anything or have any questions. Call me before you ask Jason anything, you know what he's like!'

'Grace, I promise. Now go see to that baby girl and don't worry, it's just one day!' Jayney laughed, knowing her reprimand would make little to no difference.

Grace saw she had a missed call from her mum and a text from Alice that read: *Speak soon, Gracie. Give the girl a big kiss from me and tell her I shall be thinking about her all day! Xx*

Grace replied with a quick *Will do. x* before dialling her parents' home number.

'Morning, Dad!'

'Good morning!' He did, as ever, sound delighted to hear from her. 'How's my little one doing?'

'She's a bit out of sorts, but fine really. I was just saying to Jayney, I think the biggest problem is that she can't have breakfast and hasn't had anything since late afternoon yesterday.'

'Poor little thing. I feel guilty that I've just had toast! What a lovely day we had yesterday.' Mac sighed.

'Oh it was, Dad, really lovely. So good to see everyone. I feel a bit run down myself, think I'm probably just tired. Are you and Mum okay?' Grace wondered if it might be a bug. She offered up a quick prayer: *Keep me healthy!* She had far too much to think about without having to deal with illness.

'Your mum and I are, as usual, fit as the proverbial flea!' Mac laughed.

'I might have guessed.' Grace laughed too.

'Give Chloe our love and do let us know how she gets on, won't you?'

'Will do. Promise. Love you, Dad.'

'Love you too, sweetheart.' She could tell he was smiling.

Back inside, Grace settled down on the sofa and wrapped the soft throw over herself and Chloe. 'Are you comfy?' Chloe nodded. 'Are you warm enough?' Again she nodded her response. 'Grandma and Grandad send you their love and Alice too. They all said to give you a kiss. So here goes!' Grace kissed the top of her little girl's head three times and then began.

'A mouse took a stroll through the deep dark wood. A fox saw the mouse and the mouse looked—'

'Good!' Chloe shouted. They knew the book by heart, which only added to their love of it. And this morning it was exactly what they both needed: something familiar and fun, a distraction.

Grace and Tom did their best to keep the mood light, joking and laughing as they got Chloe settled in the ward. Dr Panda insisted on lying in the middle of the pillow and Chloe had to hoick him out of the way. He then needed to use a bedpan, causing much hilarity, especially with the addition of Tom's sound effects – anything rather than give their little girl a minute to think about her rumbly tum and the fact that she was in a hospital.

Grace unpacked Chloe's little bag containing a clean

nightie and dressing gown for later. As the nurse dotted anesthetising gel to the back of her hand, Chloe instinctively cried, 'I don't like it!'

Grace watched as a single fat tear slid down her cheek.

'I know, darling, but you will soon be home and the doctor is going to make you better. Dr Ranj and Nurse Morag will be fussing around you and you will have no more sore throats!' Tom wiped away her tear and kissed her. 'Okay?'

Chloe nodded as she caught her breath and used Dr Panda to wipe away her tears.

It was now mid morning and as she lay back against the pillow, her tumble of blonde curls spread like a golden halo behind her head. With Dr Panda pushed into her cheek, she looked adorable as she succumbed to the anaesthetic. Her head lolled to one side.

Grace released her hand and kissed her cheek. 'We'll be right here waiting for you, my darling girl,' she whispered into her ear.

Tom kissed her forehead as they wheeled her through the rubberised double doors.

'Don't worry. She'll be back before you know it.' The kindly anaesthetist smiled and tucked Chloe's arm down under the blanket as she handed Dr Panda to her mum for safekeeping.

'I hate seeing her like that.'

Grace turned to her husband, who looked pale. 'Me too.

Shall we go and get a coffee?'

Tom nodded.

The two found solace in the coffee shop in the foyer. Having agreed not to eat or drink earlier, out of solidarity with their daughter, they necked their coffees fast. It was only once they'd bought second cups and had shared a rather large Belgian bun that they relaxed into conversation.

'How are you feeling, babe?' Tom looked at his wife, searching for clues.

'Bit rough actually. I said to Jayney earlier, I'd be ill if I had the time.'

'I checked your schedule and I think you have a gap next Thursday between 2.30 and 3.15, could you be ill then?' he said, tongue in cheek.

'Ha ha.' Grace ignored him and blew her nose. 'I feel a bit fluey.'

'Do you want me to go grab you some Paracetamol?' Tom offered. 'I mean, we're in a bloody hospital, there's got to be some lying around somewhere!'

She shook her head. 'No. Thanks though, love. I'll grab something at home.'

'I hate that she's up there without us. It feels crap that we're putting her through this. Maybe we should have waited,' Tom said.

'It's a bit bloody late now!' Grace smiled and placed her hand over the back of Tom's, which was toying with the little sachet of sugar that had come with his coffee. 'Just think of what this'll mean for her, think of all those horrible days with her unable to swallow or eat. Her snoring, her earaches, the whole lot gone!' She snapped her fingers. 'Just like that!'

'I know. She just looked so tiny on that trolley.' He swallowed his tears.

'When she has a baby, you are going to be banned from the building. Can you imagine if you're this bad when she's just having her tonsils out?' Grace laughed.

'I can't even think of her having a baby!' He shook his head. 'Tell you what, the bloke she marries better look after her, or I'll kill him!'

Grace giggled and sipped her coffee. '*If* she chooses to marry, I'm sure he'll be a good guy; we have to trust her to pick well. Plus they don't let just any old bloke be captain of the rowing team!'

'Good point.' He raised his mug and clinked it against hers.

Grace looked at the clock on the wall. 'Right, that's it, half an hour. Let's go back up!'

The two raced to the lift, partly in haste and partly in jest. Fuelled by coffee and sugar, they jostled each other, both keen to be the first to press the button and both a little giddy with relief that the whole affair was nearly over.

They had barely had time to sit outside the recovery area when the rubber doors opened and a porter wheeled Chloe out towards them. A nurse walked alongside in blue scrubs, her long hair wound into a tight bun and a face mask dangling onto her chest. 'It all went perfectly. Mr Portland is very pleased.'

'Oh that's great!' Tom exhaled a huge sigh.

Grace ran her hand over Chloe's hair; it was slightly sticky with sweat. Chloe opened her eyes and smiled weakly at her mum.

'Hello, little girl,' Grace whispered as they wheeled her past and into the ward.

Chloe was understandably groggy. She placed her hand on her ear and cried a little.

'They said she might have a bit of an earache after. They've given her some painkillers, so that should take the edge off.'

'Poor little thing,' Tom cooed.

Once Chloe was settled into the ward, Grace hopped onto the bed and held her daughter in her arms. 'When we get home, Chlo, we can read *The Gruffalo* again and Daddy has got you some ice cream when you feel up to it.'

Chloe nodded against her mum, turned on her side and slept for over an hour.

Grace smiled at her husband. 'I know this is a terrible thing to say, but I quite like it when she's a bit under the weather and wants to be held like this.' She kissed Chloe's hair.

'I know what you mean.' He smiled back. 'Apparently she'll be right as rain tomorrow, just a bit of a sore throat, but apart from that...' He let it trail.

'And I'll be back at work, worse luck. I feel crappy.' Grace yawned.

'You could take another day,' Tom suggested.

'I can't.' Grace shook her head. 'I'm already up against it with a couple of deadlines; I need to go and chivvy things along. Plus you know what Jason's like, the slightest whiff that I'm not coping and he'll be all over my accounts like a hungry locust. The bastard.' Grace winced as she realised she'd sworn while holding Chloe; she was usually very good about keeping her profanities for when her daughter was out of sight and earshot.

Tom tutted in mock disapproval. 'Think you got away with it, just about.'

Grace smiled. 'Do you remember when I forgot she was in the back of the car and missed the turning and said S-H-I-T and she said it for a week to everyone, as if she knew, and we kept shouting "Ship ahoy!" over her to try and stop the old ladies in the village from being traumatised?'

Tom laughed. 'We've got to be so careful!'

'We have.'

It was a little over an hour later that Chloe roused herself, stretched her arm over her head as she opened her eyes and looked at her dad. 'Stostisisipal,' she whispered.

'Yes, hostipal, Chlo!' He laughed. 'She sounds like her mother after a few gins.'

'Shall I change her nappy?' Grace wondered. After her surgery they had put her in some night-time pull-ups to save any mishaps. Grace placed a hand under her bum and pulled the waistband clear, looking down. 'Actually, no. She's perfectly dry. So no point in disturbing her.'

Chloe slept for most of the afternoon, with her parents taking turns to hold her. It was five hours after her surgery that the surgeon came to visit.

'Hello, Chloe's Mum and Dad. Good news: it all went very well earlier, no complications or surprises, which is just how we like it. How's she doing?' Mr Portland was jovial if a little rushed. Grace noticed the shiny evening shoes and black trousers visible beneath his white coat; obviously a man with somewhere to be.

'She's great, but a little groggy. Been waking up, crying, then nodding back off,' Tom explained.

'That's to be expected after an anaesthetic. Has she been drinking?' He looked at the flipchart in his hand.

'Yes, just sips,' Grace confirmed.

'Has she been chatting?' Mr Portland came closer and looked at the sleepy Chloe in her dad's arms.

Tom laughed. 'She was trying to say hospital, but it came out wrong – she's never been able to say it!'

Mr Portland laughed too. 'Well, look, take her home and make sure she keeps drinking. You've been given a leaflet, I take it, about what to expect? What to do if there are any abnormalities? Bleeds and so on?'

'Yes.' Grace patted her handbag, where the printed information sat snugly in her diary.

'Really, don't worry. It's a very routine procedure. Sleep is the best thing for her. She'll be back on track tomorrow and of course you have the ward number, so any questions or worries, just give us a shout.' Mr Portland smiled, clicked his ballpoint pen and returned it to his top pocket. 'Bye, bye, Chloe!' He waved as he strode from the ward.

'Nice man,' Tom said as he wrapped his little girl in the duvet they had brought from home.

Grace pulled the car into the driveway and killed the engine, then ran ahead to open the front door and switch on the lights.

Tom lifted Chloe from the back seat and carried her straight upstairs to her bed. She was still groggy. He laid her on the mattress. 'She's a bit shivery, Grace.'

'Well it's not surprising, it's bloody cold, Tom. Freezing out there!' she said as she rubbed her palms together. 'Don't forget, she's been in a hot hospital all day; this is probably a shock to her system. Tell you what, it's a bloody shock to my system!'

'I can't tell you how glad I am it's all over,' Tom said. 'I've been secretly quite worried, dreading it.'

'All done now, love, and for the best.' She smiled.

'Yep, definitely for the best. Mr Portland said it had all gone very well.' Tom spoke with pride, as if Chloe had passed a test.

'Yep, bless her. I'll change her nappy now so we don't have to disturb her later. 'Ssshh…' Grace whispered, to quell her daughter's whimpers as she lifted up her nightdress and removed her pull-ups. 'It's bone dry.' She laid her hand on the dry, warm nappy. 'That's odd.'

'Not really, Grace. She's hardly drunk anything, has she?' Tom said.

'No, of course, that'll be it. I guess usually she's guzzling all day, isn't she?'

'Again, like her mother!' He laughed. 'Talking of which, shall I go pop the fire on and open a bottle of red?'

'If you like. I don't feel a hundred per cent. I'm thinking I might go in a bit later tomorrow, get Chloe back into her routine in the morning, help you get her settled. I can get the 11.30 train and be in for lunchtime. That'd be okay, wouldn't it?'

'More than okay. She'll be happy.' He pointed at their sleeping beauty. 'And her daddy is certainly happy. Hello, lie-in!' Tom beamed.

'With Miss Squeaky Door on patrol at the crack of a sparrow's fart? You should be so lucky.' The two laughed as Grace placed Dr Panda by her side and tucked the duvet around her little girl. She kissed her forehead. 'Goodnight, baby. I love you, Chloe. We were so proud of you today, you did really well, my beautiful girl.'

Chloe stirred and opened her mouth. 'Aspetimeee…' She fell back again against the pillow, asleep.

Grace looked at her husband and shrugged. They both laughed.

'Definitely one over the eight!' Tom bent low and kissed his daughter. 'You were a star today, Chlo. I'll be up to check on you in a bit.'

Grace paused on the landing. 'Ha! Tom, listen!' She cupped her hand around her ear. 'No snoring!'

Tom made out to clap and twirled on the spot. 'Mr Portland, I love you, and so will the captain of the rowing team!'

Grace dug him in the ribs as they tiptoed down the stairs. While Tom gathered the bottle of wine from the kitchen, Grace switched her phone on. 'Flaming Nora, I've got a million texts from Mum and Alice and Jayney, all asking how she got on! I can't be arsed to reply to them all. Is it okay to send a group reply, do you think?' She looked up at her husband.

'Yes, do it, then we get more us-time!' He winked.

Grace laughed as she rattled off a response. *Evening all! Home! Happy to report all went very well. Chloe now soundo. Will give update in the morning. Night y'all. xxx*

Tom collapsed by her side and handed her a glass of wine. 'I'm exhausted.' He yawned as if to prove the point.

'Poor baby.' She stroked his hair. 'And there was me hoping for a bit of TLC.'

'Ooh, that feels nice. And I did offer to get you

Paracetamol earlier, that was TLC!' He nestled against her, catlike and yawned again.

'Oh, honey, yes you did. Are you too tired for sexy thoughts?' Grace nudged him with her elbow.

Tom looked up. 'Grace, I am never too tired for sexy thoughts.'

'Shame.' She sipped at her wine. 'Cos I am.'

Tom lunged forward and kissed his wife hard on the mouth, drawing away to chat. 'It's been a funny old day, horrible because of what Chloe went through, but really lovely as you've been home. I've loved it.' He kissed her again, longer this time.

'I've loved it too,' Grace whispered, feeling slightly breathless by the force of their contact. Her face glowed as she marvelled that even after all these years, they still had that magic; even when she was feeling a little under the weather, he could make her heart thud.

'Shall we take this wine upstairs?' he asked as he pulled her from the sofa.

Grace smiled, nodding as she picked up her glass and followed him back up. She poked her head into Chloe's room and stood on the landing, enjoying the silence, which would take a bit of getting used to. Gone was the snuffle-pig snore that had become Chloe's signature noise. She crept backwards, remembering Mr Portland's words. *'Sleep is the best thing for her.'*

With his clothes in a heap on the floor, Tom was already

under the duvet, trying to muster some warmth in the cool bed.

'Shall we set an alarm in case we drop off?' Grace asked. 'We need to check on Chlo in a bit.'

'No, I'm always up for the loo and to check on her anyway,' Tom said. 'Come here, I need your body for warmth, it's freezing!' He spoke through chattering teeth.

'Oh, well, if it's that cold, I'd better put my thick PJs on.'

'No!' Tom raised a palm in protest. 'Anything but those! I think I'd prefer you to talk about frozen lamb than come to bed in those passion killers.' He squirmed.

'Your mum bought me those, which means they were probably horribly expensive!' Grace smiled.

'Oh God, what is it with you? First those bloody pyjamas and now you're talking about my mother? Are you determined to put the kybosh on our love life tonight?'

'Depends – how many more minutes' sleep would I get?' Grace asked as she kicked off her jeans and peeled off her T-shirt before jumping under the duvet.

'I reckon about an extra fourteen minutes!' Tom laughed as he pulled his wife towards him.

'Fourteen minutes? How come? Are you planning on doing it twice?' She squealed as her husband bit her neck and dragged her under the covers.

It was a couple of hours later that Grace sat up and noticed she was alone in the bed. She reached to grab her T-shirt from the floor where it had fallen and slipped her arms into it. She felt the cool cotton touch her skin and shivered. Maybe those pyjamas weren't such a bad idea. Her feet touched the carpet and she rubbed her eyes, wondering whether to wake Chloe up and give her Calpol or whether to let her sleep on. *I'll see how she looks.*

Creaking the door open slowly, she saw Tom, lying on the rug by the side of Chloe's bed. The little cushion that usually sat on her bed was under his head and his dressing gown was draped over his torso for warmth.

She opened the airing cupboard and pulled out the old quilted blanket they used for picnics and tent-making with Chloe, and spread it over her husband.

He lifted his head. 'Thank you. She was a bit groggy and had a slight temperature. I've given her a slug of Calpol and she's gone back off.'

'You should have woken me up!' Grace whispered.

'I wanted you to sleep, I know you're not feeling too great.'

'Bless you. Want to swap? I'm happy to take the rug for a bit,' she offered. It reminded her of when Chloe was a little baby and they'd cared for her in shifts, sharing the feeds, the naps, taking it in turns to doze when they could. Happy times.

'No, we're fine. You go get your beauty sleep and when she gets up in the morning, you can give her her breakfast and I'll grab forty winks then.'

'Sure.' Grace bent over and laid two fingers gently against her daughter's cheek. 'Poor little thing, she does feel a bit toasty. She's been through it today.' She straightened. 'If you need me, just shout, love. I'll leave the doors open.'

'Love love, Grace.' His words cut through the darkness.

She turned and looked at the outline of her man, lying on the floor, being the best dad in the whole wide world. 'Love love, darling.'

Grace woke before her 5 a.m. alarm and patted the empty space where Tom should have been. Remembering where he was, she crept into Chloe's room. She pulled the cover up over her little girl, who looked a little flushed, then knelt on the floor and moved her hair away from her face with her fingers. Chloe began to cry. Not her usual cry, interspersed with demands or comments, but a high whine that Grace didn't recognise. She lifted her daughter and held her close as Tom sat up.

'Is she okay?'

'She's just woken up. Feels a bit hot and she's still groggy, aren't you, my darling?' Grace kissed her face as Chloe's head flopped onto her mum's shoulder.

'D'you think she might have got your bug?' Tom wondered as he yawned and stretched his back, his hands above his head.

'Oh God, Tom, I think you're right! I'll give her some more Calpol and get her changed. She's all sweaty. Clean PJs and a freshen-up will make her feel better.'

Grace carried their daughter through to their bedroom and laid her in the middle of the bed. Chloe was uncharacteristically quiet. Grace removed her nappy, which was still dry at the front, but with evidence of an upset tum.

'I need to get you drinking, little Chlo. How about a bot-bot? We haven't done that for a while. Would you like a bottle?' Grace knew if she could make it into a game, Chloe was more likely to participate.

Chloe opened her eyes briefly and seemed to look past her mum, as though still asleep, her gaze and focus a little off.

Grace changed her into a clean, fresh nightdress and ran a cool, damp sponge over her face and hands. Chloe cried quietly, her face crumpled.

'Oh, darling! Don't cry!'

'I'm a bit worried about her.' Tom leant on the bed and looked at his little girl. 'She doesn't look right.'

'Me too. What should we do? Shall I give the ward a ring?' Grace chewed her lip, not wanting to make a fuss, especially at this early hour, but wanting her mind put at rest nonetheless.

'Yeah, I think so. They did say to give them a shout, didn't they?' Tom shared her hesitancy. 'I'll lie here with her while you call them.'

Grace trod the stairs in search of her handbag. It wasn't seven o'clock yet; she hoped she'd catch them before they got too busy.

The call was answered almost immediately and Grace explained the situation.

'So you think she might have your bug?' the nurse asked.

'I think so, yes. I've been feeling groggy, bit of a temperature, just... you know, off colour.' She didn't know how to explain it.

'And Chloe is displaying the same symptoms?'

'Yes. She's just woken up and isn't really with it, if you know what I mean.' Grace gave a small laugh to cover her awkwardness.

'Has she been sick?'

'No.' Grace shook her head.

'Does she have any bleeding from her surgery?'

'No. Not as far as I can see.'

'And she's sleeping okay?'

'Yes. Yes, as I say, quite drowsy. A bit, you know, out of sorts.' Grace slapped her thigh, wishing she could find the words.

'It sounds like she might have your bug. And remember, coming into hospital can unsettle them and an anaesthetic is never nice. I expect it's probably just a combination of that. I would guard against bringing her into the ward if you think she does have a bug, but it's your call really. If you are worried, then of course bring her in and we'll get her checked over.'

'I think she just wants to sleep,' Grace concluded.

'It's the best thing for her if she's feeling poorly.' The

nurse spoke kindly; it was reassuring.

'That's what Mr Portland said,' Grace recalled.

'If her temperature gives you cause for concern or there are any other major changes, then call back or, as I say, just bring her in.'

'Okay, thank you. Hope I haven't wasted your time.'

'Not at all.' The nurse sounded sympathetic. 'Hope you both feel better soon!'

Grace relayed the news to Tom that they were best to let her sleep, then she covered them both with the duvet and made her way downstairs to the sofa. She hated feeling under par and hoped that an hour or two of shuteye would do the trick. She'd text Jayney after eight to say she was going to be a little late in.

When she woke, still in a dreamy stupor, it took a second for Grace to remember where she was and why she was on the sofa. She smiled at the sound of movement overhead. Tom was as good as his word, up every few hours with his unreliable bladder and checking on Chloe while he was at it.

They say life turns on a penny.

They say that things can change in a second.

They say that once life has changed, it is almost impossible to imagine what it was like before.

These were the seconds before.

One...

Two…

Three…

It was almost simultaneous. Grace looked at the digital display on her phone and read 9.15 at the exact moment that the deafening sound of a stranger in their house filled her head. It had to be a stranger; it was no voice she recognised, no sound that she had heard before. Was it a person? An animal? She couldn't tell. Her heart raced and felt as if it was beating in her throat. Her bowels turned to ice.

It was a scream, a guttural yell, a primal noise that came from the pit of a stomach and was intended to travel up to the highest point in the sky and down to the deepest depths of the earth.

Grace jumped and shivered. Petrified, rooted for a second or two to the spot where she sat, unsure of what to do next, unsure of how to make her legs move or how to stop her body from shaking.

'Tom?' she called, but fear had turned her voice to a whisper.

'Tom?' she called again, trying to fathom what was happening. Who was screaming? Where was that noise coming from? *What should I do? I don't know what to do.*

As if waking from a trance, Grace finally managed to stand. Gingerly she made her way upstairs to the landing.

The first thing that hit her was the smell. Vomit. She could smell sick and this made her wretch and place her hand over her mouth. She inched forward and flicked on the hall light. Her eyes darted across the space at her feet as she tried to understand what she was seeing.

Tom was kneeling on the hall floor and he was leaning over a dolly, a teddy or something, a bundle of clothes possibly, with his face buried in it. She couldn't quite make it out. He had been sick; it dripped in a stain down the front of his chest and in splashes on the wall and on the carpet.

'You've been sick,' she said, as if there was the smallest chance that he was unaware of the fact.

Grace looked more closely at the bundle and felt the strength leave her legs. She swayed. A knot of icy-cold fear gathered in her stomach and she could hear the blood racing in her head as the bile of realisation rushed into her mouth and down her T-shirt. Placing her hand on the wall, she slid down it and sat in a heap, staring not at a bundle of clothes or a dolly, but at her little girl, who was lying on the floor. She could see Chloe's small, chubby feet sticking out of the bottom of her nightdress; they were flopping inward and were a little arched.

Tom was feverishly stroking the hair away from Chloe's forehead. Chloe who was floppy. Sleeping.

'What are you doing?' Grace shouted. 'Why is she on the floor, Tom?' None of it made any sense.

'Call... call an ambulance. Call an ambulance!' he screamed in a voice she had never heard before, his tone like broken glass, spikey and painful to draw.

'What's wrong? You've been sick! What's going on?' she asked, her eyes wide.

'Get the fucking ambulance, Grace, d'you hear me? Get them now! Right now! She's not breathing, she's not breathing!' His voice got louder and louder.

Tom again placed his mouth over his little girl's and tipped her head back, trying to breathe life into her silent form.

'Call the fucking ambulance!' His voice was now high-pitched, reedy, thin and tortured. He kicked out, catching Grace on the thigh with his bare foot, kicking her as hard as he could manage from the position he was in. 'Now! For fuck's sake, Grace, come on! Now!' he shrieked.

Grace levered herself up, using her hands to steady herself against the wall as she made her way on legs that felt like sponge. She picked up the phone that Tom kept by the side of the bed and with fingers that shook she dialled 999, hoping that she would wake up from this nightmare soon. *Please, please, let me wake up now...*

Tom continued to scream, loud and high pitched. It was an animal wail of distress that he couldn't control. He stopped trying to breathe for Chloe and took his little girl into his arms, cradling her head against his front, trying not to notice the chill to her skin or the blue tinge to her beautiful, beautiful mouth. He rocked her into his chest and continued to scream her name.

'Chloe! Chloe!' he shouted. 'Help us! Help! Someone! Chlo... Baby...'

He kissed her face, her hair, her fingers.

'Please, Chloe!' He was shouting now, sounding almost angry, as if her lack of response was because she couldn't hear him or wasn't doing as she was told. 'Chloe, come on! Come on now! Chloe! Please!'

The siren snaked its way along the lane. Grace didn't know how long it took to arrive; it could have been minutes or hours. Time wasn't calibrated; it had stopped and simultaneously sped up. She managed to tread the stairs and open the front door, still shivering in her knickers and T-shirt.

The paramedic elbowed his way into the house. 'Where is she, love?'

Grace pointed to the landing overhead. The man raced up the stairs and Grace followed him.

'Hello? Hello?' the man called ahead.

Tom stared at him from the corner where he sat.

'What's his name?' he asked Grace. She looked at him uncomprehendingly. He tried again, his tone much softer. 'What's your husband's name, love?' He touched her arm, trying to get her to respond. It worked.

'It's Tom,' she whispered. *Tom. Tom and Chloe. My husband and my daughter.*

'Thank you, love. I'm going to send you off with Kelly. She'll take care of you now.'

His colleague Kelly stepped forward and took Grace by the elbow, guiding her into the bedroom, where she laid her on the bed and checked her over, making the decision that there was no treatment for a broken heart.

Kelly made her way back out to the landing to help her colleague, who was trying to remove Chloe from Tom's embrace.

'Get your hands off her!' Tom's reaction was swift and aggressive.

The paramedic spoke to Tom, bending down face to face, calm and rational, his speech controlled and slow. 'Tom...' Tom didn't respond, so he tried again. 'Tom, we need to look at your little girl. We need to look at Chloe, to see if we can help her. I need you to let her go now, Tom.' He put his hands forward to receive the bundle, but Tom only twisted his body away and held her tighter.

The man's voice was firm now. 'I need to look at her, Tom, and I need you to let her go so that I can do that. I promise you that I won't hurt her. I promise you.'

'You are not going to touch her!' His saliva ran from the corner of his mouth. 'I can't let her go. You don't understand. She's getting cold. I need to keep her warm. I woke up and tried to tuck her in, to check on her and get her a drink and she was cold. She hates being cold. I can't let her go.'

Grace could hear the chatter and commotion on the landing. She leaned up on her elbows and looked straight ahead and there was Chloe standing at the end of the bed! She was waving and she was wearing her pink mackintosh.

'Hey, Chlo…' Grace raised her hand to wave and smiled. By the time Grace had blinked, Chloe had gone.

Climbing from the bed, Grace padded across the carpet. She staggered into the hallway and sank down onto the floor to be next to the shell of her family. She tried to breathe, tried to understand what was happening.

The paramedic shone a light into Chloe's eyes, felt her wrist and touched his fingers to a small area above her breastbone. He looked at his colleague, who was now only feet away, and closed his eyes briefly for a second – their signal.

'It's all right, Tom.' The man placed his hand on Tom's bare arm. 'You hold on to her for a bit.' He too was a dad. He had a daughter. He knew.

Placing a blanket around the two of them, the paramedic sat back on his haunches, trying not to intrude as Tom held his little girl close, giving her a final hug as the last of the warmth slipped from her tiny form.

Tom rocked her back and forth. 'Ssshh. It's all right, Chlo. It's all going to be all right. Your daddy's got you.'

It was too late. Chloe's spirit was already swirling upwards, dancing among the clouds on that cold, cold, winter's morning.

Five

People suffering from sepsis often say that they feel like they might die. They often use that phrase: "I feel like I'm dying"

It was as if the house in Nettlecombe had been enveloped in a thick, thick blanket that muffled the sounds of the outside world and prevented any of their sadness from escaping or becoming diluted. Grace would not have been surprised to find the red bricks and grey roof covered in decaying, dark, woody roots of Disney proportions, with the two of them entombed inside. Even opening a window and letting the cold wind whip round the walls did nothing to dissipate the dense fug of grief that they breathed.

They too were silent. There was nothing to say, no one they wanted to see and nothing they wanted to hear. Nothing that could in any way make them feel better. Grace and Tom were fragile; they had become delicate things, as if held together with aged sellotape. Each waited to see how and when they would disintegrate. For it was only a matter of time. In truth, they both looked forward to that day, the day they wouldn't have to think any more, the day they would be released from this living hell.

Tom and Grace lurched from their bed or sofa to the bathroom and back to bed. Their days were punctuated with the taking of sleeping pills, the sipping of water and little else. They didn't answer the phone or respond to knocks on the front door. They were unaware of the flowers that lay in parched bundles in the kitchen sink or the neat pile of white envelopes, handwritten in dark ink, each bearing a card whose images could do nothing to lift their misery. They weren't aware of much.

It was as if they had entered a place above the earth and were no longer part of it. Grace existed in an altered state, where the world turned at a different pace to the one at which she operated. She was an observer, unable to participate. She and Tom had developed a bizarre dance of the macabre, waltzing around each other without talking or acknowledging each other. Sitting alone in darkened rooms, howling or muttering, falling into a wretched, unrewarding sleep, eating small amounts in silence, all without recognition of the other. No connection, no intimacy, each riven with tiny fractures; one bump and they would both have shattered.

Mac and Olive crept around them like creatures in the shadows, rinsing cups, writing and folding notes they would never read, propping them against casseroles they would never eat, before disappearing again with a yelled promise to return tomorrow.

It was after about a week that the hospital phoned. Previously, Grace's parents had been there to lift the receiver and close their eyes and nod as they absorbed the heartfelt words issued through teary mouths by acquaintances who secretly gave thanks that this was not happening to them. This caller was persistent; Grace figured she had two options, either yank the phone from the wall or answer it. Without the strength to pull the wire, she raised the phone and held it against her sallow cheek.

'Hello?' Her voice sounded husky, unfamiliar, deeper than she remembered and grainy, weak.

'Mrs Penderford...' The man paused. 'It's Mr Portland.'

She nodded, forgetting that he couldn't see her.

'Mrs Penderford?'

'Yes,' she managed, quietly.

'How are you?' He sounded concerned.

Grace opened her mouth to form a response but realised there were no words to properly explain the ache of grief that consumed her. How could she describe being filled to the brim with utter emptiness? The sadness that weighed her down like lead tied to every muscle; the desolation; the overwhelming desire to simply disappear.

'Okay,' she lied.

'I just wanted you to know that we have received the coroner's initial report and I'm afraid it's inconclusive.

They're going to conduct a second post-mortem and hopefully this will tell us more.'

Grace nodded.

'I know this is the last thing you need – more delays. I just wanted to let you know and as soon as they have the results, I'll call you again.'

'Okay.' Grace hung up the phone.

Death. Death. Dead. Dead. Gone. But we don't know why. The words sat like a bitter chant on her tongue.

Grace walked slowly across the kitchen floor and into the sitting room. She lay down on the sofa, pulled the throw over her body and folded her arms beneath it, wrapping herself in a cocoon from which she would have been happy never to emerge. Blinking her eyes, she saw the spine of a thin book, *The Gruffalo*, lying under the padded stool in front of her. Her tears came thick and fast, clogging her nose and throat, making it hard to breathe. She heard Chloe's voice – *'Gruffalo, Mummy!'* – and remembered the feel of her baby girl against her chest. She inhaled the scent of the blanket, which still held the faintest trace of Chloe. Pulling it over her head, she feigned sleep, hoping she could bring it on anyway, the escape she craved.

She and Tom had taken on the traits of injured animals, each retreating to the furthest, darkest corner of their physical space, wanting only solitude. Their contact was minimal. They were only vaguely aware of the other's presence from the telltale signs of cohabitation: the still warm kettle, the occasional sound of the loo flushing, the wailing and unfettered sobbing in the wee small hours of the morning. Normal routines of hygiene, sustenance and human interaction had long been abandoned; if they encountered each other, it was with the acute embarrassment of having been discovered lurking, out of place and filthy. Grace knew she smelt bad, but it didn't matter; nothing did. Her teeth hurt, her gut ached and her eyes were swollen, but these physical pains helped her focus, gave her something to concentrate on other than the madness that was swallowing her whole.

They had always been very good at observing the 'perfect couple' rules, never going to bed on an argument, always talking about everything, no matter how painful, being open and honest, and talking, talking and talking again. Because of that, issues had never really become problems. All the regular stuff, like jealousy of exes and anger at one-glass-too-many flirting, could be easily exorcised because they would discuss it, shout about it and make love afterwards; it was a recipe that worked for them. Both were entirely confident of the other's fidelity and support and both agreed it was a very nice way to live. No problem was insurmountable because they had each other to go home to and that always made everything better. Until now.

Neither could have envisaged an event so cataclysmic that they wouldn't be able to talk it out, support each other, get through it together. But Chloe's death had blown them apart; all that was left of their former lives was a huge crater with a few vaguely recognisable fragments poking out to taunt them. It was as though they were different people now. They were different people now.

As she lay catatonic on the sofa the following day, Grace remembered a day a few months earlier when she had sat on the side of Chloe's bed and bent down to kiss her goodnight. Tucking Chloe's hair behind her ears and cooing as she closed *The Gruffalo* for the night, she had kissed her little girl three times, once on each cheek and once on her nose. Chloe had reached up and placed her arms around her mum's neck, pulling her in for a heart-melting face-to-face hug. 'I love the way you smell, Mummy,' Chloe had whispered in the half light.

'Do you, darling? What a lovely thing to say.' Grace had smiled, delighted to know this.

Chloe nodded against her face. 'It's because you smell like bacon and I love bacon!' she had explained.

Grace had roared, instantly shattering the peace of bedtime. Tom had come running and she regaled him through her laughter. Chloe of course had then bounced up and down on the bed, her curls flying, enthused and revived by her parents' hilarity.

The memory made Grace smile, even now. It was the most curious mixture, crying unstoppable tears and swallowing the sobs that built in the base of her throat, but at the same time smiling; smiling at the very thought of her little girl and the joy she'd brought.

Tom hovered in the doorway of the sitting room, wrapped in a blanket. Grace looked and looked again; it took a second for her to place the small man with the big beard who stared at her with a slight curl to his lip. He looked awful: thin and yellow-skinned, with swollen eyes and a mouth loose, hanging open. Ugly, dishevelled, dirty.

'I spoke to Mr Portland,' he croaked.

Grace nodded.

'They have the results of the post-mortem.'

Grace sat up, slowly.

Tom walked in and sank down in the space next to her. 'They found something called sepsis in her organs. She died of sepsis.'

Grace sounded the word out in her head. *Sep-sis. Sepsis.* 'I don't know what that is,' she whispered.

Tom shook his head. 'It's an infection, I think. I could only take bits of it in. I thought we could look on the internet.'

Grace watched as Tom shed his blanket and lumbered into the kitchen, walking stiffly, as if his joints gave him physical pain. He returned and sat back down, flipping open the lid of his laptop. Up popped his screensaver: Chloe at the kitchen table with her head thrown back, laughing, eyes closed, happy.

Tears rolled down Grace's face, but she made no attempt to wipe them away or stem her running nose. She no longer noticed when she was crying; it was as natural to her now as breathing. She had forgotten what it was like not to feel this way.

Tom tapped the word into the keyboard. He misspelt it, the word that would soon become branded on his consciousness. 'Sepsis.' He said it aloud for the second time in his life.

'I've never heard of it.' Grace spoke clearly.

'I've heard of it, but I don't really know what it is.' Tom glanced at his wife and then turned his attention back to the screen. 'Sepsis Trust, here we are.' He spoke slowly, squinting at the screen through swollen eyes as he clicked on the link with his juddering hand. The first thing they saw was the fiery red logo. His finger hovered over the links and settled on 'Information'. Then, after scrolling briefly, the two were faced with the description of the disease that had come along like a thief in the night and stolen their little girl.

Tom swallowed and read out loud, slowly. 'Sepsis is a life-threatening condition that arises when the body's response to an infection injures its own tissues and organs. Sepsis leads to shock, multiple organ failure and death, especially if not recognised early and treated promptly.' He paused and looked at his wife's impassive expression before continuing. 'Sepsis is caused by the way the body responds to germs, such as bacteria, getting into your body. Sometimes the body responds abnormally to these infections and causes sepsis.'

Tom stared at the screen, reading and rereading the words, trying to make sense of them.

'How did Chloe get it?' Grace asked.

'I don't know. It must be something to do with when she had surgery. I don't know.' Tom clicked on the list of names under the heading 'Personal Stories'. The two of them skim-read one or two entries before collapsing back against the cushions, overwhelmed by the stories similar to Chloe's.

'Did I give it to her? Was it my bug?' Grace wondered.

'I don't think so. I don't think it works like that.' Tom spoke to the floor.

'Is it our fault? Should we have done something? Got her medicine?' Grace was aware her voice had gone up an octave and that she was breathing a little too quickly.

'I don't know.' Tom answered truthfully, his voice still a growl, his eyes downcast.

Grace knitted her hands in her lap and tried to let the facts crystallise. Their little girl had died from a disease they had never heard of. And she didn't know if there was something she could have done to stop it. She felt her stomach cave with a new wave of grief that hit her sharply and left her winded.

Tom reached up to place his arm around his wife, but Grace stood, unable to cope with physical comfort or any words of solace, no matter how well intentioned. She was raw, angry and hurt; no arm across the shoulders could possibly help that.

Six

People suffering from sepsis may have mottled or discoloured skin

The blinds were pulled, allowing little natural light into the room. Grace sat in front of her dressing table and stared into the mirror. She barely recognised the face that looked back at her. It was older, worn and etched with exhaustion. Her greasy hair lay limply against her skull, her skin was dull and her lips pale. It was amazing how grief had invaded every aspect of her, changed every single bit of her. Lifting her fingers, she touched them to the cool glass and ran them over the outline of the image of the woman that looked a little bit like her, but different, muted somehow. It was as if she had been scooped out, made hollow, and what was left was this flat representation of the person she used to be. She tried again to understand how in such a short space of time her entire world could have got so broken, all the joy extinguished.

It was January the twentieth. Grace tried to remember what she'd done on this date last year, or the year before that. She couldn't be sure but could hazard a guess: breakfast, work, home, supper and bed. A day pretty much like any other, and yet now this date would always be a significant one in her diary, a day that could never feel normal again. January the twentieth would always be the day that she had buried her little girl. Grace closed her eyes, taking gulps of air, trying to stay present, trying to gather the strength to make it through the day without cracking.

Reluctantly she left the solace of her room and found herself at the door of Chloe's bedroom. It would always be Chloe's bedroom, the place she had laid her beautiful head, bounced on the bed in her nightie and cuddled her toys, the walls where her snores had rippled and echoed, the creaky door that alerted them when she was on her way. Tom had beaten her to it. He sat on the tiny bed with his daughter's small pink and white duvet folded into his chest, hugging it closely and taking deep breaths through the fabric, drinking in her ever-fading scent. His eyes were red and swollen from crying, his stubble untended, his speech muffled as he whispered to himself like a madman. Grace looked at the stranger her husband had become and noticed how he, like her, was physically altered.

Leaving him alone with his grief, she returned to her room and pondered the clothes that hung in her wardrobe. She was vaguely aware of having to wear something dark.

Her suits, the costume in which she faced the world of work, held no appeal. She thought about all those mornings when she'd rushed to get to the station, always up against the clock, the minutes between the alarm going off and her leaving the house invariably disappearing far too quickly. There was never enough time and Chloe would insist on hanging around her legs while she tried to select her ensemble for the day. It used to irritate her, the continual inane questioning when she simply didn't have the time to respond. Had she tutted or snapped? Probably both. What wouldn't she give now to feel that chubby little body sitting against her leg, babbling on about something entirely irrelevant. Showing her pages from books or telling her in great detail about something funny Mr Tumble had done. Grace had only ever half listened, concentrating instead on planning her day, thinking about Jayney and Jason and work and meetings... *I'm sorry, Chloe. I'm so sorry. I thought we had all the time in the world. I thought I would always be a weekend away from spending time with you.*

Grace pulled a navy skirt from its hanger and stepped into it before fastening the zip. She let go of the waistband, only for the skirt to fall down to her hips. She knew she had lost weight and this garment was proof of just how much. Grace ran her palm over her jutting bones, hating the living, breathing body in which she was trapped. *Why couldn't it have been me? Why did it happen to her? I would have swapped, I would swap.*

Instinctively balling her hand into a fist, she thumped hard into her abdomen. The effect was intoxicating; she liked feeling the physical pain that she craved. How many times she struck herself she couldn't be sure, but it built into a frenzy of blows.

Tom seemed to appear from nowhere; he caught her by the wrists and held her fast. 'No!' he shouted at her.

His grip hurt. The thin skin of her wrist bit against the bone as he twisted. Still he didn't release her. His pupils were pinpricks as he fixed her with his gaze.

'Why are you doing that? Do you think it helps? It doesn't. Trust me.' And then his tears were flowing again.

'I've lost my little girl and I will not lose you. You are not going to cause yourself harm, do you hear me? Do you hear me?' he shouted, even though he was close.

Sinking down onto his knees, he slumped onto the carpet and she, tethered to him at the wrists, had no choice but to sink with him.

'Where is she, Grace? Where has she gone?' He was sobbing now. 'I can't bear to think of her on her own somewhere. I keep looking for her.'

There was nothing she could say to heal or console him. They sank further down until she lay with her head on his chest and they fell into a fitful sleep, welcoming the oblivion that it offered, exhausted by the outpouring.

They woke some time later to the pip-pipping of Tom's phone alarm and were surprised to find themselves in a heap on the bedroom floor, neither mentioning or recalling the drama that had led them to that point. It was nearly time for them to leave.

Grace pulled on her navy jacket, applying neither make-up to her face nor a comb to her flat hair; this, like everything else, seemed utterly pointless. Tom had managed a sports jacket and suit trousers, an odd combination, which no one would question or care about but plenty would notice.

They stood in the hallway and stared at each other. 'I wish I could fast-forward the day,' Tom mumbled.

'I wish I could fast-forward forever,' Grace replied levelly, rubbing at eyes that felt full of grit.

The front door opened to reveal a beautiful crisp blue day. Despite the cold, wisps of cloud danced in the subtle breeze. The long black shiny car sat in the middle of the frosty driveway. Grace noticed the glossy paintwork and the slick gleaming chrome of the mirrors. Two men she didn't recognise sat up front, very smartly dressed. Her eyes were drawn to the back of the vehicle, where there was a large space filled with flowers. Amid the huge daisies sat a little white wooden box.

Grace felt her knees buckle and the bile rise in her throat. Tom held her arm and kept her on her feet. She fought the overwhelming desire to run. Tom then let out a loud sob, the kind of noise a person would normally only be comfortable making when they were alone. But there was nothing normal about this day.

'Where is she, Grace? Where's she gone?' he asked again, as though she might have the answer.

She matched his tears, sobbing now. 'I don't know. I don't know where she is. I can't bear to think of her on her own somewhere. I can't. I think she might need me, but I don't know how to get to her and she won't understand why I'm not there. I'm her mummy!'

Grace heard a whimpering behind her and was aware for the first time of other people. Quite a large group of people, actually – how had she missed them? Some of them she recognised: her best friend Ruthie, Jayney, Tom's parents, the lady that owned the flower shop in the village, and some people she couldn't quite place, though they were vaguely familiar, women from pre-school maybe? How did they all know where she lived? She wished they would all go away.

Her eyes returned to the little white box that was not much more than three feet long and a foot wide. Grace could imagine the whispers. *'Apparently it can happen to anyone. What was it they said – sepsis? Never heard of it...'*

Tom guided his wife into the arms of her mother and father, one on either side, her supports. She was too distracted to acknowledge them; they were merely another two blurred faces in this surreal pantomime. She travelled to the church behind the hearse, sandwiched between Alice and Olive. Mac and Tom sat in front of them. Mac kept his steady hand on his son-in-law's shoulder. Olive made small whimpering sounds, as if she had run out of tears and this dry heave of distress was her new norm. Alice squeezed her sister's arm and whispered repeatedly, 'It's okay, Gracie. You're doing great. It will all be over soon.' But Grace knew that no matter how sincerely offered this was a lie. It would never, ever be over.

Sitting at the front of the church, Grace stared ahead. Focusing on a stained glass window of an angel with her arms outstretched, she would hold the angel's eye and leave when it was over, trying not to think about what was actually happening, because if she did, she feared she might actually lose her mind. With her parents on either side, Grace realised for the first time in her life that they could not fix everything. She felt grown up and abandoned all at once. Glancing at her mum and dad, she noticed how they had shrunk, looking every one of their combined one hundred and fifty-eight years, bowed and broken. Mac reached across and took her hand into his own. He too stared ahead, holding her hand like he used to when she was little, when it used to make everything feel better. A long, long time ago.

She was aware of the vicar standing upright and business-like, the only person who appeared unmoved, almost indifferent to the event. She tried to think of why that might be – was he so used to the disposal of bodies and the passing over of souls that the whole ghastly business had become almost matter-of-fact, routine? Or maybe he was so certain about where her little girl had gone, that 'better place' that everyone kept telling her about, that he saw no reason to feel sadness, confident that everything in the universe was as it should be. Grace allowed herself to hope so.

Throughout the service, she was aware of a light pressure against her thigh. Eventually looking down, she saw Chloe standing beside her with her hand on her leg, watching proceedings with an almost bored detachment, scuffing her pink wellington boot against the side of the pew and wearing her little raincoat.

Grace bent down at one point and whispered to her daughter, 'Not too much longer now, darling,' and her daughter smiled in response. Grace realised that every time she saw Chloe now, she was strangely silent, as though the little girl had lost her voice.

Music started playing; it was the slow segment from Tchaikovsky's *Romeo and Juliet*. It was beautiful. Grace let the sound fill her. The lilting horn and delicate, heartfelt strings cut into her like tiny daggers; she succumbed to the sorrow and desolation of the notes as they climbed.

All faces apart from Grace's turned towards the back of the church as the heavy oak door opened and Tom entered. Jack walked behind him, for no other reason than to offer moral support, stepping in the wake of his brother in a slow procession that seemed to take an eternity.

Tom's arms were outstretched, his forearms bent upwards and his fingers clasped around the small coffin that contained his little girl. A single large daisy sat on top, her favourite flower. He walked slowly, wanting the moment to last for as long as possible, wanting to hold onto her and savour this contact for the last time ever. He knew that what was coming next should be delayed. Stalling, he tried to avoid the inevitable. He spoke to her in his head. *'It's all right, my darling, you go to sleep now, baby. Go to sleep now. I am right here, Chlo. Your daddy's got you...'*

Grace kept her eyes fixed on the angel.

As the car pulled up to the house, Grace let her gaze rove over the many vehicles that were parked on the verges, crowding the lane and filling the drive.

'I don't want to see anyone. I just want to go to bed,' she murmured.

Tom nodded. This he understood. 'I don't think anyone will mind,' he whispered as he rubbed at his stubble.

She stepped from the car and pushed the front door, which was ajar. Jayney was standing by the stairs, hovering. She rushed forward, crushing her friend to her in a hug. 'Grace! Oh my God. I am so sorry. If there is anything I can do. Anything you need, anything at all, just shout.' Jayney started to cry. 'It's the worst day in the world.'

Grace nodded. *Every day is now the worst day in the world. Every single day.* She spied one of their neighbours, a sweet lady who she was on nodding terms with. They used to wave enthusiastically as their cars passed and would exchange snippets about current and future weather when collecting their bins from the top of the lane on a Tuesday evening. The woman stepped forward and handed her a white envelope, then left. Grace turned it over in her hand. She noticed Ruthie across the floor, too tearful and emotional to speak. Grace looked from person to person, room to room and felt as though she were watching everything in slow motion. Kicking off her shoes, she gathered them into her hand and in her stockinged feet trod the stairs, caring little about the eyes and comments that followed her stumbling progress to her room.

Closing the bedroom door behind her, she shrugged off her jacket and unzipped her skirt, letting them both fall to the floor where she stood. She unbuttoned her shirt, pulled on her nightshirt and pyjama bottoms and crawled under the duvet. Closing her eyes, she welcomed the escape that the soft space offered.

There was a knock on the door as it opened. Olive came in with a cup of tea. 'Here you are, darling, thought you might like a drink.' She placed it on the bedside table and sat on the edge of the bed. Her weight pushed the mattress down and Grace listed towards her. Olive's words were delivered slowly in barely more than a whisper. 'I can't tell you that it will get better, because I'm not sure it does and I have never lied to you, Gracie, but I can tell you that you are a strong woman who will find a way through this. God will—'

'Don't you mention God to me,' Gracie snapped. 'Don't you dare! There is no God!'

‘Darling, don’t—’ Olive began.

‘I mean it. There isn’t. What kind of God gives a germ to a baby girl who didn’t stand a chance?’

‘I don’t know how to answer that.’ Olive knotted her fingers in her lap and swallowed her tears.

‘Well, I don’t know either.’

They sat in silence for some minutes, both trying to erase the image of the little girl’s coffin being lowered into the soil on that sun-bright winter’s day.

‘I promised her it would all be okay. I told her we’d get ice cream and that she could watch *Frozen*. That’s what I told her. And she was hungry, Mum…’ Grace’s face crumpled as, open-mouthed, her tears flowed again. ‘She was hungry and I didn’t give her any breakfast and she was hungry and I ate a bun. I ate a bun and laughed while she was lying there…’

Olive shook her head. ‘You can’t do that, Grace. You can’t go over every detail and blame yourself.’

‘Can’t I? Why can’t I? I think you’ll find I can do what the fuck I want. And I want you to go now,’ Grace retorted.

They fell silent again.

‘I mean it. I want you to go! I don’t want to see anyone!’ She was shouting now.

Olive laid a hand on her daughter’s arm. ‘If I could take all your pain and put it into me, I would, I would do it in an instant.’ she whispered as she crept from the room.

Grace placed her head on the pillow and listened to the

murmur of conversation that floated up the stairs. Once or twice she heard laughter – how dare someone be laughing, laughing in her house, laughing today, laughing at all? Closing her eyes, she pushed her face into the soft surface of the pillow and wished for sleep. Remembering her mum's words, she whispered into the dark, 'There is no God. There is no God. There's nothing. I don't want to be any more. And yet I keep waking up. No one is listening to me, no one is helping me escape. What do I have to do to make this stop?'

An image played in her head, over and over, as it had since that morning when she'd watched her husband with vomit clinging to his skin as he bent over their little girl. It was like a movie that she couldn't switch off, on a loop. She saw herself holding her newborn, kissing her little face and whispering, 'Welcome to the world, little one. I'm Grace, I'm your mum and I love you.'

Grace must have dozed off because she woke with a start when the bedroom door opened. She recognised the outline of Tom as he shuffled in, removed his jacket and dropped it over the chair that sat in the corner. He tiptoed round the bed and slid down onto the mattress in his trousers, shirt and shoes. She could smell sweat on his skin and alcohol on his breath as he exhaled.

The two lay side by side, listening to family, friends and those they vaguely knew milling around below them. In other circumstances it would have been amusing that, in their own home, they were confined to their bedroom while strangers ate their food, sipped their wine, glugged their whisky and admired the cut of the drapes. But this wasn't other circumstances, this was January the twentieth, the day their hearts had been further ripped in two. There were no rules on how to behave and no previous experience on which they could draw; it was entirely new, raw and all-consuming.

They lay in silence as the house grew quieter and quieter. Night crept up on them and threw its dark veil over the darkest of days.

Seven

Sepsis claims 37,000 lives every year in the UK. 37,000...

Grace woke in the throes of a nightmare. The sheets were twisted about her body and she lay in a cloying film of sweat. Her heart was racing, her throat was dry and tears clogged her nose. She sat up and closed her eyes, swallowing hard, trying to picture something different, trying to make the moving image that lurked behind her eyes go away.

It was the same dream she had on a semi-regular basis, where she imagined driving up to the hospital, getting out of the car and taking Chloe by the hand. But before they walked into the building, her little girl looked up at her and said, 'Can we go home, Mummy?' Grace then laughed, packed her back into the car and drove her home in time for tea and *The Gruffalo*.

Strangely, it wasn't the dream itself that upset Grace; in fact quite the opposite: it was lovely to see Chloe again, to feel her hand in hers. It was waking up to the miserable reality that left her reeling and feeling physically sick.

Grace knew that the nightmare was a manifestation of the one obsessive thought that haunted her above all else. It was real and constant, the thought that had she acted differently, taken another decision, done... something, anything, Chloe might still be with them. She couldn't bear the idea of apportioning blame and even at her most rock-bottom she knew that this would only make things worse. But it was very hard not to, impossible to fight the questions that dogged her. How had that infection got into her daughter's body? Had someone given it to her? Was it her bug? Was it her fault? Did you catch sepsis from other people? Why hadn't Mr Portland kept Chloe in hospital just in case? Was it Tom's fault for letting her sleep? If he'd made Chloe stay awake, would she still be alive? And perhaps worst of all, there was the knowledge that while Chloe had been fighting sepsis, she and Tom had been drinking red wine and making love under the duvet. The memory made her retch.

Without Chloe, Grace felt a seismic shift in her place in the world. It confused her how something so shattering, so cataclysmic could be forgotten, but it was. At least once an hour and periodically through the night, in a break from grief, she would sit up straight and listen for Chloe, or wander the hallway in search of her and had even placed her hand to her mouth to call for her, wanting a hug and to feel her daughter's skin against her own. When her mind caught up with the reality that this was futile, so she would hurt anew. She tried to learn the fact that she no longer needed to focus her energy, finances and planning on what would be best for her daughter, pondering her daughter's future long and short term. There was no longer a future for her daughter. But this information simply would not sink in. It was too horrible to contemplate, the fact that her little life had just ended. Stopped.

It was a time of nothingness. Nothing mattered, nothing made her happy, nothing could soothe her sadness, and when she tried to picture her own future, all she could see was nothing. Grace remembered when she had a never-ending to-do list that churned inside her mind: big things and small things that filled up every second of thinking time, pointless tasks and worries that jolted her from sleep in the early hours. She used to wish it would stop, wanted a clear head. Now she knew that to be preoccupied in this way was a luxury. How she would welcome it. Now there was nothing; she was blank, like a computer that was wiped. Nothing.

When she wasn't crying, she was raging, furious at everything and everybody. A man from the church had come round one day, knocked on her door, offered his condolences and asked if she'd be interested in a visit from the vicar, or would she like a chat with the grief counsellor at the church. Grace had shivered in abhorrence and looked him squarely in the eye as he glanced past her at the mountain of used coffee cups and the growing pile of dirty laundry swamping the kitchen. 'So, this visit from your vicar or chat with your counsellor,' she'd said, 'will it bring my Chloe back?'

He had smiled uncomfortably, shifting awkwardly on the spot. 'Well, no, dear.'

'Well you can piss off then.' With that she'd closed the door. She doubted he would bother her again, but at least he wouldn't be leaving disappointed: he now had not only the state of her house to discuss, but also her extreme rudeness, which would quickly be interpreted as the first stage of a total mental breakdown. And maybe he'd be right. Who cared?

She began to question why they'd chosen to have Chloe's funeral in a church, paying lip-service to the fairy story, inadvertently supporting the myth. *It's all bollocks,* she thought furiously. *All of it.* She found it impossible to recall much of that day, as though her mind had closed off the most painful bits, but she remembered the unnatural quiet in the church, despite all those people crammed in there, shoulder to shoulder, heads bowed. *Dignified.* Grace snarled. How come there'd been so many people? Nothing else to do on a sunny morning? Were they that desperate for something to talk about? She could imagine the trite, banal comments – *'heart-breaking, it was'... 'such a tiny coffin'... 'didn't the mother look terrible'* – and it made her sick. What did they know?

She couldn't even bear to speak to her family, couldn't listen to their tears and words of remorse, couldn't cope with seeing her parents so fractured, her mum fighting to keep her emotions in check, her dad broken. She simply couldn't cope. Her mobile phone was permanently off and the landline went straight to answerphone, collecting the many messages that continued to flood in.

Untangling herself from her sheet and trying to shake the nightmare out of her head, Grace stumbled downstairs and into the kitchen. She would make some tea. The habit of tea-making, the simple, welcome ritual, punctuated the miserable hours of nothingness. It was almost a welcome diversion, to potter to the kitchen, fill the kettle. She would gather her dressing gown around her and pad down the stairs. *Time for tea*. It gave her a break, something to do and provided a small element of structure to the never-ending island of grief on which she aimlessly floated.

As she approached the kettle, she was suddenly aware of Tom sitting at the kitchen table.

'Cup of tea?' Her voice was a cracked whisper, hoarse from too many tears and lack of use.

Tom laughed dryly and held up a bottle of brandy, which he tilted from side to side. He unscrewed the lid and poured a large tumbler. Judging by the slump of his posture, it wasn't his first. Instinctively, Grace abandoned the kettle and replaced her mug on the shelf before taking a glass from the cupboard. She sat down opposite him, pouring herself a measure to match his. *Why the hell not?*

'Can't sleep?' His voice too was an unfamiliar growl; his greasy hair fell forward on his brow.

'Sleep?' She gave a wry laugh as she rubbed her eyelids. 'No.' The sleeping pills knocked them out and were good for erasing the pointless hours, but neither of them felt rested or restored afterwards. That sort of sleep was a distant memory.

Grace took a slug of the brandy and winced, hating the taste. But the warmth that spread down her throat and through her chest was far from unpleasant. She followed the first with another two large gulps; it became surprisingly more pleasant with each swig. Very soon she noticed the familiar thickening of her tongue, the slight haze to her vision and the slackness about her mouth. Alcohol had always been able to have its wicked way with Grace quickly and without too much complaint. Tom used to joke that it made her a cheap date; that didn't seem quite so funny now.

'I keep thinking I can hear her...' He held his wife's gaze.

She stared right back, knowing that they had to talk about her, but really not wanting to.

He took her silence as a cue to continue. 'You know how in the night she used to call out "Daddy, I need a drink" or "I can't find my blanky", anything just so we would go in and see her.'

Grace smiled and could hear that little voice clearly inside her head.

'It used to be a real pain in the arse, didn't it? When we were really tired and warm in bed and didn't want to get up, and I'd nudge you or you'd jab me, as though it was the other one's turn.' He paused. 'I would give anything, Grace, *anything* to get up for her now. I swear I wouldn't need any more sleep ever, if I could just get up and find her in her room all warm and crumpled and sleepy, sitting up, waiting for a hug or a drink, as if this whole thing was just some horrible nightmare.'

Grace nodded. It was the same for her.

'Occasionally I get distracted, confused, and I think, God, I can't wait for this to be over and we can all get back to normal. I can't wait to see Chloe and we can put all this behind us. But then it's like a fog lifts and I realise that we are never going to get back to normal, I am not going to see her, and this is real...' He buried his face in his hands.

She reached forward across the table and put her hand on his arm. 'It'll all be okay.' She muttered, flatly, drawing on the words that rolled around inside her head, words that others offered, words that felt hollow.

'How, Grace? How is this going to work? I can't sleep and actually I don't want to sleep because I can't cope with the nightmares and yet I don't want to be awake, so what am I supposed to do? Where am I supposed to be? *How* am I supposed to be? I keep thinking that tomorrow might be better, but then I realise days have passed and nothing's changed. I keep thinking about seriously trying to join her.'

He looked up, waiting for his wife's reaction, for her reassuring response that that would be foolish, futile, that he shouldn't be so stupid. For her to beg him not to leave her alone because she needed him. But she gave none and said nothing.

'But I don't want to leave you.' Tom drummed his fingers on the tabletop and took a slug of his drink. 'I have to believe that this will get better. I have to.'

Grace shivered, unable to take responsibility for his well-being.

Tom didn't seem to notice. 'You're so remote and closed in and I can't make anything right. I feel like I'm in a really dark place and I don't know how I'm going to climb out. I don't know if I can climb out. I'm so scared. So, so scared. I feel like I need some help. I need your help, Grace. You're the only person that knows what this feels like. Please…'

She didn't know how to begin either, and the brandy did nothing to aid her lucidity or sympathy. She tried to think of what to say. Exhausted by the exertion, she said, 'Why don't you go and stay with your parents for a bit?'

Tom laughed, a slow, derisory, wheezing chuckle. 'My parents? Is that the best you can do? That's priceless. You are kidding, right?' He slapped the table. 'I've spent my whole life trying to avoid my parents and you think when I am at my lowest, when I need support, I should go and stay with them? Jesus, Grace, you just don't get it, do you? I have worked hard to build a family that is nothing like the one I grew up in, and I had it all, I bloody had it all!' He drew breath. 'Did I tell you that they called a couple of days ago and my mother said firstly how much she had enjoyed the funeral! I kid you not. She said "enjoyed" – that was her word. She was talking about the canapés and some other complete bollocks, like she was talking about a birthday party. I couldn't bear to listen and then she suggested that I meet up with Jack in London and go out for a jolly good dinner, by which she means get totally pissed and come back smiling with a stiff upper lip. I was just waiting for her to add "worse things happen at sea!" So thanks, but no, I don't want to go and stay with my parents for a bit, even if it would make you feel more comfortable if I wasn't here.' He let the suggestion trail, hoping that she would deny it. 'I'm afraid it's just tough shit, Grace, because whether you like it or not, I live here too!' He downed his drink and reached for the bottle.

'That's not what I'm saying. God, Tom, this isn't all about you. I don't want to see *anyone* – you or anyone else. I am constantly thinking of all the things I could have done or should have done and maybe she would still be here!' She held his gaze and continued. 'Did I give her that bug? Is it because of me? I'm worried we pushed for her to have the procedure. I should never have taken her to the consultant. I should have just kept my gob shut and kept giving her Calpol and sitting with her through the night when she had a sore throat.' Her voice wavered.

'Yeah, I think that too. Why did you insist on it? Why didn't you listen to my concerns and not be so bloody pushy? Why did you do that stuff, Grace? It's typical of you to make a decision and not rest until you've driven it through without stopping to think about whether it's for the best or not. But it's all a bit too late now, isn't it?'

'What do you mean, Tom?' Her voice rose an octave in indignation. '*We* agreed it was the right thing to do – no more antibiotics, no more earache. We discussed it! Are you saying that it *was* my fault?' She didn't want to hear his response.

'I'm not saying that, but where the fuck have you been for the last three years?'

'*What?*' Her voice was thin, squeaky. She sat up straight, as though this might aid her understanding.

'Oh, come on, don't look so shocked. I mean, since Chloe was born it's all been about you and your bloody career. How's Grace doing at work? Is she okay? Is she tired? How can we make Grace happy? Let's all be quiet and let Grace have a nap. Let's make her pasta, cups of tea, iron her shirts. Gracie the great provider! And as for another baby, forget it! Forget what I wanted or what was best for Chloe, it's all about Grace, the wonderful, warm, maternal creature that she is – but she only wanted the one, what the fuck is that all about?'

‘What are you bringing that up for? What does that have to do with anything, Tom?’ she squeaked.

‘Because in my head it’s all connected, that’s why. Everything you didn’t do and everything you did. Why did you insist on her having it done? Why did you? What was wrong with her having the odd sore throat?’ He was crying now, crying hard.

‘That is so, so unfair, Tom! I didn’t insist, and it wasn’t the odd sore throat, it was every week. I thought she would suffer less and you agreed! We discussed it! You have no idea what I’ve been going through. You think you’re the only one suffering, but you’re not! I tried to keep her safe, but I couldn’t be with her twenty-four hours a day even if I wanted to; no one cou—’

He cut her short and was shouting now, shouting loudly, almost enjoying the release. ‘No, not no one, Grace, just not you. You were never with her twenty-four hours a day, that was my job. I was there for her while you were off having it all, the highflying career, the lunches with Jayney, the drinks in the city. Like anyone gives a shit about fucking pretty pictures that sell things – what you do isn’t valuable! What I did was important. It was me that looked after her, every day of her life! It was me she cried for, me that did everything for her.’ He thumped his chest. ‘Every day, Grace, that was what I did: I looked after Chloe. I was Chloe’s daddy. You just weren’t here for her ever.’

Grace felt as if she had been physically attacked. Each

word was like a punch to her gut. 'That is not true, Tom! I always wanted to be home with her, it was me that had to jump up to the alarm at five in the morning, me that had to slog it out on that shitty commute. Every day I worked myself to the point of exhaustion. And all I wanted to do was stay home and be her mum. You have no idea how many nights I cried because I wanted to be home with her—'

'Oh, poor Grace, my heart is bleeding for you! I saw the way you used to shrug her off if she came near you with dirty fingers and you were wearing one of your expensive suits. You weren't a proper mum, you were a fucking sham, a part-time mum just playing at it when it suited you, with that bloody phone never far from your hand, constantly working, checking in. You've been preoccupied since she was born, so don't give me that crying-at-night bullshit, because you never offered to stay at home, you couldn't wait to leave the confines of this house, you would never have stayed at home with her – you never did! Not Gracie – she needs to be the big career woman!'

Gracie stood from the table, scraping the chair against the floor, knowing she had to put some space between them. With trembling legs she staggered from the room, a whirling tornado of anguish, anger and hurt, stumbling up the stairs two at a time, bumping blindly into the walls. Her heart hammered inside her chest. Bitter words filled her mouth that she didn't want to swallow, knowing that if she did the taste would never leave her. She turned on the stairs and raced back into the kitchen. It was her turn to shout.

'Yes, you are right about that, Tom, I did need to be the career woman. Not through any conscious choice, but because you are totally fucking useless. Another baby? Who are you kidding! How would you have coped? You had so much help with Chloe, how would you have managed with a baby as well? Oh, imagine the luxury of being married to someone who would let me stay at home for a bit and look after my child. Imagine that, a man who could actually support his kids! We wouldn't have lasted five minutes if it had been up to you to provide for the family, or would you have just called Mummy and Daddy and got a hand-out like you've always done? God knows, you wouldn't risk pursuing a career, in case, God forbid, you might actually fail! Christ, Tom, you've spent your whole life running away! Running away from your shitty, crazy, fucking whacko parents, and from work and responsibility. Rather than deal with anything, you can just have a laugh with the boys, meet Paz for a coffee and hide somewhere; you're like some spineless creature, concealed away from the big bad world. You are nothing and you have achieved nothing – you're a joke. How proud Chloe would have been to have the only dad in school that could bake a cake from scratch! You really are pathetic!'

Tom let out a loud guttural shriek as he jumped up and charged at her. Taking her chin into his palm, he drew back his other arm, his fingers balled into a fist. Grace closed her eyes and waited, almost wanting to feel the force against her face. They stood for seconds, locked in the grotesque pose as their breathing slowed, both trying to process the accusations and damaging slurs that had been hurled.

Tom slowly lowered his hands and wrapped them around his torso. With his head bowed, he cried. Grace matched him tear for tear, gulping and swallowing her distress as she skulked from the kitchen like a wretched thing, wanting to retreat to the space under the duvet where she could be alone. Both were experiencing a new level of shock. They had gone too far and they knew it.

Eight

Sepsis is the biggest cause of maternal death worldwide

It had been a while since she'd needed to get to grips with her hair straighteners, but sitting now in front of the mirror of her dressing table, she combed her hair, letting the sections slip between the ceramic plates, smooth and kink-free. Concentrating, with the small magnifying mirror raised to her face, she dabbed the plum shade over her lids and applied two coats of lengthening mascara with her eyes wide. A slick line of black liquid liner sat close to her lashes and was finished in a neat flick upwards at the outer edge of each eye. She sucked in her cheeks and swept the pale pink blush over her cheekbones, ending in a rounded apple on the cheek, just as she'd been taught when she started wearing make-up as a teen. Her lipstick was a neutral taupe shade, brushed on and then the excess kissed off into a tissue. She looked into the mirror and practised her smile.

Grace stole out of the house, quietly closing the door behind her, not wanting to interact with Tom, whom she'd been avoiding as best she could for a while now. She climbed into her car and headed off to catch her train into London. The memory of their fight spun round her head like a halo of guilt. She couldn't rationalise what had been said and couldn't decide how much of it was true, but individual words hammered inside her skull, loud and obstinate. Every gap in thought allowed one to creep through. *'Sham'*... *'career'*... *'pathetic'*. She willed them to go away, too exhausted to sort her thoughts into any semblance of order, but this only added to the cloud of confusion that consumed her.

It might have been her imagination, but she felt that all eyes were on her, as though she was now somehow marked. Her fellow commuters, strangers on the train, people who worked in her building, it was as if they all knew that she had lost her child, were all snatching surreptitious glances, whispering behind cupped palms, or simply staring. She combed her fingers through her straightened hair and ran her middle finger around the outline of her lipstick as she felt the heat of their gaze. *I didn't lose her. She got stolen from me. Sepsis took her. It wasn't my fault. It really wasn't. It could happen to anyone. It could happen to you.*

Grace kept her eyes downcast and made her way into the Shultzheim Building, trying not to think of the person she had been when she left on that Friday night only a few weeks ago. It felt like another lifetime. It was another lifetime. She tried to remember what had filled her head before this grief filled every bit of her. She couldn't.

Jayney ended her phone call the moment she saw Grace enter the office. Placing the receiver down, she stared at her friend, blinking, palms splayed on the desk as if unsure of what to say. Slowly she wandered over, enveloping Grace in a hug and talking while patting her back. 'I can't believe you're here. It's lovely to see you, but what are you doing here? We weren't expecting you for an age. What do you need? What can I get you?'

'Nothing.' Grace shrugged her friend free and tried out a smile, before making her way to her office.

Tucking her skirt under her thighs, she sat down, staring at the squares of paper that dotted her workspace. Handwritten notes covering minutiae – Tom had been right in that respect. *'Like anyone gives a shit about fucking pretty pictures that sell things.'* What was it that had driven her to be the best at her job? What did it matter? What did any of it matter? The truth was it didn't. Not really.

She stared at the noticeboard, where some of Chloe's artwork was pinned along with a grainy printout of her beautiful face, taken by her dad on the swings. She was holding an ice cream with as much on her face and in her hair as she had eaten. *I think you're at pre-school. I think that's where you are today, and if I think that, I can carry on. Everything is just as it always was: you are at pre-school and I am at work. It's just a normal day.*

Jason entered Grace's office as he knocked, a habit she found intensely irritating. It was bolshie and presumptive, a perfunctory knock that meant he was coming in regardless, an expression of the authority which he had snatched from her hands. She couldn't count the number of times he'd strolled in and immediately offered 'Sorry to interrupt' as a kind of catch-all to excuse the inconvenience.

'There you are, Grace.'

'Yes, here I am. Who else were you expecting to find sitting behind my desk in my office?'

He smiled and was unusually hesitant as he took the chair on the client side of the desk. 'How are you?'

Broken. I am broken. 'I'm fine.' She had no desire to share her innermost feelings with this man.

'We were all so sorry to hear about Chloe. It's honestly hard to know what to say. We are all so sad. It's truly unbelievable.' He shook his head.

She thought she saw a flicker of genuine emotion, possibly discomfort.

'Thank you, Jason.' She concentrated on not crying, not here, not in front of him. Never here or in front of him.

'I thought the funeral was beautiful. It's hard to find the positive about a day that was so very sad, but it was a lovely, moving service, Grace, conducted with...' He struggled to find the word that conveyed his overriding feeling. 'Dignity.'

She stared at him, wide eyed and silent. 'Were you there?' She'd had no idea.

'Yes.' He knitted his eyebrows, convinced that she'd seen him. 'We all were.'

Grace took a deep breath. Rather than bring her comfort, this only served to make her feel exposed, vulnerable, as though the lines between her work and home life had been uncomfortably smudged. An event so personal, so upsetting, had been subject to the scrutiny of her colleagues, some of whom she merely nodded to at the water cooler. They didn't know her, they hadn't known Chloe, and yet they had seen her on that day, with her mind altered and her heart ripped open.

Jason coughed and shifted in the seat. 'To tell you the truth, Grace, we are all rather worried about you.'

She wondered if he had been practising this speech.

He continued. 'And frankly, no one was expecting to see you back at work so soon, although of course you're welcome any time, if it helps.'

Grace snorted through her nose. 'Welcome any time?' He reminded her of one of her schoolmasters, writing her annual report and detailing her lack of ability. 'You make it sound like I'm a guest! This is my job.'

Jason carried on, not allowing her derision to interrupt his flow. 'Of course it's your job.' He nodded. 'But we think it might be best if you took a bit more time. These things are so distressing and you might feel up to it one day and horrible the next.'

'Yes. These things are distressing.' She held his gaze, determined not to make it easy for him.

Jason rubbed his face, pushing his thumbs into his eye sockets to relieve some unseen pressure. His speech was quieter now, measured. He leant forward in the chair and placed his arms on her desk, his hands clasping each other in a sincere pose, imploring almost.

'Grace, look, I'm not the baddy here. If you must know, I volunteered to come and talk to you because I thought it might be a tad easier coming from me because we're friends.'

She noted his confused expression and saw that he was genuine in his assumption that they were friends. She nodded.

'You shouldn't be here. Forget the board, who are not only worried about productivity but also no doubt find the whole topic uncomfortable and unpalatable. You need to think about yourself, not them; you need to think about you and Tom. And you do need to take some time, Grace. You need to go and grieve and think about things and put some space between you and this place. If I were you, I'd bite their bloody hand off – paid time off to go and think. Please, forget the politics. I'm genuinely worried about you.'

She stared. 'I don't know what I'm supposed to do now. I can't remember anything, not even how I'm supposed to spend the day,' she confessed.

'I can't even begin to imagine…' he whispered, no doubt picturing a little one he loved.

Then you are very lucky. 'Thank you, Jason.' A trickle ran down the back of her throat; she had only recently learnt that you could cry on the inside.

'How long do they want me gone for?'

He took a deep breath. 'They have assumed that you will be non-operational for three months, but speaking off the record, I reckon you could push it to six.'

She was grateful for his honesty. 'Have they got someone to take my clients?'

'Yes, I think Roseanne has picked some up. And I'll take the rest. I'll caretaker them for you, ready for when you come back.'

Grace smiled. Roseanne – it figured. She was a climber, forever tapping into her phone, available at all hours. Tom's words flew into her head. She coughed and began to clear her papers from her desk and stuff them into her rucksack. She felt, for want of a better word, frail. 'Do me a favour, Jason.'

'Yes, of course. Just name it, anything...'

'Can you tell the board, thank you for their concern and that I will be back sooner rather than later.'

He smiled at her. 'Will do.' He meant it.

Ten minutes later, Grace stood on the grand marble steps in the dismal cold and allowed the warm fetid air from the passing traffic to waft over her. She was waiting for her pre-ordered taxi, booked on the company account as a gesture of goodwill. *Thanks a bloody bunch.* Grace felt her jaw tense. She felt embarrassed, having over the years seen people similarly signed off, nudged out of the door. The malingerers, the hypochondriacs, the weaklings, those who welcomed a bit of enforced R&R via the most spurious of ailments, ranging from frozen shoulders to anxiety over a long commute. She could never have imagined being among their ranks and yet here she was. She wondered if it was really necessary. Should she be at home? Wasn't it best to try and distract herself with work? The doctor had written a prescription for sleeping pills and anti-depressants, saying that she'd been through a lot. *No shit, Sherlock*. The little tablets had become the foundation on which she balanced. Tiny, shiny stepping stones that led to where? Stability? Normality? *Here's hoping...*

Standing with her back to the building, she could feel the collective twitching of a hundred vertical blinds behind her back. What were they all looking for? Evidence of her 'breakdown', no doubt. She was sorely tempted to run up and down the street with her pants on her head but decided against it; she didn't have the energy or the inclination when it came to it. Concentrating on the throng of people who crowded the pavement on the other side of the road, Grace was drawn to a glimpse of a pink wellington and a flash of pink raincoat. 'Chloe?' she called out.

Don't be daft. Chloe is at pre-school and I am at work. It's all okay. She is at pre-school and I am at work. I will see her when I get back. She's at pre-school, probably sticking something onto a loo-roll tube or painting another picture – we need more space to hang them. She smiled at the thought.

Jayney approached her cautiously, with the hesitation of one uncertain of the reception she might get. She edged forward with her head bowed and her body bent, as though trying not to wake her.

Grace noted her reticence, her odd stance, and it puzzled her.

'Grace?'

'Yes, Jayney?'

'How are you doing?' Her mouth curved into a smile, but her eyes remained fixed.

'I'm doing fine.' She nodded. *Chloe is at pre-school and I am at work. It's a day like any other. That's all. It's all going to be okay.*

'We're a bit worried about you.' Jayney's voice was soft; she studied Grace's face as if looking for clues.

'That's what Jason said and I told him, there's no need. I'll be back sooner rather than later.' *We discussed it, Tom and I. I asked if it was a good idea, we didn't want her to have sore throats and earaches and sleepless nights and painkillers, we discussed it as a couple. I wasn't pushy, we agreed.*

'It's just that...' Jayney bit her bottom lip.

'What is it, Jayney?'

'You haven't got any shoes on.' Jayney pointed at Grace's feet.

She looked down and saw her dirty, bare toes, wiggling them against the cold marble and feeling the winter chill for the first time. 'I must have lost them.' Grace felt confused; she ran her hand through her fringe, trying to remember, knowing she was wearing them when she left the house.

'That's okay, love, not to worry. You've got a pair upstairs under the desk. Let's go back up and pop them on and you can take my coat so you don't get cold.'

'I don't need your coat, Jayney!' Grace shook her head.

'I think you might, darling. It's a chilly old day and... and...'

'What?' She felt quite confused, afraid and overwhelmed.

'You've got your pyjama top on.'

Grace placed her hand at her throat and let her fingers run down the buttons. *How did that happen?* She stared at her friend. *It must be because I can't think straight because Chloe died. She died, Jayney, but I can't say it out loud, I can't admit to you what's happened, I can't admit it to anyone, so I need to pretend.* 'I need to get home. Chloe is at pre-school today. And I need to get home now. Everything is okay, Jayney. Everything is okay.'

Jayney could only nod, placing a hand on her friend's back, crying silently as she escorted her back up the steps to the office.

Nine

*Healthcare professionals can do six simple things in the first hour that can **double** a patient's chance of survival. These are known as the Sepsis Six*

Tom answered the front door. Grace heard their voices from the kitchen, where she was sitting looking at facts about the disease that had taken her little girl. She was jotting down information in her notebook, still trying to make sense of things, often adding her own little comments. Hushed whispers floated in from the hallway. She closed her eyes and wished she were upstairs, hiding. She didn't want to see anyone.

When her sister walked in, she was surprised at her appearance. Alice had lost a significant amount of weight in a short space of time. Her hair was now a dark auburn, making her skin look even paler, and dark circles lay beneath her eyes. She sat at the kitchen table with her hands in her lap; there was no extravagant gesture, no wave, not much sign of life. Every aspect of her was diminished.

Grace filled the kettle and took up the seat opposite her sister.

Alice looked up for the first time. 'I could never have imagined not knowing what to say to you, but I really don't. I feel like we're strangers, and that's just as upsetting as…'

'Maybe we are a bit strange to each other at the moment. We've never had to deal with anything like this, that's why. It all feels so surreal.' Grace pulled her thick cardigan around her torso and stretched the sleeves down to cover her hands. 'I lost the plot a couple of weeks ago – don't know if Tom told you? I went into work in my pyjamas. Just wasn't thinking straight. And apparently I was on the platform at the station shouting at Mr Mumble that he should stand up for himself and tell his mother he's a grown man.'

'Who's Mr Mumble?' Alice was confused.

'Just some man on my commute, who it turns out is actually called Alan and was very sweet to me, apparently.'

Alice nodded uncomprehendingly, content to listen.

Grace carried on. 'As I say, I totally lost the plot. I keep thinking that I might wake up soon or that someone will produce Chloe from behind a screen. Ta da! Like it's all been some extravagant joke.'

They were silent for some seconds, both considering how to continue. Even saying her name felt like an enormous pressure.

Alice broke the silence. 'I keep thinking about our old neighbours – that mother and daughter that used to live below Patrick and me. I think I told you at the time, about when the mother died and I went to visit the girl and tried to cheer her up by being jolly and over-enthusiastic about the adventure she was about to take. God forbid, I even took some Marks & Sparks goodies, as though some Belgian chocs could make it all better. I had no idea how she was feeling, but now, when I look at myself in the mirror, I see the same expression that she had when I first saw her and I know that instead of nice words, a big smile and a box of bloody chocolates, I should have just held her and let her grieve. I hope she forgave me. I was so naive.'

'I doubt she will have noticed. If she was as numb as me, then nothing really registers. People want to tell me about their experiences, about their loss, as though that could possibly help in some way. How could it? I just nod, switch off, don't listen. I don't care what anyone else has been through. I can't. And I know that no one fully understands what it's like for me, even if they think they do.'

'I didn't know anything could hurt this much.'

'Thankfully, Alice, I don't think any of us did.'

'I can't sleep and I can't eat. I just wish it had been me. Why, Grace? She was so small and I always felt so responsible for her whenever I was with her. And now it's like I've let her down...'

'You didn't let her down. It's just one of those things.

Sepsis took her, that's it. Sepsis, a horrible thing that can act fast and we weren't on our guard because we didn't know we had to be.' Grace felt slightly irritated that she was being called upon to offer comfort; it was her daughter, her little girl that had gone. She didn't want to have to keep going over the event in fine detail, she had enough terrible images of the day and the funeral to last a lifetime, in fact a dozen lifetimes. And she was fearful of being given a new picture to cram into her already overcrowded mind. *Please, Alice, no more.*

'I loved her, Gracie. I loved her so much.' She broke away in sobs.

'We all did, Alice. How are Mum and Dad?' Grace had noted that they'd visited less and less in the last couple of weeks, heeding her request to be left alone and probably thinking that they too should try and return to some semblance of normality.

Alice shook her head and took her time in forming a response. 'Mum's dreadful. She looks so old. She isn't speaking much and Dad doesn't know what to do, he can't make her talk and he's worried sick. I'm worried about her and worried about him worrying about her, and I'm worrying about you. The whole thing is just so awful.'

Grace had to agree, it was so awful. 'I don't know what to do next, Alice – I'm not sure how I should be and I don't have the space to worry about anyone else.' *Not you, not Mum and Dad, not even Tom, we hide from each other.*

'What can I do to help you?' Her sister leant forward.

Grace shrugged. 'I don't know. Nothing.' It was the best she could come up with.

Grace made her way into the doctor's surgery. Wary of running low, she was keen to collect her new supply of tablets: the ones that kept her afloat during the day and the others that knocked her out at night.

She took her place on a padded blue chair in the waiting room. A pregnant woman struggled to lower her bulk onto the chair opposite, exhaling loudly as though she had completed a real feat. A boy of around three toddled in, swinging his arms purposefully to help propel himself forward. He stood in front of the woman, his mum. She tutted and pulled a wet wipe from a packet, running it over his mouth. He turned his delightful large brown eyes on Grace and, smiling, handed her a red plastic car.

On any other day, in any other circumstance, Grace would have admired him, but not today. 'Thank you,' she managed and placed the toy on her lap, looking away, hoping that would be enough to placate the child and he would lose interest.

'Is he being a nuisance?' his mother asked.

She couldn't cope with seeing him and was in no mood for small talk. *Please, just take him away and leave me alone*. 'No. No, he's fine.'

She picked up a dog-eared, grubby magazine and tried to

immerse herself in the impending marriage of two reality-TV stars with matching haircuts that she had never heard of. She read and reread the same lines over and over because the information would not stick in her head. She had trouble remembering almost anything these days. There was a strange new disconnect between what her eyes saw, her ears heard and her brain registered, as if everything was out of sync. It was a similar feeling to being on a stationary train alongside another stationary train and then one suddenly moves off and for a few seconds you're not sure whether it's your train or the other one. That was how she felt, every moment of the day: disorientated and not sure of anything, even the everyday stuff. She trusted nothing; nothing was as it seemed. Because if the world could take Chloe from her, then anything could happen, anything...

Her memory loss affected even the most basic things. She would picture faces of people familiar to her, family, friends, colleagues, but could not, no matter how hard she tried, remember their names. It was pointless trying to read a prescription, an instruction, an article, and as for a book... Forget it. After finishing the second line, she would forget the first and have to go back to the beginning. She lived in a state of permanent confusion.

'It's a nightmare coming to these appointments with him, he gets so bored.' The mother was intent on making conversation. Her dungarees were taut over her distended tummy, which she showed off with pride, and her striped

T-shirt strained over her large breasts; she was ripe with child, new life. Grace could just about make out the slogan written in a jaunty script across her chest: 'Baby Under Construction!' It made her think of Alice. A multitude of wooden beads sat around the woman's ample neck.

Grace nodded. Nightmare indeed.

'My fourth.' The woman patted her stomach with self-congratulation.

Grace nodded again and tried to concentrate on the text of the article.

'Husband says this is the last, but he's said that twice before!' The woman tapped the side of her nose with her index finger and laughed, insistent on conversing. 'As if he has any say!' She chortled.

Grace thought of Tom's words. *'As for another baby, forget it! Forget what I wanted or what was best for Chloe, it's all about Grace, the wonderful, warm maternal creature that she is.'* She lowered the magazine as if she knew what was coming next. She felt a rise of panic in her throat and the familiar punch to her gut in anticipation. *Please don't ask me. Please don't...*

'Do you have any?' The woman adjusted her beads and craned her neck to look at her son, who was on the other side of the room gazing at the fish tank set into the wall.

This was the first time since Chloe's death that she had been asked this question. She swallowed nervously. Grace realised at that moment that there would be many firsts.

The dental appointment in the calendar that needed cancelling and... *Oh God...* Grace gasped at the thought of it: Chloe's first missed birthday, Christmas without her. She clenched her jaw and tried to concentrate on the woman's awful, awful question. How was she supposed to answer? What was the correct response?

I had one, Chloe, but she died. She died, my daughter died... Grace tried to say the words, pushed her tongue against the teeth, tried to sound aloud the unbearable truth. But she couldn't. To say the words out loud would be like making it true, accepting it, turning it into fact. It was an admission, something she simply couldn't do.

'A little girl.' She kept it brief. Her stomach flipped, her heart constricted and the breath caught in her throat.

'Oh, you lucky thing! I've got three boys and this is another little Herbert.' She patted her stomach again. 'We're going for a football team! Mind you, it's great for hand-me-downs, saves us a fortune. How old?' The woman sounded delighted: a common link, the bond of motherhood. From here they could progress to the benefits of breast-feeding and the merits of disposable versus terry when it came to nappies.

'Three.' Grace swallowed, wondering if this was how she would feel for the rest of her life, wondering if there might ever come a day when this dark gauze of total distress might be lifted. *You will always be three, Chlo. Always three...*

'Oh! Same age as Alfie! Are you thinking of St Saviour's? My older boys are there and it's wonderful. Bit of advice, though: try and get her name down now, as places are like hen's teeth.' The woman spoke out of the side of her mouth as though she were imparting a secret.

I miss you, Chloe. I miss you now and I miss your future. I used to picture you starting school, pictured you at university. I wondered who you might marry. I pictured it all...

'Grace Penderford.' The tannoy system called her name and she was thankful. She stood and placed the little red car on the table before walking into the consulting room without looking back.

Ten

In the UK, sepsis kills more people than breast cancer

Grace hovered on the landing with one hand on the suitcase and the other on the door, steeling herself. She took a deep breath and turned the handle, closing the bedroom door behind her. The creak of the door made her cringe, ashamed and upset by what it used to represent.

Letting her eyes dance from wall to wall, she studied the room that had been her little girl's favourite place. They had chosen the sugar-pink paint when she was born. The miniature white furniture with heart-shaped cushions, a later addition, had turned it into a real fairy-tale palace. Framed photos of family, friends and special days out sat at jaunty angles on the windowsill. There was one of Chloe with her grandma; one of her sitting between Grace and Tom in a pub garden; and, her particular favourite, one of Chloe on a trampoline, wearing fairy wings and holding a wand. She pictured that day, saw Tom carefully reaching into the back seat when they arrived home, lifting Chloe from her car seat, remembering how she'd flopped over his shoulder as he carried her up the stairs. She was exhausted by the day at Paz and Polly's housewarming. Tom had pulled off her sandals and laid her on this very bed, as Grace watched, smiling and freshly sun-kissed, from the doorway.

Grace placed her hand on Chloe's duvet and felt warm at the memory of the little bundle, snoring safely in her beautiful room. She picked up the silver building blocks that spelt out her name, a christening gift from Tom's parents, and folded them into the bubble wrap, before putting them into the open suitcase that she had set on the little bed. Next she carefully unhooked the mobile, which probably should have come down a year or so ago anyway, a bit too babyish with its cartoon-like fish. She then turned to the bookshelf that occupied a recess by the fireplace, lifting from it the cherished editions of stories that had been hers: *Alice in Wonderland*, *Tom's Midnight Garden* and others. Grace wrapped them all, deciding to protect them and stow them away in the loft. She pictured Chloe sitting up in her bed – *'Another story! Mummy, I need another one!'* – as she thumped the little pink comforter that kept her warm in the night. Had she made time? Could she have read to her some more? Had she let work take priority? Again, she felt sick at the thought.

Opening the wardrobe doors, she surveyed the tiny

wooden hangers holding the garments that were all in various shades of pink and purple and ran her fingers over the little items that her daughter had loved. Grace removed a party dress and a dress-up fairy frock and began folding them methodically, inhaling the scent from each one as she wrapped them in tissue and placed them in the suitcase, as if packing for a family holiday. Her mind drifted to Chloe in the swimming pool on their vacation last year, jumping into the pool with abandon. There had been no hesitancy or concern about being in water too deep; she knew that she'd be safe, that her daddy would catch her, he would always catch her.

'What are you doing?' Tom's voice boomed from the doorway, startling her.

They'd had no contact for days, both still smarting from the hurt they'd inflicted on each other in the preceding weeks, both preferring to be alone rather than risk greater pain.

Her response didn't come quickly enough and so he repeated his demand, more loudly this time, as though volume would help her comprehension.

'Grace, I said, what are you doing?'

She looked at him as if to say a response was unnecessary. Wasn't it obvious what she was doing?

'I'm packing some of Chloe's things away, her precious bits and pieces, to keep them safe. I thought that would be better than letting them gather dust in here.'

'You are *what*?' His tone was incredulous. 'How could you do that?' He shook his head, looking at her as though she was committing a heinous sin.

She felt her cheeks flame, ashamed and awkward. She hadn't thought she was doing anything wrong. There were some things she wanted preserved – not that she needed objects to remind her of Chloe, she never stopped thinking about her, picturing her, not for a single second.

'I... I thought I'd pack some things away, keep them safe and dust free in the loft,' she repeated quietly.

'No! No you are not! You are not going to do that! How dare you!' Tom spat, his eyes darting around the room, as if trying to spot what she had taken.

Grace felt like a thief caught in the act.

'You put it all back! You put it all back *now*! Do you hear me?' His anger made his voice waver. She felt mildly afraid. Before she had the chance to act, Tom rushed forward from the doorway, thrust his hands into the suitcase and removed the books, shoving them back on the shelf, at least one of them upside down. She resisted the temptation to turn it the right way up. He pushed the small clothes onto the hangers haphazardly and was muttering under his breath, indeterminate mumbling that made little sense.

Grace backed out of the room and left him to wrestle with what was left of Chloe, all that represented her, her little dresses and toys, so many inanimate objects that for him had taken on extra meaning.

She held on to the bannister and listened from the landing as Tom worked like a whirling dervish. It was as if every second was of the essence: the quicker he could get things back into place, the sooner he could restore... what? Chloe? Order? He could restore neither of those things, never Chloe and not even order, not in the present circumstances. Grace felt a wave of pity for her husband as he grappled for control over Chloe's things, simply because he could, when everything else around him was in chaos. She looked down at the carpet and saw Chloe's little feet falling inwards as they poked from beneath her nightdress.

Grace made her way to their bedroom and sat on the end of the bed, her shoulders slumped in utter weariness. She stared at her face in the distant mirror, barely recognising the person that glanced back, who seemed lost and ill at ease, like a visitor in that environment, not at all relaxed. She looked around the room, at the carefully placed faux-Victorian fauna prints, the bespoke handmade Roman blinds that hung artfully at the windows, the much-deliberated-over duvet cover and the vintage bedside tables with their boudoir-chic lamps, and she felt nothing. When she'd put the room together, with its myriad accessories, it had all felt so important. She'd spent hours poring over fabric swatches, canvassing the opinions of friends, rejecting shades on a mere whim and reworking ideas and combinations until she'd been certain that it was just about as perfect as it could be. Getting each detail right had been what mattered. She remembered coming home and entering the room with something akin to pride, standing at the grand entrance each night before bed and surveying her perfect kingdom. No corner or ensemble would have been out of place in a glossy magazine; she had achieved the tasteful and the enviable. It gave her great satisfaction.

Now, however, there was no temptation to turn a candle so that it faced the 'right' way, or to plump a cushion, or to make the dishevelled bed, or even to wash the greasy bed linen. The whole place looked neglected and unloved. The photos were covered in a layer of grey dust, random piles of laundry, both dirty and clean, littered the floor, and the blinds were pulled unevenly, a fact that would have driven her to distraction in her previous life, the life before, when she had the energy to be concerned with the smallest detail. She could no longer imagine the luxury of existing without the pain in her chest and behind her eyes, without the huge rocks of grief that weighed down her stomach and made her breathing laboured. Couldn't imagine living without having to consciously remember how to walk and how to talk. She couldn't imagine living in a world where the perfect decor of her bedroom mattered at all.

Grace felt as though she wanted to go home. She wanted to twist her key in the lock, shut the door behind her and feel safe, but therein lay the problem: she *was* home and yet it didn't feel like home any more. She wanted to get away, far away, and she wanted to go as quickly as possible. She felt as if she might literally suffocate on the atmosphere within the house; she wanted to be somewhere that Chloe had never been. Jason had been right; she needed to go somewhere where she could think, where she could grieve.

Flipping open her laptop, she searched for 'places to get away'. That seemed to be synonymous with romance, she realised, as she trawled through the numerous advertisements for remote hotels with swim-up bars, the promise of 'new experiences' at couples-only resorts and, God forbid, 'fun!' Grace wanted none of these; she wanted to be alone, somewhere quiet where she could hide from the world. She dug deeper, until something caught her eye. She stumbled across the ad by accident – it was a small, insignificant placement as a link to a bigger site offering outdoor pursuits and she'd nearly missed it.

The wording was simple and drew her in: *Compact, private, no-frills, self-contained studio. The Old Sheep Shed at Gael Ffydd Cottage offers peace and quiet in the beautiful Welsh countryside...*

It sounded perfect, intimate, a place where she could choose not to participate, could hide away, somewhere to spend time alone and think. Even making the decision gave her a flash of mental clarity, as if confirming that she was doing the right thing. She clicked open the link and read some more.

Eleven

In the UK, sepsis kills more people than breast and bowel cancer combined

Grace flicked the indicator and turned right onto yet another winding country road, driving at a snail's pace. She hoped that the satnav would soon catch up, watching as it struggled to find a signal.

She was grateful for her sturdy 4x4 and its elevated driving position. With each turn, the hedgerows grew thicker, the lanes narrower and the view more breathtaking. She found herself climbing slowly up one side of a steep valley. The fields rolled down to her left in a glorious verdant patchwork until they met the wide twist of a river, where full and ancient trees stooped and flourished at the water's edge. In a mirror image, on the other side of the river, fields edged with hedgerows sloped upwards to the top of the ridge, and beyond, the crests of dark, imposing mountains framed the picture. The big sky was blue and despite the chill of the April day, the sun sat high, glinting off the water that foamed where it hit boulders or clusters of twigs gathered against the bank.

'It's beautiful,' she whispered.

It was all she'd needed to read in the description: 'peace and quiet'. Grace didn't doubt it would be quiet, but peace? That was another thing entirely. She had booked it there and then, for a month.

Dusting off her suitcase from under the bed, she'd thrown some clothes into it, along with one of Chloe's nighties, which lived under her pillow; she always slept with her hand on the fabric, keeping a small part of her daughter close. The next day, as she'd zipped up her travel bag, she'd realised there was something she'd forgotten to do, but couldn't for the life of her remember what. Her memory was still very sketchy. Evidence of this lay in the half-drunk cups of tea that littered the surfaces in the house. Daily, she would put one down, forget where, and plod to the kitchen on autopilot to make another.

'Money, car keys, toothbrush, pyjamas, pills. Money, car keys, toothbrush, pyjamas, pills.' She slowly ran through the list of essentials, touching her hand to each thing, trying to spot what might be missing, like the party game she'd played as a child, where objects were removed from a tray.

'What are you doing?' His deep, croaky voice startled her from the bedroom door.

Grace had to look twice at the hunched, growly man who had walked into the bedroom – recognition took a fraction longer than was comfortable for them both. *It's okay, it's Tom. Don't be scared, it's just Tom, the new Tom, different...* Her interior monologue quieted her nerves. And with this, it came to her. Of course! That was it! That was the thing! She had forgotten to tell Tom that she was going away.

Without enough time to think of any preamble or soften her words, she made her statement. 'I'm going away. I need to go away. I'm going to Wales.' It sounded more matter-of-fact than she'd intended.

'You're going to Wales?' His tone held the accusatory note that she could now identify as the forerunner of an argument. She felt her spirit flag at the prospect.

'Yes. To a studio, actually.'

'"A studio, actually."' His imitation of her tone both irritated and upset her. 'How lovely for you, Grace, a holiday in Wales. Your timing really is impeccable.'

She hung her head and tried to summon the strength for the exchange, wishing he would just go away. 'I'm not going on holiday, Tom. I just need to get some thinking time, some space. I'm going mad here.'

He snorted in derision. 'That's perfect. You think you're the only one? We are falling apart. The world has turned to rat shit and you are going to drink wine and stroll the hills? Fucking marvellous!'

'I told you, it's not like that. I need to keep sane, Tom. I need to go somewhere that I can think because I'm sinking and I'm scared.'

He shook his head. 'Listen to yourself, Grace. "I... I... I..." Here's a newsflash for you: we have both lost her, *we*, us.' He pounded his fist against his chest. 'This thing happened to both of us and now I'm losing you. Have you any idea how shit my life is? How low *I* am?'

She reluctantly looked into his sunken eyes and knew that he spoke the truth. It saddened her to hear his next words.

'There used to be a time when we would have sunk together. I am so, so lonely, you have no idea.' He couldn't stop the tears.

She hated to admit that to see him like that angered and repulsed her. She didn't have the capacity to help him, he was right. She was way too busy looking after herself. Grace knew it was a pivotal moment, as he stood some two feet away with his head hung forward, begging her to hold him, imploring her to join him in a circle of grief. But she had turned away from the sight of his distress and continued to pack.

The memory of that conversation came to her now as, instructed by the satnav, which had finally located her, she turned the car onto a narrow, bumpy track signposted 'Gael Ffydd Cottage'. The five-bar gate was wedged open and she continued slowly along the potholed, pebble-strewn driveway, which had been built along a ridge that dropped away by a foot on each side. Eventually she pulled up on a tarmac apron, next to a battered, square caravan whose windows were missing, and an equally sorry-looking Land Rover, the open flatbed of which was partly covered in rather moth-eaten faded green canvas.

To the right of the apron was the side of a house – a cottage, to be more precise – made of pale, rough, irregular stone, which seemed to have a greenish tinge, beautiful against the lush setting. One solitary window sat below the apex of the roof, and smoke curled from a single chimneypot above that. Grace inhaled the scent that reminded her of childhood, of bonfire nights and sitting in front of her grandma's real fire with her parents on either side, while Alice danced in the firelight. She had felt happy and safe. Safe – unlike Chloe. Grace shook her head, not wanting to succumb to tears, not here, not now.

To her left was an open-fronted workshop in which she could see a workbench scattered with various tools and a pile of logs neatly stacked in one corner. The sagging, rust-coloured pantile roof was tightly bound with ivy.

Turning her head, she listened. There was nothing bar the babble of water in the valley, the crow of birds overhead and the far-off bleat of sheep in the distance. It was just as the advert had said: quiet.

'Hello.'

She hadn't heard the man or his fat blonde Labrador approach. She jumped a little.

'Sorry, didn't mean to startle you.' He raised his palm as if to show he came in peace. 'I tried making a noise, but you were miles away.' He clicked his fingers and patted his thigh. The dog sidled up to him and stood by his leg. 'Good boy, Monty.' He splayed his flattened palm in front of the dog.

Grace turned to face the middle-aged man, noting his bushy, wild beard, curly dark hair and muddy Rigger boots. His thick red plaid shirt was unbuttoned over a once-white T-shirt and his oil-covered jeans were tucked into his boots.

'I was just, looking... the view... it's incredible.' She blushed, hating having been caught unawares, wondering if she'd been talking to herself, as she often did.

He nodded. 'You found us okay then?'

Grace suspected visitors were scarce as he'd correctly surmised that she was his guest. 'Yes. The satnav went on strike a couple of times, but I've arrived, so...' She let this trail, in no mood for making small talk with this stranger.

'Let me grab your bag for you.' Without waiting for a response, he took a step closer. Grace realised he wasn't as old as she had first assumed; his clear, hazel eyes were those of someone closer to her own age.

'Oh!' She was more than capable of carrying her own bag but didn't want to offend with a rebuttal.

She opened the boot and watched as he grabbed her suitcase. Then she gathered up her pashmina and rucksack from the back seat and followed him down a rather precarious path that wound around the back of the workshop.

A few steps across a muddy field sat a single-storey rectangular building, made from the same green-tinged stone as the main cottage. Grace gulped, wondering where on earth she was heading, alone in the middle of nowhere with the bearded man. She looked back towards the track and realised she was miles from the road. *You can always jump in the car and disappear if you don't like it. Just make your excuses and leave, say you're going to fetch milk or whatever and just go.*

'I'm Huw by the way.' He turned towards her and offered this a little gruffly, as if remembering that such information might be useful. 'And this, as you might have gathered, is Monty.' He patted the dog's head, his tone flat and formal.

'I'm Grace.' She nodded, her response indicating that, like him, she was not interested in making friends – of the human or dog kind. She had to admit, it was rather nice to be in the company of someone who didn't talk to her as though she were going deaf or was wounded, someone who didn't know to ask quietly how she was doing, someone who didn't define her by her grief or her daughter. The frisson she felt at this realisation was instantly replaced by a spike of guilt that lanced her gut. *Happy? Relieved? How dare you.*

Huw placed the case on the small flagstone terrace at the front of the property and paused at the bottom of the three steps that led up to the green front door.

Grace was busy taking in the details of her home for the next few weeks. 'I can't believe how quiet it is here. It's another world.'

'That's the idea.' He turned towards her, smiling briefly and seeming to appraise his guest's face for the first time.

She did likewise. He looked kind behind his rather bluff exterior.

She noticed the brightly coloured pottery that was inlaid in the concrete tread of the steps, a kind of haphazard mosaic that made a stunning pattern. 'I like the steps.'

His response was slow and considered. 'I made them.'

'How?' Her interest was genuine.

'I take pots and jugs, cups, any old bits and pieces that belonged to my mother-in-law and my aunts, and I smash them—'

'You smash them?' she interrupted, trying to imagine taking her mum's or gran's china and deliberately breaking it. Her heart constricted at the thought of the pretty cups and saucers that she had inherited from her great-gran, which she'd thought she would pass on to Chloe. *Pointless now... all pointless.* That was how her mind worked: every topic, every thought, no matter how disconnected from the discussion in hand, led her back to Chloe, and every time her thoughts turned to Chloe, she pictured her little girl, lying on the hall floor in her nightdress as Tom shrieked and howled, and each time this happened her heart split and slowed a little bit more. She longed for the day it would simply stop.

'Yes, I smash them up and then pick out pieces at random as I work, so it's authentic and not too ordered.'

Grace studied the shards of floral china, the squares of green glaze and the dazzling blue willow-pattern fragments that turned the ugly concrete steps into things of beauty, works of art.

'They look lovely,' she said as Huw climbed to the front door.

'I see no point in hiding them inside a closet, gathering dust. This way, I get to look at them every day and my guests get to enjoy them too.'

'What does your mother-in-law think?' She pictured Olive's face on being told this was how her beloved china had ended up, smashed for the sole purpose of putting it into a step.

'She knows I'm a little crazy. Trust me, it's not the maddest thing I've done.' He flashed her a smile; his teeth were white and even. His thick hair was curly and almost black and he had to run his hand through it every so often to remove it from his eyes. His skin had the natural dark tan of someone that worked outside in all weathers.

Huw lifted the latch of the door that Grace noticed had neither lock nor keyhole. He pushed the door open and stepped away, gesturing for her to enter. She trod past him and found herself inside The Old Sheep Shed.

Huw leant in and placed her bag inside the front door. 'I'll leave you to it. Feed Bertha when she's hungry. She's like a child: if you keep her fuelled and give her a bit of attention, she'll cause you no trouble.' He pointed at the log burner.

His words took Grace to a fraught autumn morning and Chloe jumping up and down on the spot. 'I want my breakfast! I want my breakfast! I want...' she had chanted over and over as Grace searched high and low for her car keys, in danger of missing her train. She couldn't be late, not that day. Their German clients were in town and she couldn't afford to muck up the day or the pitch that she'd been working on for the last month. She knew Jason was desperate to intervene.

Her tone had been sharp, impatient. 'For God's sake, Chloe, I know! Daddy will be down in two seconds and he'll get you your breakfast,' she'd snapped.

Chloe's bottom lip had trembled. 'But I... I... want Mummy to get it,' she'd stuttered through her tears.

'Well, Chlo, Mummy would love to be able to stand here and cook you scrambled eggs and watch a bit of Mr Tumble, but some of us have to go out into the big wide world and earn the cash to buy the bloody breakfast!' She spoke as she tore around the kitchen, peering under newspapers, delving into the fruit bowl and raking through Lego. 'Where the hell are my keys?' she shouted.

Tom trotted down the stairs, scooped Chloe up onto his arm and kissed away her tears. 'Hey! Come on, Chlo! No tears, we've got Shanta's birthday party today, you can't cry on a party day!'

His ability to calmly soothe had made Grace's jaw tighten. 'Have you seen my car keys?' she barked, hands on hips, hearing the tick of every second that passed on the kitchen clock.

'On the windowsill in the cloakroom.' He smiled.

Yes, of course! She had rushed in the night before, desperate for the loo...

Grace tried to remember what had happened next; had she said goodbye to Chloe? Had she kissed her? *Did I say 'bye, Chloe? Did I hug you, make sure you were okay? Were you happy when I left? Did you have a nice party? I can't remember! I remember the meeting and the pitch; they were pleased. That made me happy, but I can't remember leaving you that morning. I'm sorry, Chlo. I'm sorry I snapped at you. I wish I'd stayed and made you breakfast, I really do, but I didn't know. I thought I had all the time in the world to make it up to you...*

'You okay?' Huw asked, a little awkward in the company of her fixed stare and agitated fingers.

She nodded, not trusting herself to speak. She wasn't okay, but it was nothing that he or anyone else could fix.

'If you need anything, I'm around.' With that, Huw closed the door and disappeared.

Grace looked around at the stone walls, which had been painted brilliant white, making the long, low room bright and clean. There were no windows, but at the far end, wide French doors with red gingham curtains pulled back on either side framed the most incredible view. It was a clear, uninterrupted panorama of the valley, with a large mountain behind and the river in the centre, like a moving work of art and one she knew she wouldn't tire of staring at. Beyond the doors, Grace could make out a deck on stilts, with two wooden steamer chairs positioned at angles to make the most of the view.

On the right side of The Old Sheep Shed was the lounge area. A low, soft, linen-coloured sofa stood in front of the window with a coir rug alongside. A multitude of cushions in reds and creams, some with ornate appliqué and others in checks, littered the back of the sofa. The kitchen area was to the left of that. One small grey French dresser sat against the wall, holding a collection of grey and white fluted plates, cups and bowls; table linen was folded neatly on its top, along with a tray that held four fat wine glasses. To the left of this and forming an L-shape was a length of scrubbed wooden work surface, where there was a sink, a small drainer with a fridge underneath, and a hob and microwave. Two bar stools sat on the other side.

At the far left end of the room, pushed up against the wall, was a very grand, if slightly dented and rusted, black wrought-iron bed. Here too a plethora of red and cream cushions in various shapes jostled for position on top of the heavy white lace counterpane. In the corner was an opaque glass shower cubicle behind a screen, and a loo. The only mirror was behind the washbasin next to the loo, a vast, ornate, gold mirror that would have looked more at home in a fancy hallway than in this small bathroom space inside The Old Sheep Shed.

Opposite the door and in the middle of the wall stood the centrepiece, a round, white, log burner with intricate scrollwork on its heavy iron door and a flue pipe that exited via a neat hole in the ceiling. Next to the fire sat a tall wicker basket full of logs and hooked over the side of the basket was a pair of black wrought-iron tongs.

Grace sank down onto the bed, suddenly overcome with exhaustion. As her breathing slowed and her blinks grew longer, her gaze fell on the tin, Shaker-style side tables with cutaway star designs on the top, and their simple candle lamps with red gingham shades. The place was perfect. The Old Sheep Shed was pretty, quiet and everything she'd hoped it would be. She let her head fall heavily into the bolster pillow and fell into a deep, deep, restful sleep.

She woke suddenly; a noise had disturbed her, which on reflection could have been a dog barking. Sitting bolt upright on the bed with her heart racing, she realised she was in her clothes and in the dark; day seemed to have slipped into night and she had no idea where she was. She swallowed as she placed her arms behind her on the creaking bed, remembering that she had travelled to Wales. Reaching over, she flicked on the lamp and let her pulse settle as her eyes roved over her new surroundings, now softly lit by the creamy glow from the lamp. It was cold and she was more than moderately hungry. A quick poke around the fridge and cupboard revealed milk, bread, butter, jam, coffee and a bottle of red wine. That was kind of the man. *Huw – that was it. Huw.*

Grace decided against food, finding the idea of wine far more appealing. She pulled the cork and removed the duvet from the bed. Making her way out of the French doors, she settled herself on one of the steamer chairs on the deck and tucked the duvet around her legs. As she swigged from the neck of the bottle, she stared into the darkness and wished she had a packet of cigarettes; she hadn't smoked since college, but that didn't stop the craving that came over her suddenly.

Gazing at the landscape, she tried to focus but could only see the black outline of trees and mountains against the inky-blue night sky. Animal noises, hoots and rustles drifted up from the valley below. She had no idea of the time. Her phone was still on the front seat of the car; she would fetch it later. She should probably drop Tom a text to say that she'd arrived safely, not that he was speaking to her, but that didn't really matter, not in the grand scheme of things.

The stars seemed closer there, as she lay back on the recliner. 'Where are you, Chloe? Where did you go?' She spoke aloud as her tears came. The ferocity of her sobs took her by surprise and she howled, gulping for air and releasing the pent-up anguish that had swirled inside her for too long. *Chloe died!* Those words, all these weeks later, still felt like a lie. It couldn't be true. But it was and Grace knew that it would always feel that way. She would never, ever get used to it.

'Hello?' A voice cut through the darkness.

She looked to the right of the deck and could see a beam of light making its way across the field. She didn't answer but tried to stem her tears as she trembled inside the duvet, a little confused and unsettled.

'Grace?' It was the man from the cottage.

'Yes,' she confirmed, as if it might be someone else sitting on the deck in the middle of nowhere.

Monty lumbered up to the deck and barked at the figure huddled in the darkness.

''S'all right, Mont. Good boy.' Huw calmed his companion. 'Can I come up?'

Grace noted his outline, the curly hair and bushy beard. She nodded; it made little difference to her.

'Grace?' He clearly hadn't seen her nodding.

'Sure,' she managed, sniffing her distress down her throat.

Huw climbed the three wide stairs of the deck and sat on the end of the empty steamer chair opposite. It was a moment before he spoke. She wondered what he wanted but had to admit, having someone else sit with her in the darkness was quite comforting.

‘I heard you from the cottage, you sounded upset, so I thought I’d come and see if you were okay.’

‘I’m fine,’ she lied.

‘Would you like me to get Bertha going? It’s a cold night.’

‘Huh?’

‘The log burner?’

‘Sure, thanks.’

She watched as Huw made his way inside and switched on the kitchen lamp, letting more light filter out over the deck. He took some logs from the basket, dropped them on top of the old embers, stoked the flickering blaze and fiddled with the grate in the burner’s door. He wiped his hands together before sitting back down. ‘She’ll be roaring in a bit and that’ll cosy up the shed.’

‘Thank you,’ she whispered. ‘I fell asleep and when I woke up I didn’t know where I was,’ she offered by way of explanation for her tears and the half-drunk bottle of wine.

‘Righto, well, as long as you’re okay. You startled Monty, he’s a crap guard dog really, more likely to bring you a shoe and wag his tail than savage you.’

‘That’s good to know.’ She smiled towards the dog. *Go now, please, and leave me alone…*

‘Forgive me for asking, but you seemed very distressed. You sure everything’s okay?’ He picked at his nail, avoiding eye contact.

‘Yes, thank you.’ She too looked towards the floor. ‘I’ll be fine after a good night’s sleep.’

Huw stood and made his way off the deck. He clicked his tongue and patted his thigh and Monty ambled into step beside him. 'Well, you better get a move on, night's almost done, it's nearly four o'clock in the morning.' He strode across the field back towards the cottage, fading into the dawn.

Grace shook her head; she'd thought it was early evening. No wonder her howls had carried across the silent countryside. Lying back on the recliner, she wrapped the duvet around her form and reached for what remained of the bottle of wine.

She stayed there, watching the dawn break over the valley, saw the rumbling, smoky mist roll along the river, kissing the bank as it went. The sky turned from inky blue to pale mauve, with shafts of golden light firing from the sun as it rose, bathing the fields and all it touched in a beautiful glow. Long shadows stretched and yawned across the meadows, alerting every living thing that it was time to wake. She found herself reduced to tears again, but this time by the sheer beauty of her surroundings. Eventually she shuffled inside, still wrapped in her duvet, and sank into the soft bed, where she slept until mid morning.

Freshly showered and in her jeans and sweatshirt, she reached into the car for her phone. There were no missed calls, no messages – and no signal. It was odd not to see the usual texts from her mum and Alice, sending love and reiterating their availability, should she want to chat, which she didn't. Nor was there a rant from Tom for her to ignore, telling her how sad he was and how selfish she was.

'Morning,' Huw called from the workshop.

Grace lifted her hand in a wave as she extricated herself from the car. *Please don't come out and talk to me, please just stay where you are...*

Huw stepped out into the sunshine, wiping his hands on a rag. 'How are you feeling this morning?' he asked, without embarrassment but sounding concerned.

'Good. Thanks.' She felt her cheeks colour. 'Sorry about, erm...'

'Don't mention it.' He avoided her eyes. 'It's sometimes the best medicine to howl at the moon, quite literally. It means you're looking for guidance and wisdom and facing your deepest fears. It can lead to the resolution of problems. Least that's what I find.'

'Right.' Grace nodded. *Bloke's a bit of a nutter.*

'It worked for me, anyway.' He smiled awkwardly before turning and walking back into the workshop.

Grace spent the day walking, tramping high and low, concentrating on putting one foot in front of the other and not stumbling as she navigated tracks that led down to the river. She hiked briskly through the mud and overgrown grass of the bank. With her walking boots clogged with soft clay, she ploughed on, working up a sweat inside her ski jacket and enjoying the mindless roaming that made a perfect diversion. She didn't have to think; she just had to keep walking.

Eventually her legs tired and she stopped to rest on a hillock to catch her breath. With her arms braced against her knees and her breathing rapid, she looked up in time to see a flash of pink disappearing behind a tree. Her heart raced as she narrowed her eyes, staring at the space. She reached across thin air and was about to call out when her phone let out a volley of beeps and rings as it found its signal. An avalanche of messages poured in.

Grace pulled the phone from her pocket. She deleted the countless texts from her mother; the first few were full of wordy sentiments of encouragement, then they decreased in frequency and length, culminating in a single kiss. There were two from Jason, one sending her good wishes and another giving a brief update, informing her that Angharad had approved the costs for their project; she deleted them both. Tom had sent a single message. This she read slowly. *Hope you are having fun. Courtesy would dictate some contact, if you get the time. Tom (husband).*

She read and reread the lines, absorbing the sarcasm. She knew he was hurting and that thought alone made her feel sick with guilt. She had left her husband alone with his grief, how could she begin to explain that this was necessary for her very sanity? She pictured him sitting on Chloe's bed, inhaling the scent from her duvet, and she felt a wave of love for him. Closing her eyes, she then saw him sitting at the kitchen table, a fug of brandy fumes hovering in the air and his face twisted with hatred as he fired his poisonous darts at her. '*Where the fuck have you been for the last three years? Since Chloe was born, it's all been about you and your bloody career.*'

'I really can't cope with you, Tom, I can't cope with anything.' She spoke to the river that burbled and flowed two feet from where she sat. Grace let her breathing steady and unzipped her jacket; too warm now as the sun sparkled its diamonds through the branches of the huge trees that made a hazy canopy overhead. Her eyes scoured the trunks and branches over the water, searching for a flash of pink. She looked to the right as twigs cracked and something scampered through the undergrowth.

'Monty!' She heard Huw's voice before she saw him.

Monty halted at the sight of her and pushed his nose into her hand.

'Hello, Monty.' She smiled. The dog barked loudly.

'Monty! Shush!' Huw yelled, before catching up. 'Oh, hello! Are you stalking me?' He gave his hesitant smile.

Grace shook her head.

'I was joking.' He swallowed, his humour squashed by her blank stare. 'We've been fishing.' He held up a hook with three fat fish hanging from the end.

'What are they?'

'Brown trout.' He smiled, clearly happy with his catch.

Grace looked at the majestic fish, each a good thirty

centimetres in length. They had shiny orangey-brown underbellies and a stunning pattern of little black orbs in slivery orange rings on their backs. They were beautiful. Their dorsal fins were fanned and fragile, their eyes were blank and their mouths hung open. Grace felt her tears gather.

'I didn't mean to upset you.' Huw hid the fish behind his back, like a crap magician.

'It's okay, it's not your fault. Everything upsets me,' she said, her voice a monotone.

Huw joined her, staring at the water in silence, unsure of the correct response. When he eventually found his voice, his suggestion was practical. 'Would you like a lift back? I've got the Landy up the top.' He pointed up to the ridge above them.

Grace stood and dusted the damp from her bottom with her flattened palms, not sure if she could face the tramp back.

She climbed into the filthy Land Rover and Monty barked and lay in the space at her feet, clearly put out at having been ousted from his usual seat. Huw placed the fish in a cool box in the back and started the engine. Grace, as a passenger, was able to look out at the countryside, free from having to stare at the satnav.

'It's so beautiful here. Do you still think so, or do you take it for granted?'

Huw shot her a sideways glance. 'I never take anything for granted. Every day when I wake up I take a minute to look out of the window or stand in the yard and just drink it all in.'

'You're lucky,' she whispered, thinking of the rat race in the city, the rushing along crowded pavements, the elbowing onto packed trains, standing cheek by jowl in the fierce heat of summer or wet through in the winter rain.

Huw gave a snort of laughter. 'That's me – lucky.' He stared ahead.

'Have you always lived here?' she asked as they slowed and pulled into a shallow lay-by to let a vehicle similar to their own pass.

'Huw!' The man in the flat cap nodded and waved his palm in thanks.

'Richard!' Huw waved back.

'No. I grew up in Winchester and moved here six years ago.'

'Oh, I thought you'd been here forever.'

'Why?'

She shrugged. 'Don't know. It just seems to suit you and you seem very at home. With your dog and your fishing and your steps.'

'I've always been at home here. Gael Ffydd Cottage was my grandmother's home, where my mum grew up, so I spent all my childhood holidays here.'

'Lucky you.'

'Yes, again, lucky me.' He kept his eyes on the road.

'It must be a lovely life,' she mused.

'It's the life we want.' He smiled.

'Does your wife work?' She couldn't imagine having to get into work everyday from there; it made her own semi-rural commute seem like a doddle.

'No. She doesn't.' His voice was flat.

Grace decided to remain quiet and enjoy the view. It was fifteen minutes later that Huw turned into Gael Ffydd Cottage.

Grace jumped down from the cab. 'Thanks for the lift.'

Huw disappeared round the back of the Land Rover. 'We're cooking these up on the bonfire tonight, if you want to join us.'

Grace was unsure if she wanted company and stared at him, rather lost for an answer.

'Tell you what...' He eased the awkward silence. 'You'll know when they're cooked because you'll smell them. So if you want to come over, great. If not, more for us!' With that he clicked his tongue, tapped his thigh and walked across the apron towards the cottage with his dog trotting faithfully by his side.

After her second hot shower of the day, Grace sank down onto the duvet, feeling the ache in muscles that had been underused in the past weeks. It had felt good to get her body moving again.

It was late evening when the smell of the barbecue wafted over to The Old Sheep Shed. Grace inhaled the scent of the trout roasting on the open fire and began to salivate. She'd had little appetite of late and to want food was a new and welcome sensation.

Looking into the mirror above the sink, she was surprised by what she saw. Old mascara sat caked beneath her eyes and her hair was unbrushed, ratty at the back. She pulled her fingers through her bob and pushed it behind her ears before giving her face a good scrub with soap and water. It looked clean at least, if a little flushed. Throwing on a cardigan under her ski jacket, she tied her pashmina around her neck and headed into the encroaching darkness, across the field towards the back of the cottage, where the orange flames of the bonfire flickered up into the night sky.

'Hi,' she called as she approached.

Huw was sitting on a fishing stool a little way back from the fire, in the middle of which was a metal brazier with the fish on a pole dangling over the flames. He looked up and waved, then indicated an empty stool by his side. A lantern on a hooked stick stood behind him, throwing out a dim arc of light.

'That's a great fire.' She sat down, holding her palms up towards the heat, instantly mesmerised by the dancing licks of flame and the embers that crackled, spat and glowed against the dark sky.

'I've had a bit of practice.' He smiled. 'I'm renovating the old cowshed.' With his thumb he pointed over his head, behind the cottage. 'And when the work gets tough or I'm tired, I remind myself that this will be my reward: a bonfire with the old timber and rubbish from the site. It's something I love to do.'

'I can see why. It's hypnotic, isn't it?' She stared at the flames, watching as tiny ash fairies flew from the pyre and danced up into the blackness. Spiralling upwards one by one, elegant in their grand ascension.

'Yep. It's the thing I remember most about my holidays here – great fires and that smoky smell in all my clothes. They always seemed to smell more smoky the closer I got to Winchester. I hated it when my mum washed my jumpers and the smoke was gone. I knew it meant I was going back to school and that my fun was over.'

'Where's your wife? I'm sorry, I don't know her name.' Grace picked up a stick and snapped off the end, hurling it into the centre where the colour glowed amber.

Huw hesitated. 'Her name is Leanne. And she died.' He prodded the logs and lumps of cardboard in the fire with an old railing spike that was perfect for the job.

There was a respectful silence while both adjusted to this new level of openness.

'Oh. I didn't know.' She swallowed. 'When you spoke about "us", I assumed...'

'I meant Monty and me,' he explained. 'Although I do still think of her here, of course, think of her with me.'

'I feel terrible. I didn't know. I'm sorry,' she repeated,

pulling the sleeves of her cardigan over her hands, watching his face, which was lit by the orange firelight.

'Well, no, why would you? No harm done. I like talking about her.' He forced a smile.

'You do?' This surprised her; she was still unable to mention Chloe without feeling her insides fold in on themselves in grief.

'Yes. She's my wife, it would feel odd not to mention her.' He blinked.

'When did she die?' she whispered, wondering if this was prying or taking an interest.

'Six years ago. Hence the move.'

'I'm sorry, Huw.'

'Thanks.' He nodded. 'You don't have to keep saying sorry, you know.' He paused. 'She was killed by a car. It mounted the pavement as she walked home. It was quite a rainy day and the driver was old. He fumbled with the windscreen wipers, couldn't really see in the downpour, got confused, lost control, panicked and that was that. She was thirty-four.'

Grace steeled herself. 'I lost my little girl. She died too.' It was the first time she'd said the words, the first time she'd been able to. The phrases sat like slivers of glass on her tongue; once she'd launched them from her lips, she stared at the ground where they'd fallen, shiny among the dust and cinders.

There was silence while she recovered from the shock of

having said the words out loud and he recovered from having heard them.

'When was that?' Huw looked up from the fire.

'Three months ago. She was three.'

'Oh God.' Huw sighed. 'I'm so sorry.'

Grace nodded. 'She was killed by sepsis.'

'Is that septicaemia? Sorry, I don't know.' He shook his head.

'No, that's okay, not everyone does know. I didn't. I had to look it up. When they told me about it, I wasn't really listening, I couldn't take anything in.'

'I remember that.' He sighed again.

'I've been looking up facts and bits and pieces and writing them down in my notebook.'

'What kind of thing?'

Grace pictured her first entry. 'Things like "People suffering from sepsis might have slurred speech, just as people do when they have a stroke." It helps me to understand what happened. It used to be called septicaemia, but apparently that term's not accurate for what happens, so now it's sepsis. It's when the body responds badly to an infection. So, bacteria – an infection – makes the immune system react, but, instead of just controlling the infection to make you better, the body goes into overdrive and creates a storm of reactions that damages its own organs. And they can shut down. That's what happened to Chloe. Her organs shut down and she died.'

'Chloe.' He repeated the name. 'I could tell you were grieving when you arrived; you have that look, like you died but are still here. I can spot it.'

'That's exactly what it's like. Part of me did die,' she admitted for the first time.

He nodded and raised his eyebrows in acknowledgement.

'Does it get any easier?' she asked hopefully, conscious that he had a six-year advance on her.

His response was slow in coming. 'Truthfully? No it doesn't, not really. It will always be hard, no matter how much time has passed. It will always hurt you, shock you, take your breath away when you wake in the middle of the night and realise it's not some horrible nightmare. Even now there are days when I don't want to get out of bed, don't want to see anyone and so I don't, I just stay there and let the day roll over me. That's a freedom I have here.'

She was grateful for his honesty. 'What did you do before you came here to burn things?'

'I was an English teacher.'

'Oh, lucky you. I toyed with that as a career. I studied English and I love books, reading and writing... But I didn't want to be a student any longer. I think I was impatient to start earning and I kind of fell into my job.' She inhaled the smoky fumes, trying to think back to the time when she'd made that decision. 'And you resigned to come here?'

'No, they sacked me. I lost the plot on more than one occasion and the final straw was when a colleague and supposed friend took me to one side and reminded me that it had been six months. As if I needed reminding!'

Three months, one week, four days. She saw the calendar in her head.

Huw coughed to clear his throat. 'He suggested that I try and pull myself together because it was bad for morale and made other people feel uncomfortable. I already knew it made him feel uncomfortable – he hadn't talked to me properly, couldn't look me in the eye, as if what I was going through was infectious. He hadn't said a word about Leanne until that point, not one, nothing, like she'd never existed, like he hadn't been to our house and she hadn't made him cups of coffee.' He sucked his teeth and jabbed the pole at the fire.

Grace thought about her own friends. They fell into two camps: those who worried about her, dropped her a line, called her, offered help or just sat with her in silence in the kitchen, and those who had simply disappeared, silently receding into thin air, hidden behind a cloak of discomfort. 'What did you say to him?'

'Nothing.' Huw shook his head. 'I just punched him, punched him in the face, and then I left.'

She found his frankness shocking and yet strangely reassuring. It was almost a relief that he wasn't trying to tell her it would all be better in time, that time was a great healer. He was acknowledging quite the opposite and she appreciated his honesty. That sort of insight could only come from someone who spoke from experience.

'Do you miss teaching English?' She pulled her pashmina tighter around her neck to block the cold whistle of wind that blew up from the river.

'Yes, sometimes I do. I used to love it. I write now, that's how I spend my evenings when I'm not burning things.' He poked the fire and the flames roared.

'What do you write?'

He shifted on the canvas seat. 'All sorts – poetry, ideas, plans. I'm still waiting for inspiration for the great novel.'

'They say we all have one in us.'

'They do and I think that's true. Don't you?' he asked.

'Sometimes. I think it takes courage to put your thoughts and ideas on paper and show them to strangers. It takes a confidence I know I don't have – it'd be like opening up my diary and inviting the world to take a look. I'm not sure I could do that. Not sure if what I write could ever be good enough or if anyone would want to read it.' She shrugged.

'What *do* you write?' She had caught Huw's interest.

'Oh...' She sat up straight. 'Not novels, or even stories, really. More snippets, ideas, funny things. Things to make Chloe laugh or because sometimes it feels like the easiest way to make sense of stuff.'

'I get that.' He nodded. 'Do you have other kids?' he asked as he pulled the pole from the fire and removed the fish, using a fork to skewer them onto two paper plates.

Grace took the plate he offered and put it on her lap. 'No. I didn't fall pregnant with Chloe until I was a little older. I thought it would be good to get further up the career ladder before I had children. I guess that's part of my sadness, that I didn't have her earlier, get to be her mum for longer. I keep thinking about that. I thought it was important that we had a house and a pretty room for her and all that stuff, but actually I just wish I'd had her younger and held her more.'

'Ah, the great "if only"... Trust me, that can send you mad.'

'I think I'm already there,' she admitted. 'I don't know if having other children would make it better or worse right now. I think I would hold *them* that little bit tighter and be distracted by them and they would be a reason to keep going, give me hope, I suppose. But also I like the fact that I can just curl up and switch off; there's no one relying on me or needing me to keep it together.' Tom's image flashed into her mind. 'It's so recent; it's still very hard for me. It's very hard for me to talk about or even to think about it. I'm numb.'

'That doesn't really change with time; you just get better at hiding it. I've learnt not to punch people, no matter how much better it might make me feel.'

Grace let out a laugh, a short burst of joyfulness that flew from her. It was a sound that she'd forgotten; it felt alien. Immediately, she placed her hand guiltily over her mouth. *I'm sorry I laughed, Chloe. I'm not happy, I'm not! I miss you. I'm sorry.*

Huw clearly felt no pressure to fill each silence with noise or meaningless small talk. He simply let her cry. His words, when they came, were carefully chosen.

'It doesn't get easier, Grace, so I'm not going to tell you that it does. It will never be easy. It's like living with a big black hole in your world, but it gets okay for you to remember, not so painful.' He unconsciously placed his hand over his heart. 'It's as if the you that you were before gets replaced with a new you. How you feel, the hurt, the pain, the longing, the sadness, it becomes part of you and you kind of grow to fit the new you, where all those terrible feelings and that energy-sapping grief are your new normal.' He looked across at her. 'Does that make any sense?'

Grace nodded. This was kind of what she expected: never to recover, but that time would take away the sour smell of grief that right now invaded her every breath.

'Are you married?' he asked nonchalantly.

The question floored her rather more than it should have. A simple yes or no would have sufficed.

'Yes, to Tom. He's at home.' She thought for a second about how best to describe the state they were in. 'We've kind of fallen apart. It's as if we're too injured to help each other. I can't take on caring for him, helping him. I know how terrible that sounds, and it makes me *feel* terrible. I don't like myself for it, but it's like I don't have anything spare.'

'Because you don't,' Huw said. He sat up straight. 'You should eat your fish and then go to sleep.'

He sounded concerned in a paternal way. Grace was touched. She felt a flicker of guilt as she pictured Tom.

Biting into the blackened flesh of the trout, she knew that if her heart weren't so heavy and her mind so distracted, it might taste good. But all food turned to ash in her mouth these days. She didn't want to enjoy food, she didn't want to enjoy anything. How had he phrased it? *'I don't want to get out of bed, don't want to see anyone.'* That was exactly how she felt, all the time. It was some comfort to be with someone who understood this, someone who wasn't Tom.

Grace laid the empty plate on the ground and patted Monty on the flank. 'Night night, Monty.' He was a little too close to the fire and she could smell the slight singe to his fur.

'Thanks for supper.' She spoke over her shoulder as she made her way across the field, leaving the warm orange glow behind her.

'Don't forget to feed Bertha!' he called after her into the darkness.

Grace nodded and let herself into The Old Sheep Shed.

Twelve

In the UK, sepsis kills more people than breast, bowel and prostate cancer combined

A few days later, Grace was woken by a light rapping on the door. She stumbled from the bed, gathering her cardigan around her trunk and lifted the latch to see Huw standing on the steps.

'Thought you might like to come with me,' he said with an edge of indifference that she'd learnt was just his manner. He began to back away from the building.

'Where are you going?' she asked, yawning.

'Into Hay-on-Wye.' He gestured down the valley. 'Got to pick up some bits and bobs, and I usually have a fry-up. If you fancy it.'

Grace nodded. *Why not.*

'Leaving in ten minutes,' he called, without looking at her, as he strode across the field towards the cottage.

Eleven minutes later, with her hair still damp from her

speedy shower, Grace climbed into the Land Rover, zipped up her fleece and put her rucksack on her lap. 'Where's Monty?'

'In the back. I think he's sulking cos you're coming along.' He shook his head in mock exasperation.

'Oh. I thought he liked me.'

'Don't take it personally, but he prefers it when it's just the two of us. Prefers it when I only have him to talk to. Plus you ate his fish.'

Grace smiled. She wound down the window, which juddered. Clogged, she suspected, by muck, judging by the smears of muddy water and paw marks on the glass.

There was something purifying about the air in the valley; it tasted sweet and as it flowed through her body and dried her hair in its gentle breeze, she felt calm, clearer-headed than she had in an age. It was as if she was hidden away from the real world, without the intrusion of email or television, or family members popping by. Not that she hadn't appreciated her mum and dad's concern, she had of course, but it was a relief not to have to sit quietly around the kitchen table with them like she had back home, a relief to be left alone with her thoughts.

'I was thinking about what you said the other night. In fact I spent all day yesterday thinking about my life now, and about what you said, how feeling like this is my new normal.'

He gave a small nod, started the engine and swung the Land Rover round.

Grace let out a deep sigh. 'And it helped. I've been waiting to feel... *better*, if you like. But knowing that I might never feel better has made me accept it and, strangely, that's actually made me feel less desperate, a bit. You know, like having a bad, bad pain and you can't function because of it, but then you find out it's never going to go away, so you have two choices. You can either lie in a darkened room and do nothing, forever. Or you can try and carry on, and learn to live with it.'

'That's pretty much the size of it.' Huw glanced at her before turning out onto the drive. 'And you do look a bit better, you've got a bit of colour.'

'I'm going to call Tom later. I need to speak to him. He thinks I ran out on him. I guess he was right.' She felt a little embarrassed; this man was a stranger and yet she felt comfortable sharing her innermost thoughts with him. She decided that it was because he was a stranger that this was possible.

'Oh, wow! That's a little more than a cowshed – it's a massive barn!' Grace stared at the shell of the building Huw was restoring. She couldn't see it from The Old Sheep Shed because it was hidden from view by the cottage and the copse. It sat at the top of the ridge, a long, low structure whose wooden rafters formed intricate patterns and were currently patched with tarpaulin.

'Yes, but it's what we used to call the cowshed. It's going to be beautiful, with a huge inglenook fireplace, a Welsh-slate floor, an Aga in the open-plan kitchen and a mezzanine library deck. There'll be a couple of bedrooms and a huge terrace with a view over the whole valley. Plus a herb garden out the back in raised planters that will provide colour from wherever you look from inside. Leanne always wanted raised planters. She drew pictures and wrote a list of all the flowers she wanted and why.'

'That sounds amazing. What will you do – live in it?' she asked as she gazed at it.

Huw shook his head. 'I'm not sure really. It's about six months away from being finished so I've got time to decide. I was going to live in it, but I'm thinking maybe I'll sell it and live off the proceeds while I write that great novel. Plus I kind of like living in my nan's house. It's where all my memories are. It'd be weird for me to abandon the cottage; I don't think she'd like it.'

'That sounds like a plan then.' Grace liked the simplicity of it.

Huw didn't respond. He was a man wary of making plans, knowing how quickly they could go awry.

The Land Rover trundled towards the town, between hedgerows that allowed only occasional glimpses of the valley below. Huw raised his hand in a wave at nearly every car they passed, the drivers of which did likewise. It felt like a proper community.

When they reached Hay-on-Wye, Grace craned her neck to peer out of the window at the steep and winding cobbled streets. She spotted several inviting-looking teashops and coffee houses among the higgledy-piggledy buildings that were clustered along the pavements. Signs swung from iron arrows or chains, nearly all of them advertising books of some sort – antique books, collectable books, children's books, historical books.

'What do you do here if you don't like cake or books?' she asked with a small smile.

'You move,' Huw said dryly.

He pulled up and parked the Land Rover next to the pretty clocktower with its distinctive ornate bellcote. The whole place was picture-postcard perfect.

Huw jumped from the cab and whistled as he tapped his thigh. Monty fell into step. 'I need to go up to Jones's Hardware and pick up some strimmer lines. Do you want to take a wander and I'll see you back here, and then if you like we can go get some breakfast?'

'Sure. I need a supermarket.' Grace pictured the empty bread bag, the contents of which had kept her in toast since she'd arrived. 'Thanks for getting that food in for me by the way.'

'There's Pugh's up round the corner, best bread in Hay.'

Grace watched his waxed jacket disappear up the road as she slung her rucksack onto her shoulder and set off to explore. She voluntarily stepped off the kerb to allow walkers in their heavy boots and spattered gaiters to pass, and she gazed into several bookshop windows, wishing she had the concentration to read. She liked the anonymity of being in a strange town. No one here knew who she was or what she'd been through; no one was whispering about her or nudging their friends with their elbows, and there was no morbid fascination about how she looked or acted. It was a relief not to have to worry about her effect on others, how, just by catching sight of her, people who knew her would be forced to contemplate what would happen if the shadow of sepsis fell over their lives.

Grace pottered in Pugh's lovely store, filling her basket with two freshly baked sourdough loaves, three bottles of wine, a couple of warm cherry bakewell muffins and a large wheel of soft Welsh goat's cheese wrapped in waxed paper. Carrying her cargo, she made her way back towards the car, thinking that actually she could eat breakfast. The bite of her hip bone against her palm that morning had reminded her that she needed to eat; she was thin, too thin. She arrived at the car and leant on the passenger door, happy to feel the rays of spring sunshine on her face.

A woman stopped on the pavement in front of her; she looked tired. Her greasy blonde hair was pulled into a tight ponytail and loose tendrils fell about her pallid face. She was pushing a buggy with a little girl, a toddler, sitting back against the curve of the chair. Grace found the distraction of the woman irresistible, wanting to watch her with a strange curiosity. *I used to be a mum like you. I had a little girl like that.*

She watched as the young mother suddenly bent forward, screeching at the top of the toddler's head. The child, as far as Grace could decipher, was guilty of asking repeatedly for sweets. In her anger the mother jerked the pushchair handles to the right once or twice, to make the pushchair shake. Grace had to restrain herself from intervening, from marching up to the woman and explaining that her daughter had been taken from her and that she would give anything to have her with her, demanding sweets, chattering inanely about nothing much in particular. Even if that meant she ate a ton of sweets, she would give anything, anything in the whole wide world to be in that situation.

Grace remembered the morning before Chloe had gone into hospital; she had wanted something to eat. Tom had reassured her with promises of ice cream when it was all over. She pictured Chloe nodding against her dad's T-shirt, gripping Dr Panda in her little fist. *And what did you do, Grace? You went to call Jayney. You put work first. She was hungry and a little nervous and you went outside to make a call. Why didn't you hold her tight, stay with her? Why didn't you tell her she didn't have to go? Why didn't you listen to her, properly listen and keep her home?*

Grace watched as the little girl in the buggy began to cry, before defiantly pulling off one of her flashing trainers along with her pink sock and flinging them onto the pavement.

And that was all it took. The sight of a chubby little foot with five perfect toes dangling in the air – it was enough to transport her back to the hall floor in the early morning, where vomit sat in a triangular stain across the wall and Tom was shouting, screaming. She saw the soft edge of Chloe's nightdress, resting on her shins, and those little feet…

'I'm sorry, Chloe! I should have just held you and kept you with me, but I didn't know! I didn't know!' Grace was only vaguely aware that she was shouting as she cried. As the strength left her legs, she slid down the side of the car and ended up slumped on the cold pavement with her head leaning towards the front wheel.

The young mother stared at her, then yanked at her little girl's pushchair to get her away from the strange woman on the ground. Grace placed her head in her hands and sobbed, unable to control the sadness that flowed from her.

She was suddenly conscious of Monty's soft muzzle against her arm. She opened her eyes as Huw ran towards her.

Huw dropped down onto the ground and placed his arm around her back. 'Come on, let's get you into the car. It's okay.'

He seemed to care little that people had gathered on the pavement, confused and fascinated by the spectacle. Monty barked in concern and backed away from the duo. Huw helped Grace stand and manhandled her up into the passenger seat. Grace flopped over until her head was practically on her knees and continued to cry, oblivious to anything else.

Huw drove steadily without speaking until he turned into Gael Ffydd Cottage and killed the engine. He jumped down and whistled for Monty, who knew the drill. Opening the passenger door, Huw undid the seatbelt and took her arm.

'Come on, Grace, let's get you inside.' He caught her as, with her eyes closed, she almost fell from the cab. With his arm across her back, he guided her along the path towards The Old Sheep Shed one last time. She leant heavily against him as he helped her up the pretty steps and pushed the door.

Stumbling towards the bed, Grace let herself tumble onto the soft mattress. She lay where she fell, uncaring about the hair that spread in a tawny sheet across her face, or the fact the she was still wearing her trainers.

Huw pottered in the kitchen area, putting the cheese in the fridge and the rest of the produce on the sideboard. He fed Bertha with several fat logs and flicked the grate before disappearing outside and returning almost immediately with the fishing stool from the garden. Monty loped in and lay on the floor at the end of the bed and Huw closed the door behind him.

Slowly Huw unfolded the fishing stool by the side of the bed, sat down, leant his back against the wall and stretched out his legs. 'Go to sleep, Grace. I shall sit here until you wake up.'

She felt her shoulders sink. There was something very comforting about knowing that someone would be watching over her as she slept. 'I miss her. I miss her so much. And I just can't accept that I won't see her again. I can't!' she mumbled as hot tears slid across her face and down into the duvet.

'I know,' he whispered. 'I know.'

Grace wasn't sure how long she'd slept, but as her eyes flickered open, she saw that Huw was dozing, his head resting on his chest, his breath even. Bertha was pushing a soft orange light into the room.

Grace scraped the hair from her eyes and sat up. The bed creaked and woke Huw.

'How are you feeling?'

'Bit better.' She answered honestly and with a clearer head, more than a little embarrassed by the situation in which they found themselves. 'I'm sorry, Huw. I don't know what happened. I just suddenly couldn't cope.'

'It's okay. You don't have to say sorry.' He took a deep breath.

'I'm a bit hungry.'

He stood and stretched his arms over his head. 'I'll let you get on.' Monty lifted his head in case they were on the move.

'Stay and have some cheese. If you'd like to.' She was suddenly nervous, not wanting to impose her friendship on him, but feeling quite fearful of being alone.

'Sure,' he said noncommittally as he made his way over to the kitchen area.

'Sit yourself down. It feels weird saying that to you in your house on your sofa, but you know what I mean.'

Huw nodded and sat.

Grace walked to the dresser and collected plates, which she placed on the breakfast bar, followed by the wheel of cheese, the sourdough loaf and the muffins. 'Wine?' She lifted the bottle of red in his direction.

'Sure.' He shrugged.

She plonked two of the fat wine glasses by the plates and fished in the drawer for a corkscrew.

'Here.' Huw stood and took the bottle from her. Removing his keys from his pocket, he unfurled a natty penknife and used it to twist and lever the cork. Then he took his place on one of the stools.

Grace sat next to him and cut the bread. 'Bread and cheese – not much of a supper, I'm afraid.' She smiled.

'Do you like to cook?'

'Not really, I bake occasionally with Chloe...' She swallowed. 'Used to bake... but not really. Tom does the cooking and I go to work. At least that's how it used to be, but I'm not sure now.' She drank the wine he'd poured for her. 'I'm sorry about today.' She stared at her glass.

'As I said nothing to be sorry about. It can hit you like that, suddenly and without warning, and it can be the smallest thing.'

'Does that still happen to you?'

'Yes.' He raked his beard. 'Leanne was a stickler for

lists, she was always consulting a list, or transferring things to a different list or ticking things off…' He paused and sipped his wine. 'I was going through a box of stuff I found in the garage a few weeks ago and I found one of her lists.' He stopped and briefly clenched his teeth. 'It was one she'd made for our wedding – you know, check flower ribbon colour, write the table plan, hire cake stand, loads of detail.' He shook his head, clearly having memorised it. 'And then the last thing on the list was…' He paused. 'Marry Huw and live happily ever after!' He downed his wine. 'And it reminded me of how she used to make me feel, how we used to laugh and laugh because we were so happy; how sunny she was, how excited, not just about the wedding, about everything, and how she made *me* sunny and excited. And now I'm not; I'm cloudy and miserable.'

'I think you're lucky to have had someone who loved you that much.'

'As I said before, that's me – lucky!' He gave a snort of laughter.

'Was she a teacher too?'

Huw shook his head and took a slice of bread. 'No, she was learning about horticulture, she wanted to be a gardener and a florist. She had grand plans to landscape places in the city, make urban environments more beautiful. She replanted the whole garden up here when my nan died – not just shoving plants in to fill gaps, she knew what plants should go where. She put a lot of thought into it. What job do you do?'

'I work for a marketing agency. I'm on leave – enforced leave, but I didn't punch anyone—'

'Good, because punching someone is never the answer.'

'No. I went to work with no shoes on and practically wearing my pyjamas and I didn't even notice.'

Huw gave a small laugh. 'Weren't your feet cold?'

It was Grace's turn to smile. 'No, not really. As I said, I didn't even notice.'

'What are we like?' Huw said, reaching for the bottle and refilling her glass and then his own. 'It's not the solution either, getting drunk, but sometimes it sure feels like it!'

They clinked glasses and sipped their medicine.

With half the cheese eaten, a large chunk of the loaf missing, the muffins reduced to crumbs and two empty wine bottles lying in the sink, Huw nipped to the cottage and reappeared with a bottle of port. He sloshed large measures into their wine glasses, then pulled the steamer chairs together on the deck. They sat in one each, with the duvet thrown over their legs.

'I've never done this, never sat outside in the cold and dark and had a drink!' He lifted his glass to the early evening sky.

'Me either, but it feels good, like I'm connected to something bigger than this shitty little life.' She took some more sips.

'It's not shitty or little, you're just at the cliff edge and it's scary and uncomfortable.'

'Are you saying I should jump?' She slurred slightly; the wine and port mixture was doing its job.

'I guess it's the only way you'll know if you can fly.' He threw his head back and laughed. 'Why is it so easy to give you advice I can't take myself!'

'Ah, well, that's the million-dollar question. If I was looking at my mates' lives, looking at their marriages, and they lived like me, I'd know what to say, but I can't see through the fog. It clouds everything.'

'Do you love him, Grace? Do you love your husband?' His inhibitions had departed with the last of the daylight. Sitting in the darkness, he felt comfortable asking.

Her response was slow and considered. 'I did. I do. I don't know. It used to be perfect and I thought we were happy. No, that's not fair, we *were* happy for a very long time. But if I'm being honest, the cracks were there before we lost Chloe. I work so hard, and I guess I resent that sometimes, it doesn't feel fair. We had a terrible row and we both said some terrible things. Not just heat-of-the-moment stuff, but as though we'd been storing up the bad things and that was the time to say it all. And, boy, did we!'

Grace sipped the warming liquor. 'It's as if we've been twisted apart and got so badly broken that no matter how hard we try, we can't fit back together because we're different shapes now.'

'Have you tried to fit back together?' he asked.

She shook her head. 'No. No, we haven't. We've been avoiding each other and now I'm here, I've run away. But there is nowhere else I want to be, Huw. I can cope here, away from everything and with you here to bundle me off the streets when I lose the plot. Thank you for that.'

She put her free hand under the duvet and sought out his fingers. Taking them into her palm, she squeezed them tightly. It felt strangely familiar and comfortable.

He responded by knitting his fingers with hers and laying them entwined against his thigh. 'I can't imagine not trying, not fighting for Leanne.'

They sat in silence for a moment, each reflecting on the other's words and enjoying the physical closeness of their joined hands.

It was nearly midnight when Grace felt her head loll against her chest. 'I need to go to sleep.'

She jumped up, pulled the duvet from them both and stumbled across the deck. Her feet caught in the quilt cover, which was hanging loosely around her toes, and she pitched forward and hit her head on the handrail for the stairs. Tumbling forward through the dark, with her hands outstretched, she landed in a crumpled heap in the mud.

She truly didn't know whether to laugh or cry. The alcohol had numbed her sufficiently so that she wasn't in pain, but when she put her hand to her forehead and pulled it away, it was wet. She sniffed the liquid that was falling in a warm trickle down her face and recognised it as blood.

Monty barked through the French doors, not liking the disturbance outside.

'Shit! Grace!' Huw leapt up and hurried to her side. Crouching down, he tried to assess the damage in his slightly sloshed state. 'Are you okay? Talk to me! Have you broken anything?'

'I think I've cut my face,' she whispered.

'Heaven's above!' He sighed. 'Come up to the cottage. I need to look at that in the light – you might need stitches.'

Grace stared to cry. 'I don't believe in heaven above. I don't believe in anything. So where is she, where is she now, if not in heaven?' She wiped her hand over her nose and face, smearing tears and blood into her hair and over her cheeks and fingers.

'I don't know. I don't know.' He put his arms around her and cradled her to his chest. 'But I do know that I need to get you cleaned up. Come on, come up to the cottage, there's a first-aid kit somewhere.'

Gingerly she stood, clinging on to him for fear of falling again and finding it hard to see through the blood, tears, snot and hair that clogged her eyes.

Monty circled them, sniffing and whining. 'It's okay, Mont. Good boy.' Huw slapped his thigh and the dog stayed close.

The inside of the cottage was very different to The Old

Sheep Shed. It wasn't pretty by intent, there was no particular design to it and nothing matched. It looked like the sagging, cotton-covered furniture, fringed standard lamps and dark-wood bureau had been there since it was built. Large potted plants took up space on the deep window sills and the floral wallpaper had long since faded to sepia, though it remained firmly glued to the thick walls. A large fireplace had coal and ashes spilling from it onto the flagstone hearth and a tarnished companion set stood like a sentinel to the side of the tiled surround. Small watercolours, capturing the bend in the river and the mountain tops, hung in clusters in the wall space between the dado rail and the sloped ceiling. A thick wool rug lay on the flags in front of the fire.

Monty flopped down onto another rug and sighed, indicating that this was his home, taking ownership, as if the carpet of dog hair wasn't proof enough. Huw lowered Grace gently onto the sofa and thundered up a narrow twist of wooden stairs, only to return minutes later with a tartan wool blanket, a large green first-aid kit and a glass bowl full of water.

'Lie down,' he instructed.

Grace did as she was told, twisting on the cushions until her head rested on one arm of the sofa and her feet, from which she had kicked her trainers, on the other. She inched her bottom across the base until she was comfy.

Huw flipped open the box and pulled out some cotton wool that he dipped into the bowl of water. He patted her face, chin and eyes; the cotton wool came away red. He squeezed it dry and dipped it into the bowl again, repeating the process before reaching once again into the tin and pulling out a bottle of TCP.

'This might sting a bit.'

Grace kept her eyes closed.

He tipped the strong-smelling disinfectant onto a fresh piece of cotton wool and dabbed it around her forehead, hesitating as he got closer to the gash on her forehead. It was a curved cut about an inch in length.

'Owwww!' She screwed up her nose and scrunched her eyes even tighter, which helped ease the pain.

'Sorry.' He winced. 'I've got some butterfly sutures, they might hold it, otherwise we'll have to get you to casualty. I'm in no state to drive, Grace. I'm sorry.'

''S'not your fault. And now it's your turn to stop saying sorry.'

Huw peeled the sutures from their backing and pushed one over the cut and then another and another. She grimaced again.

'We'll see how these hold and if they aren't up to the job, I'll take you to the hospital in the morning.'

Grace nodded. 'Are all your guests as much of a pain in the arse as me?'

'No.' Huw sat back against the sofa. 'I don't usually see them, not really. Maybe a quick hello when they arrive and a bye when they leave, but that's it.'

'Why do you think it's different for us?' she asked as Huw began screwing up sheets of newspaper and laying them in twisted bundles in the fireplace.

He sat back as if considering this. 'I guess we're kindred spirits.' He smiled.

Grace smiled too as she pulled the blanket up to her chin, ready to let sleep overcome her. 'I like that. Kindred spirits,' she whispered as her breathing turned to snoring and Huw lit the fire.

Thirteen

In the UK, sepsis kills more people than road accidents, breast, bowel and prostate cancer combined

The scab on her forehead healed in barely more than a week, leaving a thin white line that amused Huw no end. He delighted in pointing at it and saying, 'You're a wizard, Penderford!' But she cared little about the scar; her appearance was no longer of interest to her.

It was now the end of a long day in which Grace had hiked the river trail, stocked up on wine, olives and more of that fabulous sourdough bread, and cleaned her car with a sponge and some washing-up liquid. Monty had helped by barking and chasing the water from the hose, making the whole exercise a darn sight messier and more complicated than she had envisaged; she ended up drenched.

She sat in her sparklingly clean car with the engine purring, parked in a lay-by up on the road, drinking in the incredible views down over the valley. She exhaled and swiped the screen of her phone, feeling ridiculously nervous. It was hard for her to fully understand how she and Tom had fallen into this state, hard to picture how they'd been before, when they were happy. Happy parents. She was apprehensive about making the connection, but knew that the longer she left it, the more difficult it would be. Her finger hovered over the icon that meant home. As she closed her eyes, pressed the button and waited, she half wished there'd be no reply.

It took Tom a good thirty seconds to register that the phone was ringing – it had been days since he'd last spoken to anyone – and then to negotiate his way to the handset in the kitchen. The place was barely recognisable as the room he'd once kept in such immaculate condition. Every inch of available surface was now covered with dirty crockery and the foil containers and detritus of a dozen takeaways, and there was actually fungus growing on the tiles behind the sink.

He eventually located the phone and answered. 'Yup.'

'Tom?' Grace couldn't be sure that it was him; he had given her too little to go on. Was that the voice she had woken up to on countless mornings? The voice that had made those heartfelt vows on their wedding day?

'Grace.' He sighed. She couldn't tell if this was in irritation or relief.

'Yes, it's me. I'm sorry, Tom, this isn't a very good line. The signal here is a bit sketchy.'

'Yes, I figured that must be it. Why I got no answer or return call when I phoned. At least I hoped it was that and not just that you're avoiding me.'

There were a few silent seconds while she made the decision to ignore the jibe. She didn't want to spar with him, had no energy for verbal jousting.

'How are you?' she asked.

He laughed at her enquiry and surveyed the empty bottles of wine, crushed beer cans and stinking bin bags that surrounded him. 'Oh, you know, Grace, peachy, living the life...'

She had prayed that this conversation would go differently. 'I just wanted to see how you are.'

'Well, that's good of you. I'm still here.' He laughed again.

'Tom, I don't want to fight.' *I can't. I don't have the strength or the will.*

His tone changed. 'I don't want to fight either.'

There was another pause while both considered how to continue. It was Tom who spoke first.

'To be completely honest with you, I don't know how I am, Grace. Sometimes I can get by okay for hours and the next minute I fall apart – you know?' He hesitated. 'And it can hit me at the oddest of times, over the smallest of things.'

'Yes, I do know. I'm the same.' She thought about sliding to the ground in the middle of Hay, the way people had ushered their children past, afraid of the wailing lady. She felt a flush of embarrassment.

'You're the same, but doing it with a prettier view!' He sounded genuinely amused and she smiled.

'Yeah, something like that...'

'Where are you?'

'Wales. I told you.'

'Yes, I know it's Wales, but whereabouts? It's a big country.'

'I'm staying in a kind of shed, but fancier than a shed. It's nice. Near Hay, on the River Wye. The Old Sheep Shed. It's pretty and peaceful.'

It was hard to explain her reluctance to give him too much detail, but she felt that this was her refuge and she wanted to protect it. She was also wary of giving too much away, in case he picked up a hint, a nuance in her voice, that she was enjoying someone else's company as well as the location. Not that she and Huw had any reason to feel guilty, none at all. They had simply become friends, linked by grief, members of the worst club in the world. There was no more to it than that.

'It sounds lovely.' There was an awkward pause. 'When do you think you might come home?'

When are you going home? she asked herself. 'I'm not sure. I've got the shed booked for another couple of weeks yet, so we'll see.'

She was aware that she sounded distant and it had little

to do with her geographical location. This level of formality and awkwardness was odd for them both.

'Yes, Grace, I know, another couple of weeks, but I'm wondering if that will be the end of it, will you be coming home then?'

His insight was quite alarming, but her answer was immediate, automatic. 'Of course I will, Tom.'

'Righto. Well, that's good news.' She could tell by his tone that his relief was superficial. 'I guess I'll see you then.'

'Yes, I'll see you then.'

It was as if she was talking to a stranger – how had this happened to them? They had both consciously avoided mentioning Chloe, unable to talk about their little girl. She had always been central to every conversation they had, every decision they made. *'Is she still up? Has she eaten? Would Chloe like it? Kiss her for me...'*

'Oh, and Grace...'

'Yes, Tom?' She had been keen to end the call, dreading and predicting what was going to come next.

'Love love.'

She didn't want to reply, but she felt backed into a corner. It was a test, a test that she was too afraid to fail. The simple words that held so much meaning and seemed to belong to another lifetime.

'Yes, Tom. Love love.'

With a click he was gone.

Grace sat in her smart, shiny car and shivered at the

prospect of going home and at the thought that she would have to say goodbye to Huw. It was ridiculous, really, how she had latched on to this stranger and how she felt better knowing he was around.

She pictured Tom holding the phone for some time after their call had finished, in the way she had seen him do after speaking to his parents, feeling crestfallen and unsettled; only this time she wasn't smiling at him from the kitchen, trying to make everything better, supplying him with a cup of tea or a glass of wine and telling him that it didn't matter, he had to ignore his mum and dad, they didn't know him and what counted was the three of them, safe and snug inside their lovely home. She heard his thoughts, drifting to her like soundwaves across the miles. *My Grace, where are you? How could this have happened to us?* It was as if they were on opposite sides of a chasm with neither knowing how to reach the other, and even if they could, the task felt too huge to undertake with the sparse reserves they had left. She hadn't recognised the timbre to his voice; his words had sounded forced and unnatural.

While she had a strong phone signal, Grace took the opportunity to send her mum, dad and Alice a text. *Staying in peaceful, peaceful Wales and loving the solitude. Here I can think. Sending love. X* She knew they would appreciate this contact, which carried more than a whiff of positivity. She started the engine, switched on her lights and made her way along the lanes to The Old Sheep Shed.

The conversation with Tom had left her spent. She fed Bertha and, still in her jeans and sweatshirt, flopped face down on the bed, pulling the duvet over her legs and feet. She let her thoughts meander and began wondering about Leanne, what she'd been like; she felt a punch of envy that Huw would fight to keep her, make her happy. Not that she wanted Huw, of course not, but had she and Tom ever felt that way? They must have.

She closed her eyes and remembered a time when they were newly married and on holiday in Spain. Sitting hand in hand by the edge of the pool in a budget hotel as the hot sun dipped, they'd sipped at their sangria, smarting from their sunburn and making plans for the house they wanted to buy. Tom had suddenly rolled his top lip up to his gum, where it stuck, exposing his teeth. 'Look, Grace, I'm Wallace from *Wallace and Gromit*!' He then proceeded to wave and say hello to everyone that passed, even attempting to drink sangria, which spilled down his shirt. Grace had giggled like a teen, screwing her eyes shut and begging him to stop. 'Please, Tom, don't! I'm literally going to wet myself!' she'd wheezed. But he hadn't. Couples and families sauntered past on their way to the dining room and Tom greeted them all with his top lip tucked away and the point of his tongue sticking through his teeth. He then stood and with his arms spread wide shouted 'Cheese!' in his best Wallace voice. Grace had felt her bladder constrict. 'Tom! Tom! Oh my God, I'm going to pee!' She'd laughed until she'd almost cried, barely able to get the words out. Without a word, he grabbed her hand and sprinted with her towards the pool. They had jumped together, hand in hand and fully clothed, landing with a loud splash and shrieks of laughter, free to pee without detection. With her floaty white skirt billowing around her, she had trod water, hand in hand with the man who knew how to fix things.

Apart from this, he couldn't fix this. No one could.

A small bark made her heart jump as Monty alerted her to the fact that he was on the floor on the other side of the bed.

'Jesus, Monty! You scared me! I didn't know you were there.'

He whined and breathed out through his nose. It sounded like an exasperated sigh.

'It's okay. Go back to sleep.'

She closed her eyes and spoke to the dog, whose company was reassuring. 'Chloe would love you,' she murmured, picturing her little girl petting the placid animal. This was quickly replaced by the memory of her daughter's podgy bare feet poking from beneath her nightdress on the hall floor. It was this image that replayed in her mind, on a loop, over and over. She wished it would stop.

Grace pulled the spare pillow down into her chest as she rolled onto her side, hugging it close. Her tears came thick and fast, filling her throat and nose. She cried silently and deeply, swallowing the saltiness. 'I miss you, darling. I miss your little hand in mine, I miss your voice and I miss the way I could hug you into me and smell your hair. Chloe... My little Chloe...'

The sleep that followed these tearful episodes was always deep if short. Sometime later, she let her eyes flicker open at the sound of creaking.

'Sorry, Grace,' Huw whispered as he tentatively pushed the door wide. 'Is Monty in here?'

She nodded her cheek against the pillow. As if on cue, Monty whined.

'There you are.' Huw's voice was hushed, his tone a mixture of relief and amusement.

'Stay with me,' she whispered in her half-sleeping state.

'What?' He needed it repeating; the awkwardness that would ensue if he'd misheard would be devastating.

She raised her head slightly. 'I said, stay with me. Please.'

Huw shut the door behind him, crept towards the bed and sat on his fishing stool beside her.

Grace closed her eyes, happy to know he was there. She heard the groan of the fabric against the wooden frame as he leant forward and gently placed his hand on her back. Her skin pulsed beneath the weight of his touch.

'Do you think... do you think you might hold me, Huw?' she whispered into the darkness.

Slowly, hesitantly, he rose from the stool, walked to the other side of the bed and stepped over the snoring Monty. Grace heard him pull off his heavy work boots and remove his thick, plaid shirt before folding back the duvet and easing his body into the bed. He edged closer to her and wrapped his muscled arms around her. The backs of her legs rested against his thighs and her head lay on his chest. She placed her palm on his forearm; her heart beat fast at the thrill of being close to another person, a man. A man that wasn't Tom.

Huw tried to arrange the pillow and as his hand reached beneath it, he touched a small, soft item. Pulling it from the shadows, he saw it was a child's nightdress. He tucked it under Grace's hand. She was vaguely aware of the lightest kiss on her temple before she drifted off, unable to fight the sleep that pulled her under, into another world, her escape tunnel.

She floated away and, like an observer, saw herself standing in a beautiful garden, which she instinctively knew was Huw's garden in full bloom. It was the way the light fell and the sound of the river burbling in the distance. She was wearing dungarees that were taut over her pregnant stomach. She stood in the garden, inhaling the intoxicating scent of a plant she couldn't quite identify. She felt happy, light, as if the wearying yoke of grief had been lifted. Grace could sense that her mother was not very far away; her reading glasses and an open novel lay abandoned on a table behind her, but where was Mac? She couldn't see him. Try as she might, she could not locate her dad. Unaccustomed to seeing Olive without Mac, and vice-versa, it felt most odd. Suddenly, her husband's arms were around her. She knew with absolute certainty that this was her husband, could even feel her wedding band pressing against his, and yet she felt an overwhelming joy, a feeling that she hadn't associated with Tom for a long time. She smiled, relishing the happiness, the contentment. It felt wonderful. Maybe there was hope for her and Tom after all. She tried to turn around but was stuck fast, unable to look into the face of the man who held her.

She awoke with a start and found herself anchored by the duvet, which had twisted around her form. No wonder she hadn't been able to turn around. Huw had gone, and Monty too. The dull light meant that dawn was but a breath away; even so, there was time for more sleep, thankfully. Repositioning her body in the middle of the bed, she quickly slipped into a deeper sleep – without the dreams but just as blissful.

A while later she woke again, to find Huw standing at the foot of the bed. Rather than feel alarmed, she welcomed his presence, not least because he was bearing coffee and several huge, warm, plump, almond croissants.

'Good morning, Grace.'

She smiled; she liked the way he spoke her name. 'Good morning, Huw.'

'You slept well?'

'Yes, yes I did. Thank you for holding me last night. It felt so lovely. It's been a long time since someone did something so wonderful just for me.' She was sincere in her gratitude; there was none of the anticipated awkwardness.

'You are very welcome. It was good for me too. It's been a long time since I felt another person so close. I liked it very much.' He smiled.

They were both quiet as they recollected the previous evening. To have described it to an outsider would have made it sound tawdry, wanton, but it had been neither of those things. It was as if they had transcended the physical and formed a strong spiritual bond; in the short space of a couple of weeks, they'd built trust and deep mutual affection.

Huw placed the coffee and croissants on the breakfast bar. Grace clambered out of bed and ambled over, taking a large gulp of the restorative liquid and a bite of one of the croissants.

'Ooh, delicious, thank you!'

She had done it without thinking – welcomed the sweet, sugary pastry into her mouth and let her tastebuds feel the joy! She stood still for a second, chewing slowly and trying to gauge the significance of this small thing, which felt like a very big thing, a step towards recovery. But it was laced with guilt. She had enjoyed food in a world where her little girl would never eat again.

Huw had noted her expression. 'You okay?'

'Yes.' She nodded and gave a small, cautious smile. 'Can I ask you a question?' She spoke through her mouthful.

'Yes, of course. You can ask me anything.'

'Did you ever want children?'

Huw took a bite from his croissant and looked at her. 'I did. We did. I guess we were waiting for the right time. And then...' He shrugged.

'I think you'd have been a great dad.' She spoke softly and considered his gentle, patient, caring nature, applying sutures and swabbing her cut in her hour of need. She pressed croissant crumbs into the pad of her index finger and transferred them to her mouth. When she looked up, she was aghast to see Huw's face contorted with tears. 'Oh God! Huw, I'm so sorry! I should never have asked.'

'I thought I would be a dad and I know she would have made the best mum. She'd have taught our little one about the plants and they'd have grown vegetables together. Our plan was to end up here eventually. It would have been perfect.' He exhaled, wiped his nose and eyes on the long sleeve of his shirt and faked a smile.

'It would have been.' She squeezed his hand.

'Well, this is a turn-up for the books, eh?' He laughed. 'Me falling apart and you keeping strong.'

Grace nodded. 'Reckon that bump on the head did me a bit of good.' Monty barked from the deck as if in agreement.

'Right – come on, I'm taking you out to lunch!' He slapped the countertop and sniffed, taking deep breaths.

'We're only just having breakfast,' she pointed out.

'No matter. You need feeding up and I can eat any time. Be ready to go in ten minutes.' He jumped from the bar stool and left, whistling for Monty as he went.

Ten minutes later, Huw was standing at the door of The Old Sheep Shed dressed in clean dark jeans and a pale blue denim shirt.

'You look smart,' she commented as she grabbed her rucksack.

'Hardly.' Huw blushed, rubbing his beard. 'But smarter, possibly. In fact, probably just clean.'

'Have you always had a beard?' she asked.

He shook his head. 'No. I couldn't be bothered to shave when I first lost Leanne and this just grew.' He tugged at his chin. 'I trim it occasionally, but I've kind of made a pact that I will only be clean-shaven when I feel I'm ready to face the world properly, when I make a fresh start. I guess then I'll feel able to remove my mask.'

Grace shut the door and hiked up the field towards the workshop. 'Oh my word!' Huw had parked the car outside the cottage: a vintage Mercedes 230SL. Its paintwork was the original colour, a glorious burnished gold.

'Oh, Huw, she is really beautiful.'

'Yes, she is.' He looked at the car with pride. 'It was my grandad's. He loved her very much and I told him I would look after her.'

'Well, you've kept your word.'

Huw opened the passenger door and she slid onto the

cracked leather seat, its scent evocative of a bygone era, cigar smoke and musky aftershave.

'It'll do her good to have a run,' Huw said as the engine purred.

'Where are we going?' Grace asked, only mildly curious.

'The Saracens Head at Symonds Yat.' Huw pumped the accelerator and smiled at the sound. 'Best lunch in a top spot – you'll love it. It'll make a change from bread and cheese.'

They navigated the winding lanes, which quickly gave way to wider country roads, passing signs for enticing-sounding villages like Mansell Gamage and Stretton Sugwas. Broad, sweeping fields bordered the meandering river and every so often they'd see a clearing peppered with a cluster of huge trees and a deer or two grazing nearby.

They drove in amiable silence with the windows rolled down and the radio dipping in and out of various different music channels. Grace thought about her drive home from the train station that Friday evening not so long ago, before her whole world had unravelled. She saw herself zipping down the high-hedged lanes to Nettlecombe, singing along to Ryan Adams and then arriving home, dipping the headlights and watching Chloe and Tom together in the kitchen for a bit. She hadn't realised that she had it all, had not fully appreciated that she was staring at perfection.

She took a deep breath. 'You know, Huw, I keep thinking that if I'd read up properly about all the possible complications, or if I'd known what to look out for, things might have turned out differently. Tom blames me. He kind of said so.' She toyed with the hem of her sweatshirt. 'And I keep thinking that perhaps he's right. It was me that assured everyone that the procedure was nothing – I even told Chloe it'd make her better. We used to joke about her terrible snoring. I understand that he blames me.'

'He doesn't blame you, Grace, he blames himself.'

She sighed. 'Oh, I'm not so sure, I think he does blame me. I didn't know about sepsis. I didn't know what to look for, but the signs were there: her confusion, diarrhoea, slurred speech and flu-like symptoms, and she hadn't done a wee in a long while. All the things you should be looking out for, especially if there's a risk of infection.'

Huw worked his way down the gears, slowing the car as he looked at her. 'I think a lot of people would struggle to identify it.'

'Well they should be bloody taught. Everyone should know what to look for – it kills over thirty-five thousand people a year in this country alone! That's about a hundred a day, every day! Why didn't I know about it? No wonder he blames me...'

'Trust me, no matter what he says, he blames himself. It was the same for me, when Leanne was killed.' He paused, struggling to find the vocabulary. 'I kept thinking that if only I'd met her from town like I used to sometimes, walked her home, then that car might have seen me walking by her side and swerved, or it would have hit me and that would have been preferable. Why didn't I make her wear a high-vis vest? Why didn't I insist on her getting a cab in the rain? Why didn't I go and pick her up? I have a million questions that all lead back to me and things I could have or should have done.'

'It doesn't work like that though, does it?' She stared ahead as her eyes blurred behind a curtain of tears, a sensation that was now as familiar to her as breathing.

Huw hadn't finished. 'You know, Grace, I have a head-start on you. I've had a long time to think about everything and ponder the reasons why. And I'm sure these terrible things that almost destroy us, they are decisions made by something or someone bigger than us, and we can't understand it, and we are certainly not meant to change it...'

'Decisions made by who or what, Huw? Do you mean a god?' Her tone was a little sharper than intended.

'If you like.' He focused on the lane ahead.

Grace could see the comfort in the abdication of responsibility and blame, in acting as if there were some omnipotent being playing chess with her life so that no matter what she did, said or thought, it was all scripted and decided. That might work for some people, might even work for Huw, but it wasn't how she saw the world.

They continued the drive in silence, each playing out the scenario in which things had happened differently. Then the car rounded a bend and an owl swooped overhead.

'Wow!' Huw yelled. 'Did you see that?'

Grace nodded. 'Beautiful.'

'Is it one of yours, sent from Hogwarts with your post?'

Grace touched her fingers to the scar on her forehead and let out a burst of laughter. She immediately felt a pang of guilt – how could she be laughing? How could she be feeling a moment of happiness? It was wrong and it was too soon. She had a very real fear that it would always be 'too soon'. The image of Chloe's coffin being carried into the church instantly filled her mind. She shook her head and placed her hand over her eyes.

Huw looked at her and allowed her a moment of reflection.

'Obviously I never knew Chloe, but I can bet that she wouldn't want her beautiful mum to be sad, not forever...'

Grace didn't trust herself to speak, not knowing what was going to pop out of her mouth next. It was as though he had insight into her mind and it both frightened and comforted her.

He spoke to ease the silence, trying to comfort her with his own experience. 'I cried every day for a whole year after I lost Leanne and I still cry now. I think of her maybe once or twice a day. It's the small things that remind me the most – a song on the radio or if I see her favourite programme – but thinking of her once or twice a day is a good thing. It's a good thing because I used to only be able to think of her twenty-four/seven. She filled up all of the space in my head.'

Grace smiled at his expression; it was literally perfect and a feeling she knew only too well. 'I feel guilty if I don't think about Chloe, I feel guilty if I do, but most of all I miss her. I miss her now and I miss what she will never become. Does that make sense?'

He nodded; it made absolute sense. He too missed the child that was never going to be born and the wife who never got the chance to be a mum. He mourned the missed opportunities.

His understanding gave her the confidence to continue.

'I feel as if I'm mourning what I will never have. And...' She hesitated, having never spoken these thoughts aloud and anxious as to how they might be interpreted. 'I keep thinking of the times I was less than patient with her. Like when I hoped she would just go back to sleep so I didn't have to get up for her, or when I was working and just wished she would be quiet so I could crack on. I wish I'd played with her more, talked to her more, held her...' She swallowed the bitter-tasting words. 'I can hear her little voice saying, "Mummy do this" and "Mummy do that" and how sometimes I would be so exhausted I would feel like shouting, "For God's sake, just leave me alone! Just for a minute, please let me think!" And I want to say sorry to her for that, I want her to know that I would give anything for one minute to hold her and hear her voice again.'

'You can't beat yourself up forever about being a normal, busy mum. A mum who was working hard and doing her best to give her daughter a lovely life.'

'Can't I?' She sniffed.

Huw indicated and pulled into a lay-by. 'Shall we turn around, go back to Gael Ffydd?'

Grace nodded. 'Yes. Sorry, Huw. I don't feel up to lunch. I don't want to see anyone.'

'You don't have to say sorry to me, remember?' He smiled and swung the car round.

Back at the cottages, Monty came running up to greet Grace as she climbed out of the car. 'Hello, Mont.' She smoothed his coat and scratched at his neck, which he seemed to love.

'You've got a fan there.'

'Think I've won him over. He wasn't too keen on me when I arrived.'

'That makes two of us.' Huw laughed.

'Charming! Grace smiled. 'Thanks for taking me out today. Sorry we didn't make the pub, but it was lovely to be out in your car.'

'Any excuse! I love driving her. Tell you what, I've got a few chores to do this afternoon, but how about I grab a couple of ciders a bit later and we sit on the deck?'

'Sure,' Grace said, noting how animated he seemed.

It was after two bottles each that their tongues loosened and their inhibitions shrank away.

'I liked you holding me, Huw. Thank you for that.'

'Jheesh, it's not every day I get asked! It was nice to feel someone close.'

Grace looked out across the horizon, taking in the mountains against the clouds and watching the birds swoop and dive around the riverbank. 'I think I see her, you know,' she confessed.

'Maybe you do.' He stared ahead.

'Do you see Leanne?'

'Yes, everywhere. Whether it's in my imagination or it really is her, doesn't matter, it's lovely just the same.' He smiled.

'I don't like being this broken,' she whispered. 'I wish it would stop.'

Huw almost leapt from his chair. He dropped to his knees on the deck and enveloped her form with his own. He was crushing her to him and smoothing her hair as he kissed the crown of her head. 'Oh, Grace, you're not broken, you're just bruised, and you will get better, I promise. I promise!'

'There's too much going on in my head,' she cried.

'And I don't want to add to that confusion, but it's obvious, isn't it? You and I have clicked. There's something going on here, it's like some good is coming out of this whole terrible, bloody situation. I swear to you, I hadn't smiled or felt hope for six years, until you pulled up on that driveway.'

Grace kissed his palm where it rested against her cheek. 'You are wonderful, Huw. You really are. And this place... It makes me feel safe and so much happier than I have any right to be at this time in my life. But I am married and grieving for my little girl and with a messed-up husband waiting to pounce on me the moment I get back.' She shook her head; it all suddenly felt very overwhelming.

'So don't go back. Don't go back, Grace. Stay here, where you can see clearly and you're happy. Stay here with Monty and me.'

She laughed. 'Oh, Huw, you don't know how good that sounds, but I can't just pack up and start over.'

'Why can't you? Why can't you just pack up and start over?'

'Because… Because…'

'Because what? Because why?'

'I don't know! I don't know why.'

She stood up, shrugging him off. He rose too, and embraced her in another hug. It was confusing. The familiar feel of Tom beneath her palms, and the smell of him, was all she'd known for so long. She was so accustomed to her husband's height and stature that she knew exactly where to place her hands, rest her head, position her feet. With Huw, she smelt the unfamiliar scent of a human that wasn't known to her; he smelt of bonfires, trees and paint, with a hint of turpentine.

They swayed in the gentle breeze that drifted up to them from the river.

Huw took her hand and led her through the French doors. They didn't switch the lights on, preferring the dark as they fell onto the bed and pulled the large quilt over their slightly chilled bodies. Huw kissed her full on the mouth and ran his fingers through her hair. She responded hungrily and tugged at his shirt, feeling the soft matting of curls that covered his chest. She arched upwards to meet him, not wanting to think, not wanting to feel, but happy at the prospect of losing herself for an hour, a minute, whatever she could grab. This wasn't about sex, it wasn't about Tom, it was about a distraction, a moment of escape from the misery and the sadness. She lay on top of him and he ran his hands down over her waist and hips as she pushed against him, not caring about anything or anyone but driven by the feel of him, the scent of him. He flipped her over and laid his head against her chest, holding her arms by the wrists, slowing the proceedings. Their breath came in shallow pants.

'Grace... Beautiful Grace...'

'Oh God.' She felt tears of humiliation and regret. 'Oh no!'

He put his face close to hers and spoke directly to her. 'No... No, not "Oh no!" Please don't look like that.'

She hid her face in her hands. 'Huw, I'm so embarrassed.'

'Embarrassed? No, Grace. This is too important to me. You're the first... You're the first... everything since Leanne, and the circumstances aren't right. I never want you to regret anything and I never want to take advantage of you and I know that your head is a mess. I need you to be so, so sure.' He held her tightly.

He was right; there was too much hurt, too much unfinished business, between her and the outside world.

'Huw, I—'

'Ssshhh.'

They didn't need any words; instead, they held each other until the small hours, each locked in private contemplation of how it all might end, each hoping that what they were feeling right then wouldn't be taken from them, not just yet.

Grace fell into a deep sleep with her head against Huw's chest, rising and falling to the slow rhythm of his breathing. His arms were clasped tightly around her. It was the sweetest sleep she'd had in a very long time.

When morning came, there was less embarrassment than she'd expected; their chaste embrace had been spiritually binding, comforting. Nonetheless, Tom's face swam into her head, accompanied by the ache of disloyalty.

The smell of coffee being brewed stirred her into activity and as she swung her legs over the side of the bed she felt a certain sense of peace, albeit tinged with guilt, that was new to her, as if the diversion of Huw had indeed taken her away from grief, just for one night.

'I watched you sleeping,' Huw said from the breakfast bar.

'That sounds boring.' She smiled.

'It wasn't. It was lovely. You had your arms up around your face. I never knew the way someone's eyelashes lay against their cheeks could hold so much fascination.'

'You need to get out more!'

'Christ, don't I know it. My only friend is a bloody dog.' He smiled and handed her a mug of coffee. 'I think I've figured out what the problem is, Grace.'

'What's that?' she asked, sipping the hot drink.

'This is not our time. You are someone else's wife and I still feel like someone else's husband, and as much as I want more...' He let this trail.

'You're a great bloke, Huw. You deserve to be happy. But I don't think your happiness lies with me.' She meant it, every word. 'Having you to confide in has changed me, helped me.'

'I'm glad.' He nodded. 'I'd wait for you, Grace. I'd wait until you were less—'

'Broken?' she offered.

'Bruised.'

She shook her head. 'I don't want last night to change our friendship, and I don't want us to confuse friendship with anything else.' She looked away.

'I agree. Business as normal – we can go for our walks, eat cheese and sit in the bloody dark on the deck!' He tried to lighten the mood. 'But I'd be a liar if I didn't admit that I'm hoping that when you are ready, you'll maybe give us a chance.'

'No promises.' Grace held his gaze.

'No promises.' Huw stared back at her.

Monty barked loudly from the field. Both were glad of the diversion.

'He's probably found a rabbit.' Huw made for the door.

Grace followed him in her crumpled clothes and with her hair mussed from sleep. They stood on the step, looking down towards the river, where the dog was scampering about. Grace looked up towards the workshop, where her car was parked.

She saw him instantly.

Her voice was quiet, resigned almost, but with a slight edge of panic. 'Oh my God! Huw! You have to go to the cottage. You have to get out of here! Now!'

'What's the matter with you?'

'It's Tom… Tom's here!' She felt a dizzying combination of nervousness, excitement and sadness that her adventure was over.

Huw looked at her as he prepared to stride across the field and put as much distance as possible between the two of them. Guilt dripped off him. There was no time to tie up loose ends; they had just a few seconds in which to try and sum up all that the last couple of weeks had meant.

He reached backwards and interlaced her fingers with his. They spoke almost simultaneously, in a rush of words.

'I feel like I've woken up,' Huw said, swallowing hard. 'Like I've been sleepwalking since I lost Lee. You've helped me realise that I might find happiness again. You've given me the greatest gift, Grace and I want you to know that I won't ever forget this terrible, special time…'

'Thank you… Thank you, Huw, for everything,' Grace

stuttered as she looked into his eyes. 'You will never, ever know...'

It was inadequate and unsatisfactory, but she didn't trust herself to say more. One thing she definitely didn't need was more complications.

With a last squeeze of Huw's hand, Grace almost jumped from the steps and ran towards the driveway, not wanting to be seen in his company. The last she saw of him was the back of his head as he disappeared into the cottage, banging his thigh and whistling for Monty.

Fourteen

In the UK, sepsis kills more people than AIDS, road accidents, breast, bowel and prostate cancer combined

Grace had the advantage of being able to study her husband unseen. She felt instantly guilty that his clothing and pale skin irritated her. His trademark striped shirt with its button-down collar beneath his V-neck jersey was out of place in such a rustic setting, far better suited to drinks in the local pub or a country walk. It wasn't his fault, he just wasn't the person that she wanted him to be right then. He just wasn't Huw. Huw, who had taken her to the river, who had fed her bread and cheese at the peaceful close of day, as iridescent kingfishers swooped on the water.

She was almost upon him when he turned and saw her. He smiled at his wife and appraised her form, nodding almost imperceptibly. She smiled back, comfortable and familiar. He looked a bit better, fuller in the face, as if he'd resumed eating. He'd shaved, his skin had lost some of its sallow pallor and his eyes were brighter, like a cloudy film had lifted.

'I could kill a beer.'

Typical Tom: start with a joke, break the ice, get everyone to relax. So familiar was she with his modus operandi that it now appeared corny, even contrived.

'Come on then. I haven't got beer, but there's wine.'

He followed her across the field towards the steps that led to The Old Sheep Shed. She looked around, feeling like a local, which was simultaneously exhilarating and embarrassing. They walked shoulder to shoulder without touching and for that she was grateful.

Grace showed him into the studio, deliberately choosing not to sit on the deck, where she and Huw had shared so many confidences.

Tom stood with his hands on his hips and looked out at the view. The breeze was making the trees at the river's edge bend and creak. 'This really is lovely, Grace.'

She smiled in agreement. 'I wasn't expecting to see you. It's a lovely surprise, Tom.'

He walked over to where she was standing in the kitchen area and grabbed the opportunity to take her by the hand. His family ring sat on his little finger, emblazoned with its crest and reminding her so much of another world, another home, another life.

'Is it really a lovely surprise?' He looked at her with childlike expectancy, willing her to want him.

Her stomach flipped. 'Yes, of course.' There it was, another lie, so easy.

'I've missed you, Gracie, and I came here because I wanted to tell you that I don't know where we're heading, but I do know that until you come home and we talk, I mean really talk, like we used to, we're never going to get back into any routine, we're never going to find our path out of this dark place that we've stumbled into.'

She nodded as she discreetly pulled her hand from beneath his. Sitting on the sofa, she tucked it into her lap and out of his reach.

'I know you're right.' She refrained from adding, *'But I don't want to get back into a routine with you, I don't want to find a path. I like being here, I like this peace.'* She was thinking how this place had switched on her senses. It had been nice to have her own space, as if at Gael Ffydd she had time and space to grieve, without having to worry about Tom's feelings all the time. She remembered a time when he would have been the first person she reached for in her hour of need. How had it all changed so much in such a short time? The answer came back into her mind fast and clear. *It's not him that's changed, Grace; it's you. You're a different person now, a completely different person. Part of you died when Chloe did. Remember?*

'You look so much better than when I last saw you, Grace – apart from your head. What on earth have you done?' He touched his finger to the scar on her forehead.

'I fell down some stairs in the dark. Stupid, really. Apart from that, physically I feel quite well.' She nodded.

'You don't need to say any more. I'm going through it too and that's why we'll be okay, Grace, because we're going through the same thing. We're the same.'

She looked into her lap and focused on her cuticles, as was her habit. There was a pause while they both gathered their thoughts, familiar and yet strangers.

'Gracie?'

'Mmmn?'

Tom took a deep breath, wiped his nervous palms on his thighs. 'I didn't mean what I said about you not being there for Chloe. I was just so, so angry and I wanted to be as horrid as I could.'

'I think we both achieved that,' she conceded.

'It's been bothering me; I keep replaying the things I said to you. I didn't mean it. I really didn't. You were and you are a great mum. Chloe was very lucky to have you and she was very, very happy, always. She was.' He sniffed up his tears. 'I know that for a fact. She was happy, Grace! Chloe loved you, loved us, and she was always happy. That thought gives me comfort and it should give you comfort too.'

She looked at her broken man and felt a weight lift from her. His words were like balm, lightening her spirit and sending a flicker of hope through the tangle of grief.

'Thank you for that, Tom. Thank you. That means everything. And I didn't mean it either.' He looked at her and nodded, accepting the apology he had hoped for. She nudged him with her elbow. 'I mean, obviously I didn't mean it. We both know that you could *not* make a cake from scratch!'

They laughed and Tom sipped and then raised his glass of wine. 'Cheers, Grace.'

She raised hers too. 'Cheers.'

'So, what's the plan?'

She thought about how she should answer. What was the plan? Both immediate and longer term? She really didn't know. She tried to picture the future for them, but inspiration was thin on the ground. She breathed deeply and looked into his eyes.

'I guess it's one day at a time, Tom.'

She held his gaze and he smiled. It was a smile of relief.

'That sounds good, babe. One day at a time...'

It was somehow agreed that they would spend one night at The Old Sheep Shed and then drive back early the following day. Grace wasn't sure how she would survive a night on the same property as Huw with Tom by her side; the prospect made her feel awkward, embarrassed. But she needn't have worried. Huw didn't appear, neither that night nor early the next day. She wasn't going to see him again; their whole liaison, the lovely friendship that had sprung from the darkest of springs, was over.

As she packed her suitcase with her belongings, his scent

and the memory of him still imprinted on them, she couldn't stop the tears from falling. Grace pictured him striding away from her in haste the day before, eager to put distance between them. She knew, however, that this was not the image that she would carry with her; instead, it would be Huw in profile, sitting on the deck in the fading light, relaxing in his plaid shirt and dirty jeans, sipping wine or swigging cider from the neck of the bottle as the sun set behind the mountain. Huw, her lovely, lovely friend. She felt like a teenager again, being wrenched from her first love after the summer holidays – pitiful, really, for a woman of her age.

Tom misconstrued her tears. 'Please don't cry, love. We'll be home soon. It will all be okay.'

Home soon. The thought made her cry even harder.

She couldn't even leave a note; her husband's presence and attentions were predictably constant. She gathered her stuff together quickly, not caring too much that she might have missed a few items lurking under the bed or in the bathroom. In truth, she hadn't thought about leaving, not properly, like a teen planning for the next day on the beach who can't bear to look too far ahead and feels like the holiday might last forever, this was similar. She knew in her heart that a date was red ringed in the diary when she would have to pack up and return to Nettlecombe, but picturing it was another thing entirely. There was so much that scared her about returning home, having to face the knowing looks, the tight lipped nods and the tearful, well-meant interrogations around the kitchen table, and not least what it would feel like to see that spot on the landing, the very place that was branded in her memory. How could she simply step over it every day with armfuls of laundry or holding a cup of coffee, as if it held no significance? She didn't know if she could.

As she cast her eyes over the Sheep Shed one last time her heart felt like it might burst with all that it tried to contain. She was wary of leaving this place where she had felt a semblance of peace and had tasted the beginnings of happiness, like the first raindrops after a drought, sweet and life-giving.

Grace felt a familiar exhaustion return to her limbs as she turned her car onto the lane, heading home. She scrutinised the contours of the beautiful land that she was leaving – what did she expect to see, Huw waving? The very idea made her laugh. *Pathetic, Grace.* She felt her heart sinking as she hit the main road, covering the miles that would take her away from Gael Ffydd and back to the sadness that awaited her. She hadn't slept the previous evening, feeling a mixture of guilt and distress in equal measure. Guilt because she felt something akin to anger as her husband lay on the bed that had been her sanctuary, how could she ever explain that a part of her resented him gate crashing this precious retreat, wrenching her from her escape. And distress because she knew her adventure was coming to an end, it was time to go home. Not that she could ever imagine it feeling like home again. She was already missing Huw, missing the balm of his words and his steady, reassuring manner, having to say goodbye to their friendship saddened her. Grace knew that she would not see him again and the pain this caused her was immense.

Fifteen

Sepsis claims 6 million children's lives every year across the world

Tom stood by the side of the bed and gently shook her shoulder, calling her name to wake her. She reluctantly prised open her eyes and stretched.

'Mmmmn? What?' The sleeping tablets knocked her out, meaning that when she woke there was always a second or two where she felt a little muddle-headed, dozy. Had she had a nightmare? What time was it? She wasn't fully aware.

'Are you okay?' He sounded concerned, bending over the bed.

Through the fog of sleep, she registered her husband as the shape that loomed over her. 'Yes. Yes, I'm fine. What's wrong?'

'Nothing. You were just shouting out. Who's Monty?' he asked.

'What?' She was surprised to hear the name, having tried to expunge it from her thoughts for so many days now.

'Monty?' he repeated.

'I... I don't know what you're talking about, Tom.' She closed her eyes to demonstrate that she wasn't fully awake, and in an attempt to make him go away.

'You were saying, "Come on, Monty," and you were patting the duvet.'

'I have no idea, Tom. I don't know anyone called Monty and I don't remember the dream at all.' She yawned and pretended to doze.

As he disappeared from the room, she rolled over and buried her face in the pillow, trying to recapture the dream, the vision, the feeling. It had felt blissful to be back at Gael Ffydd, with the sun coming up over the valley. She had been taking breakfast on the deck. The sun was warm on her skin as the river burbled in the valley below and, again, in her dream she was pregnant. She had even been able to smell the garden – all her senses contributed to the great deception. She had been transported to that special place, where part of her spirit still roamed, where she could breathe deeply and she had felt free.

Tom broke into her thoughts and her daydream as he stepped through the door, forcing her back to where she didn't want to be, into the bedroom they shared, in the quiet house where childhood laughter no longer rang out, where happiness had been stretchered out one cold, cold morning, along with the heart of the house.

'Happy birthday, Grace.'

'What?' She sat up. 'Oh God! It isn't, is it?'

She looked up uncomprehendingly as he stood at the foot of the bed with a tray, complete with Earl Grey tea in her favourite dotty mug, and toast with honey. She gazed at his efforts and swallowed a yearning for sharp black coffee and fresh, organic, sourdough loaves. *Stop it, Grace, just stop it! This helps no one; he is trying his very best.* A small bud vase held a single bloom from the garden. Her instant reaction was to laugh, which she managed to suppress.

She hadn't even realised her birthday was looming, hadn't thought about it, but it was of course inevitable. A birthday was the last thing she wanted and the last thing that she felt she could cope with. It was, however, one of many anniversaries, milestones that were to be endured without her little girl, and she knew the first of each would always be the hardest. The day held no appeal; wishing she could fast forward, she just wanted it to be over.

'Oh, Tom, thank you. That's really lovely.' She sat up, leant against the headboard, dug deep and found a smile as he placed the tray on the bedclothes.

He smiled back at her. 'Did you forget?'

'I did, yes,' she replied meekly, slightly embarrassed by the admission, as if this were further proof that she wasn't firing on all cylinders. 'I had no idea.'

'Don't worry, it's not like you haven't got enough other stuff to think about.' He was holding something behind his back and his manner was hesitant. 'I don't know whether to give you this or not.'

He fingered a brown-paper parcel, which he now bought into view. It was a flattish rectangle tied up with kitchen string; clearly, the purchasing of gift-wrap had not been high on the agenda. It mattered little; she was in no mood for a birthday or the frippery that went with it. Didn't need the marker, proof that, for her, life went on. Didn't want to have to draw the obvious comparisons with the previous year, when Chloe had bounced on the bed with a fistful of wilted flowers and a birthday muffin with a bite out of the top, yelling, 'Happy birthday, Mummy! I help you open your presents.' She'd then set to, ripping open the gifts, flinging strips of paper high into the air like confetti, completely disinterested in the contents, hurling them this way and that while reaching for the next one.

'Oh, do! Give it here – you know I love pressies!' Grace feigned enthusiasm and grabbed at the package. It was almost as if Tom was holding it out of her reach. There was a split-second tussle when she had to stretch further to grip it and then pull slightly to get him to release it. 'Tom!' Grace smiled at his curious behaviour.

She crossed her legs under the duvet and placed the parcel on her lap. She pulled at the string, ripping open the paper until it was shredded, and there she sat, staring in wonder and silence at the most beautiful thing she had ever seen. It was a handmade photo frame. She didn't move or speak for some seconds. Tom rested on the side of the bed. They were both silent.

The frame was uneven, lumpy and grey in texture, and adorned with stickers of animals and tiny stars. Plastic jewels of various shapes had been pushed into the cast and someone had scrawled into the edge of the plaster with a stick the words 'For my mummy'.

It was the beautiful effort of a three-year-old with the help of a patient nursery assistant. Grace had a vague recollection of Chloe having told her that she'd made her a present, but couldn't quite remember where or when that had been. Tom had placed a print of Chloe inside the frame; it was one Grace hadn't seen before and therefore all the more beguiling. She studied her daughter, who had been caught unawares, looking into the middle distance with her gorgeous curls obscuring half her face. She looked thoughtful, her large eyes clear and concentrating. It was perfect.

'Oh, Chloe! Thank you, Chlo, thank you, Tom! I couldn't love anything more! It's brilliant, really brilliant.'

Tom fell forward, catching his wife in his arms as he slumped next to her on the bed. They cried together as they held the frame that their little girl had made with such care and attention for her mummy.

Grace spoke to the ether and kissed the print. 'Thank you, my darling. It's beautiful, my clever, clever little girl. I love it.'

She felt a physical pain in her heart. She missed her daughter with a tangible ache that didn't seem to dull with time. She slid back under the duvet and Tom crept in alongside her. This was where they spent most of the day, hiding themselves away, not wanting to compare it with April the twenty-sixth of the previous year.

The two of them lay together in a loose, passionless embrace. Grace realised that the strongest emotion she felt for Tom just then was indifference. She couldn't begin to imagine a life without him, but at the same time she couldn't figure out how to live a life with him. She felt trapped, made even worse because the one person she would usually confide in about such a matter was Tom. Therein lay her problem.

The day ticked by and neither Grace nor Tom demonstrated any real desire to move. Tom occasionally lifted his head to ask, 'Are you okay?' in response to which Grace would nod, keeping her eyes closed, incapable of much more.

With her head submerged beneath the duvet, she allowed a montage of fragmented memories to replay in her mind; they were out of chronological order and often confused reality with the imagined. Most of all, she heard the stirring sounds of Tchaikovsky's strings at Chloe's funeral and saw the stained-glass window where an angel with her arms outstretched smiled down at her.

At some point she felt herself waking and stuck her head above the duvet. Tom, disturbed by her movement, roused himself into a sitting position. She sat up too, with her back against the headboard.

'Are you okay?' he asked again.

'No. No, I'm not.' She wedged her hands into her hair and brought her knees up to her chin.

'What's up?' He placed a hand on her back.

'I think I'm going mad.'

Tom considered his response. 'I think we both are, at least a little bit. But I don't think it's permanent, at least I bloody well hope not.'

'I think I'm going crazier than you.'

'Come on, Grace, you don't seriously want to play "who's going the craziest", do you?'

She managed a laugh. 'Not really.'

She thought about how to phrase the next question and whether she should raise it at all. 'Can I ask you something, Tom?'

'Of course you can. Anything.' He settled his hands in his lap and gave her his full attention.

'Do you ever see her?' she whispered with her thumb nail against her teeth.

There was no need for her to explain who the 'she' in question was. Tom smiled and closed his eyes. 'Yes. Yes, I do.'

'Where do you see her?' Again, her voice was small.

'I see her in the garden, I see her at the supermarket and I see her in the back of the car when I'm driving along. And I see her on the landing.'

'Does she ever talk when you see her?' Grace asked, wide eyed.

Tom pondered this, then shook his head. 'No. I haven't thought about it until now, but no, she never speaks. She's always silent.'

'What is she wearing when you see her?' Grace whispered.

Tom sniffed back his tears and rubbed his prickly beard. 'She's wearing her pink mac and her little pink wellies.'

Grace nodded. 'Yes. Yes, she is! Her pink mac and her little wellies.'

They both cried then, miserable wretched tears for the miserable wretched predicament in which they found themselves.

Sixteen

Sepsis can occur following chest or water infections, problems in the abdomen like burst ulcers, or even from minor skin injuries like cuts and bites

The little green Austin chugged into the driveway and there it sat as the engine shuddered to a halt. Its occupants stayed inside, trying to find the strength to leave its familiar confines. The house looked decidedly gloomy without its usual array of lamps and lights beckoning to them from within. The curtains were drawn and the windows no longer sparkled. It was a house in mourning, unloved and slipping further into decay with each passing day.

Olive released her rather ineffective seatbelt and breathed deeply. Mac patted her hand. 'You all right, old girl?'

She nodded and placed her hand over his, still drawing strength and comfort from physical contact with him, even after all these years. 'Less of the "old", if you don't mind.'

She loped from the car and knocked hesitantly on the front door. She felt tentative, unconfident; her stomach sat somewhere just below her throat. She could never have envisaged being made to feel unwelcome at her daughter's front door, but today of all days, she wasn't so sure. It had been many days since she'd last had any contact – the family had decided that it might be best to give Grace the space she seemed to crave – but enough was enough. This was the day Olive had given birth and she considered it her right to celebrate too.

Tom made his way down the stairs and spied Olive through the glass pane in the top half of the door. She raised her palm in a wave and he called back up to the bedroom, 'Grace, your parents are here!'

Crawling out from beneath the warm duvet, Grace glanced at the bedside clock. It was nearly 4 p.m. They had slept and cried away most of the day. She pulled the comforter from the end of the bed and wrapped it around her shoulders; it didn't occur to her to put on clothes or to shower, and the mirror was just another wall-hanging, not something by which to gauge her appearance. She sloped down the stairs, allowing her bed-socks to slip off the final bit of tread with every step, and arrived in the hallway as Tom unbolted and unlocked the front door.

It was hard to say who made the first move, but Olive and Grace fell into each other's arms as Grace wrapped the quilt around them both. They stood in a soft floral pyramid, weeping and holding onto each other as if their lives depended on it. Olive whispered in her ear, 'You know what it's like to lose a daughter, Grace, and I cannot begin to imagine the pain you're in. But I love you, I love you so much. I'm your mum and I'm not going to lose my daughter, do you understand?'

Grace nodded inside her mum's embrace.

Minutes later, Mac appeared at the front door, in his standard costume of cricket jersey and striped tie. Tom was shocked at how much he'd aged; his eyes had retreated into their sockets and his skin had the grey pallor of the terminally ill. Tom chose not to comment.

Mac stepped past his wife and daughter, almost ignoring the duck-down-covered lump that crowded the hallway, and brandished a birthday cake in Tom's direction. 'Got some tea to go with this then, young man?'

Tom nodded and welcomed Mac's warm hand on his back. He'd missed him. Tom indicated the large Victoria sponge. 'Did you make it, Mac?'

'Of course,' the old man lied, raising his chin.

'From scratch?' Tom added, and he and Grace both gave a small giggle. Mac and Olive joined in, not sure what they were smiling at, but relieved to be able to show a happy face in the presence of those they loved.

Olive placed her hands on either side of her daughter's face. 'Happy birthday, my darling girl.'

'Thank you, Mum.' And once again she was enveloped in her mother's strong arms.

Eventually the quartet moved into the kitchen. They ate

the cake with as much relish as they could muster and drank large quantities of hot tea.

Mac was the first to break the taboo; the oldest and the bravest, the head of the family. He coughed. 'I know that losing Chloe has blown us all apart, shattered everything that we thought we knew, and I know that none of us will ever be totally complete again. We will carry a Chloe-shaped hole in our hearts forever...'

The group was silent, each of them swallowing hard and listening attentively.

'But I for one would go through it all again in exchange for the three glorious years that we had with her. She was my little one, our little ray of sunshine, our pure joy and our pleasure.'

It was the perfect eulogy and a much-needed public acknowledgement. For a while afterwards, the four sat in quiet reflection. Then Tom nodded and left the table.

Grace reached out and patted her dad's hand. 'I know you're right, Dad, but I'm still bogged down by how bloody unfair it all is.'

Olive concurred. 'I agree with you, my darling. I'm old and I've had my life. It is so, so unfair.'

Grace could tell by her mother's new pattern of lines that she had pondered the injustice of it every night until the daylight brought her some relief. She knew she would have lain in her bed, repeating over and over that it should have been her, not her darling granddaughter. No words of comfort could change that for Olive, so Grace offered none. Instead, she simply placed her hand over the back of her mother's.

Tom returned to the room, holding the photo frame. He tried to hand it to Olive. 'This is Grace's birthday present – from Chloe.'

Olive stuffed her handkerchief into her mouth and wept. Mac took the frame from his son-in-law and ran his fingers over the uneven bumps; he even chuckled at the garish collection of jewels and beads. 'Well, well. It is truly beautiful and very Chloe. Why have one jewel when you can have forty?'

Grace smiled as she nodded at her dad. He held her gaze. 'And you, my girl, are you looking after yourself?'

'Oh, you know, Dad, everything is sort of carrying on regardless. The world turns, even if I don't want it to. I haven't had the energy to think or plan, I'm just being carried along like so much flotsam on the tide.'

Mac closed his eyes briefly at his brave daughter. 'Oh, darling, I would never liken you to flotsam. A fine rare seaweed maybe.'

Grace smiled again. She loved her dad.

Olive chipped in. 'I'm more of a reed – I sway between crying and feeling fucking furious!'

Tom positively choked on his tea and Mac thought that he must have misheard his wife of fifty years. Olive didn't care.

Grace shook her head as she wiped her tears on her pyjama sleeve. 'Oh God, Mum! Alice wouldn't believe me if I told her what you'd just said.' She looked up. 'Is she still afraid to come and see me?'

'Yes, a little, I think,' Olive said. 'But she's coming anyway.'

'Today?' Grace was surprised.

'Yes.' Olive glanced knowingly at her husband.

Grace sighed. She knew she didn't have the energy to fix Alice, but she was glad of the chance to move forward. 'It'll be nice to see her, Mum. It really will.' She noted the relief in her mum's expression.

It was an hour later that Alice pulled into the driveway. 'Happy birthday,' she whispered as she entered the kitchen.

Grace stood and took her little sister in her arms. She looked her up and down, noting her cheesecloth smocked top and her ripped jeans. 'How are you, Alice?'

'I'm... Oh God, Gracie, I don't quite know how to start!'

'Well, come and sit down. There's cake, so that's a good start – one of Mum's Victoria sponges, though Dad's been trying to take credit for it!' Grace flashed a smile at Mac as she tried to put her sister at her ease.

Alice kissed everyone around the table before taking up a chair. 'There's something I need to tell you, Gracie.' She exhaled sharply.

Grace stared at her, knowing in that instant what her little sister was going to say. She noted the bloom to her cheek, the slight swell to her already ample bosom. She placed her head on one side and let her tears slide from her nose. 'It's okay, Alice. It's okay!' She waved her hand, trying to catch her breath. 'These are happy tears, I promise. You're having a baby, aren't you?'

Alice nodded as she rummaged in her bag and produced a grainy grey scan picture.

Mac reached out and held the image flat in his large hand. 'What would our little Chloe make of *this* news, I wonder?'

Mac was and would continue to be unafraid of talking about his beloved granddaughter. Grace was happy and reassured that, within her family, Chloe would never disappear, would never sink without trace; they would keep her alive in their minds and imaginations and would not succumb to the temptation to never mention her, however much pain that might save them. Avoiding talking about her would mean that she really was gone, gone from the earth and gone from their lives. They would never – could never – let that happen.

'Not much, I suspect.' Tom smiled.

Olive laughed, thinking about how her granddaughter would have reacted. 'Oh my goodness, yes, quite right. She'd have hated the whole idea! She would not have liked it one bit! Chloe was always the baby and our only baby

– can you imagine asking her to share her grandpa with this little thing?' Olive pointed at the image, a copy of which she had been gazing at for the past few days. 'She would be having none of it. She'd say, "You are porridgeable, Grandma!"'

They all tittered, knowing this to be true. Darling, darling Chloe.

'I did ask her if she'd like a baby sister or brother.' Grace recalled the day – like all ordinary days with her daughter, now extraordinary; a precious day, one which she stored away, its details and memories like hidden jewels that she kept close to her chest, taking comfort from the feel of the treasure against her skin. 'And she said she'd rather have a green bike with a basket. She was quite adamant.'

They all gave small, soft laughs, picturing her cherubic mouth forming the words.

Grace smiled at her sister. 'Congratulations, clever Alice. I'm so happy for you, after all those tears…'

Alice shrugged her shoulders. 'I know! We gave up, completely gave up. After being told it would never happen, I accepted it, reluctantly, but I did, and the next thing, here we are!' She rubbed her tummy. 'I feel…' Alice chose her words carefully. 'I feel delighted, over the moon, obviously, but also guilty. I was nervous about telling you.'

'I'd feel a bit like that too, if the shoe were on the other foot.' Grace spoke openly. 'I understand. But how sad it would be if losing Chlo were to take the joy from everything good to come. We can't let that happen. We must celebrate your news, Alice. It's wonderful! I bet Patrick is beside himself.'

'He is.' Alice beamed. 'I've had to stop him redecorating and buying all sorts of contraptions that we can't afford and I'm sure we don't need.'

Olive gazed lovingly at her incredible daughters; fine, strong, compassionate women. She knew her job was done.

'You'll be a great mum.' Tom smiled, speaking the truth but finding it hard to share his wife's magnanimity. It felt like he was handing the mantle on to Alice and Patrick and that thought left him feeling empty. 'And you must let Patrick redecorate and buy his contraptions. Let him enjoy every single second.'

Alice nodded. 'I will. I promise.'

'Do you know what you're having?' Grace hardly dared ask.

Alice shook her head. 'No, not yet. It's too soon.'

'Doesn't matter though, does it – a baby's a baby. It will be wonderful.' Grace stood and held her sister tightly. 'It will, it will be wonderful.' She closed her eyes and remembered the moment they'd placed her little girl in her arms. '*Welcome to the world, little one.*'

The evening stole up on them too fast. It had been a day of healing; the cathartic musings over the kitchen table had been restorative, with tea and birthday cake as the salve.

It was worth more than therapy and left all involved with a feeling that they had moved forward a little, and had laid some ghosts to rest.

Tom and Grace were still in their pyjamas, having waved Mac and Olive off in their little car only an hour before. They had somehow forgotten to get showered and dressed and now there was no point; as if by magic, it was night-time again. They sat in the sitting room, nursing mugs of cocoa on the sofa. For the first time in as long as they could remember, the silence was far from uncomfortable.

'I can't believe she wanted a bike over a brother or sister.' Tom sipped the foam from his drink.

'Not just any bike – a green one with a basket. She was very specific.'

'I can imagine!'

'It's incredible and horrible, Tom, how much our lives have changed in one year. I can see us all so clearly this time last year. You'd both decorated me that fab cake and cooked supper, Chloe was so excited, and everyone drank too much wine. It was amazing.'

'Our lives didn't change in a year, Gracie. They were changed in a matter of minutes. When we brought her home from hospital, sat on this sofa, chatted, tended to her, we had a life, a family. I had it all...' He shook his head in disbelief. 'And by nine o'clock in the morning, it was all gone. My daughter, my marriage as I knew it, everything.'

Grace wanted to offer some warmth, some kindness. She sidled closer to him. Perhaps she could offer physical comfort through proximity.

Tom continued without registering her actions, as if afraid that if he reached for her, like a hesitant bird, she might fly away. 'Even though she was only a little girl, Chloe managed to make this place into a home, didn't she? Her routine kept us busy. It was the little things that made the difference. There was always noise, activity, mess – even her physical presence, singing or humming, like a comfortable background noise. And now...'

Grace was silent. It was true.

He continued. 'Recently, I've been missing much more than just her. Missing the things that she used to do and missing the way that our home used to feel.'

'I'm sorry, Tom. I'm sorry that I'm so crap at making things better. I just feel so preoccupied.' It was the grossest of understatements.

'Grace, I don't expect anything from you. I wasn't saying it for that reason. I know you've got a lot to contend with; more than most people will ever have to endure. I think you're amazing and I think you're doing a great job of keeping going. A lot would have thrown the towel in.'

'Don't think I haven't considered it.' She smiled at Tom. Poor, sweet Tom. He, like her, had had his life turned upside down and was trying to cling on to the wreckage of what remained. But she was trying so hard to stay afloat herself that she couldn't deal with his sinking as well. It was every man for himself, women and children first.

'That's some news from Alice.' He sniffed.

'Yes. I'm pleased for her and I'm happy for Mum and Dad. This will be a lovely diversion for them.'

'You don't feel odd about it?' he asked, cautiously.

Grace rubbed her eyes. 'Yes, of course I do. Even a bit jealous, if I'm being honest. But would I want to deny her the joys of being a mum? No, of course not. I know how brilliant it will be.'

'You are one amazing lady, Grace Penderford.'

'I don't feel like an amazing lady, I feel like one who's trying not to drown.'

'Happy birthday,' he whispered, still unsure if he should kiss or touch her.

She sighed, grateful that he did neither. 'Oh God, yes, my birthday. I had quite forgotten. Thanks, Tom. And I really love my frame.'

Grace ran her fingers over the jewelled edge and smiled at the blobs of glue that an enthusiastic Chloe had daubed on the edges. And, just like that, she pictured her working dextrously with her little tongue poking from the side of her mouth. And, just like that, she was back to crying, folded over and inconsolable at her loss.

These tears, however, felt a bit different, tasted different. They'd lost their metallic sour notes and seemed fresher, lighter, almost cathartic.

Seventeen

Sepsis – if you suspect it, say so. Effective treatment in the first hour can double the patient's chance of survival

Grace opened and closed the cupboards, searching for something to make for supper. Her appetite had improved a little in recent weeks and she had lost a little of the sharp-edged emaciation that had altered her face in the immediate aftermath of Chloe's death.

'Do you want me to make something?' Tom offered as he came into the kitchen.

'Don't think there's much to make anything from.' She looked over her shoulder at the man she cohabited with and sometimes ate with, but didn't sleep with; sex and any real physical contact were still too much to contemplate.

'I think there might be fish fingers in the freezer,' he said.

'We had them for lunch the day before yesterday,' she reminded him, knowing how easy it was to lose track.

'So we did,' Tom said. 'How about we go to the pub?'

'The pub?' Grace furrowed her brow. They hadn't been out socially for a long, long time and to do so felt like a big step. 'I'm not sure...'

'Come on, it'll be nice. We can just go grab a table in the corner, order scampi and chips and walk home afterwards. What do you say?' He gave a brief smile.

'I suppose so.'

'Don't look so worried. I promise if at any point you feel uncomfortable or want to come home, we can. No questions, we can just pick up and leave. Okay?'

'Okay.' She nodded, still far from convinced.

The White Hart was their local. It did a roaring trade in the summer, when the spacious garden heaved with visitors wielding order numbers as they waited for their pub grub, and kids ran amok around the tables, fuelled by bags of crisps and squeezy bottles of fruit juice. But the season hadn't quite started yet, so it was a little quieter. There was always a cluster of locals around the bar that they knew by sight, and one or two kids from the local sixth form, chancing their arm, ordering pints of beer with Jägermeister chasers, which they then distributed to their mates who were a mere pint's froth away from being eighteen.

Grace brushed her hair and cleaned her teeth but was still disinclined to put any make-up on. She slipped into her boots and grabbed a cardigan to go over her T-shirt should it get chilly.

She and Tom walked there in amiable silence. Listening

to the birdsong as the light dipped. The pub was nearly in sight when, on rounding the corner, she looked up in time to see a flash of pink disappear by the large oak tree on the bend. Grace stared at the tree, quickening her pace until she reached it.

'Grace?' He called after her.

She placed her hand on the nodes and cracks of the oak's gnarly bark, peering behind the trunk.

'What are you doing?' Tom asked.

Grace scanned the grass and tumble of weeds that had gathered between the edge of the field and the tree. She ran her hand over the tree trunk before staring up into the thick branches that blocked the sky overhead.

'Is it just me, Tom, or do you think about her every second of every day?' She lowered her gaze and studied her husband, waiting for his response.

'I do.' He looked at his feet, his hands shoved in his pockets. 'Every second of every day. And if I wake up in the night, there might be a brief moment when I forget, but then it hits me like a stab to the chest – boom!' He took his hands from his pockets and flared his splayed fingers as though revealing a magic trick. 'And there she is, bobbing about in my head, and I want to reach for her, so badly.'

'Sorry, Tom, I didn't mean to start the evening off like this. Let's go inside and have supper, like we used to.' She slipped her arm through his. Tom patted her hand, glad of the contact.

Grace found a quiet table by the fireplace in the corner and sidled onto the padded bench along the wall. She clenched her hands and placed them on the sticky tabletop in front of her. Tom navigated his way to the bar and nodded at a neighbour while waiting to be served. Grace saw a man to his right lean close into his companion and whisper, holding his half-empty pint against his chest, obscuring the logo on his rugby shirt; he let his gaze flick in her direction. His companion arched his neck slowly as if taking in a panoramic view, swept her with his eyes and looked away instantly.

Yes, it's me. I'm her mum… She picked up a beer mat and read about the Red Squirrel range of beers; anything for a distraction.

'Here you go.' Tom placed a large glass of red in front of her and slurped the top from his ale. 'Cheers!' He smiled, speaking jovially.

'Cheers.' She nodded.

He took up the seat opposite and the two sat, quietly thinking of what to say. Both sipped their drinks, glad of the prop. It was Grace who found her voice first.

'I told someone quite recently that we've become bent out of shape.'

'Like a car, you mean? That's been bashed?' He smiled nervously.

'Kind of. But more like we used to be smooth…' She ran her palms slowly against each other. 'Sliding together to form a whole, but now we're spiky, different, and we can't fit together, because we're so changed.' She held his eye, her tone steady.

'Who did you say that to?' he asked, interested.

'To Huw, the man who owned Gael Ffydd, where The Old Sheep Shed is. I spoke to him a lot. It's a special place.' She flicked the edge of the beer mat between her thumb and forefinger. 'It really helped, actually, having him to talk to.'

Tom downed his pint. 'Well, that's good to know.' His anger flared. 'You couldn't talk to me, but you were okay sharing details of our life with a fucking stranger.'

'Please don't be angry, Tom. I needed someone to talk to and he was there.'

'Good for him. No wonder you were reluctant to come home. I could tell.' He nodded, his teeth gritted.

'I came home early!' she reminded him.

'Only because I drove all the way to bloody Wales to get you.'

Grace stared at her wine, feeling as if all eyes and ears in the room were tuned into their discussion. She instinctively ran her finger over the neat pink scar on her forehead.

'It wasn't like that. It was more about the place than him. It's so peaceful, beautiful; it was as if I could breathe, start over. I felt calm, better than that, I felt the beginnings of happiness, I could see it.'

'Lucky you.' He stood and went to the bar.

'Yep, that's me – lucky.'

Tom returned. He hadn't bought her another drink. Grace wanted to get this topic straight, wanted to be able to talk about Gael Ffydd without it turning into a row.

'I think it was *because* he was a stranger that I found it easier to talk to him. And he understood. He lost his wife.'

'How convenient – single, then?' Tom snorted.

'Tom! How can you say that? He gave me good advice because he's grieving for her and knew what I was going through.'

'No, Grace, he didn't know what you were going through. *I* knew what you were going through because I'm Chloe's dad, remember? Or was that easier to forget too?'

Grace shook her head and picked up her cardigan.

'Did you sleep with him?' Tom asked, his voice low, eyes steady.

'No!' She stared at her husband, mightily relieved that she could at least answer that question honestly, acutely aware of how, if she had, it would have cleaved her and Tom even further apart, would have hurt him still more at a time when he was just beginning to show signs of healing. For that she would never have forgiven herself.

She stood, unwilling to have this argument in public. She rested her cardigan on her shoulders, wearing it like a little cape.

'Don't go, Grace, please! I've ordered scampi and chips.'

She glowered at him and whispered, 'You can shove

your scampi and chips up your arse.' Then she squeezed through the gap between the table and the wall and made her way to the exit.

Stomping along the lane, Grace had only made it a few hundred yards when Tom called out behind her. 'Grace! Wait up!'

She duly stopped and watched him trot towards her.

'Did you just say shove the scampi and chips up my arse?' he asked with the twitch of a smile to his mouth.

'Yes.' She nodded, feeling her face bloom with suppressed laughter.

'Up my arse?' he repeated, giggling.

'I couldn't think what else to say!' She laughed too, covering her mouth.

Tom reached out and held her arm as he bent backwards, letting out a huge guffaw, which spilled from him. 'I told the landlord you'd lost your appetite, but what I wanted to say was, "We no longer require our scampi and chips, you can put them up your arse!"' He laughed until he cried, wheezing and puffing as he clung to his wife, who was similarly affected.

'I'm sorry, Tom!' she said as she snickered.

'I'm sorry too.' Her threw his arm around her shoulders and the two continued along the lane, laughing and shouting 'Arse!' as they did so.

To laugh without feeling immediately guilty or sad was new for both of them and they quickly realised it was special, something precious to be protected and nurtured.

Grace flicked the lamp on in the sitting room and flopped down on the soft sofa. Tom sat down too and did as he had done a million times before, placed her feet on his lap and sank back against the cushions.

'Why was it a special place?' he asked, as though they were mid conversation.

She considered her response. 'I think because I didn't have to do anything. Didn't feel the pressure of work or having to do chores around the house, didn't have to worry about avoiding people who knew me, who knew Chloe. I felt freer and that gave me space to think, to try and get my head straight.' She paused and wiggled her toes inside his warm palm; that always felt so good. 'But it wasn't only that. There's something about the actual place. It has a different feel from anywhere I've ever been, a different pace; even the light is unusual. It's quite magical.'

'It certainly looked it,' Tom whispered.

'Yes, yes of course!' She'd forgotten that he'd been there for one night and had seen for himself the sweep of the valley, the green fields sloping down to meet the River Wye.

'It is, Tom, it really is. I would love to show you more of it; I'd love you to feel how I felt. It was as if I was connected to nature in a way that I haven't been before. I had no interest in watching telly or anything like that; I was more than happy to sit and look at the landscape. And I did, for hours. I was a stranger there, but I felt... welcome.' She smiled.

'What are we going to do, Grace?' he asked earnestly.

'I don't know,' she answered truthfully.

'Do you still love me?'

'I don't know.' Again the truth left her lips. It felt now like there was no point in anything other than honesty. 'I want everything to be like it was before, but I know it can't be, and it seems like the best solution might be to make everything different, new job, new start, new house...'

'New husband?'

'I don't know.'

The two sat in silence, both trying to navigate this difficult path, unsure not only of what steps to take but also of their destination.

'I think you're right, we have bent out of shape. But fundamentally, we are still Chloe's mum and dad, and as long as we don't ever forget that, we can keep part of her here.'

'I feel her, Tom.' Grace placed her hand on her chest.

'Me too.' He smiled. 'Maybe that is the answer, love – to move, change your job, start over. Although I don't know how I'd feel about leaving here, where I see her everywhere.'

Grace nodded. 'I see her everywhere, whether she's been there or not. I saw her in Wales—'

'With the single, grieving bloke who helped you,' he sniped.

'Yes, even there.' Grace pictured her little pink mac and her wellington boots disappearing behind the tree. 'His name is Huw and I don't want you to be off about him, Tom, because he helped me make sense of things. He was the reason I felt able to come home.'

He considered this. 'I guess anyone that helped you return to me can't be all bad.'

She smiled. 'I thought I might have had feelings for him—'

'Jesus Christ, Grace!' He interrupted her, throwing his head back on the cushions and gazing upwards.

'No! Don't shout! Please.' She raised her palm. 'But I think it was because I was so low. I was just happy to have someone to lean on for a bit, and he is kind, and as I said, has been through it, sort of.'

'I honestly don't know whether I want to shake his hand or punch him in the face.' Tom sniffed.

'*Punching someone is never the answer...*' She smiled again. 'As I said, nothing happened, not really. He was just a very good friend to me. He was what I needed at that time and I know how that sounds and I know how that must make you feel, but if we're going to go forward, we have to be straight with each other. There's no point in holding back, is there?' She looked at her husband.

'I guess not,' he replied levelly.

'You know, Tom, most people go through their whole lives hoping that the worst thing doesn't happen, but it has happened to us and if we can survive it, I think we'll be stronger than anyone because we'll have plummeted to the lowest depths and to come back up after that takes something really special.'

He nodded. 'If... I guess that's the big question.'

'It is,' she agreed. 'And I've been thinking that Chloe's not here in these bricks or in the air – she's in us, in here.' She patted her heart. 'And that won't change, ever. We don't need to be here.'

'Would you like to move?' He looked at her. 'Because if that would make you happy, if that's what it's going to take, then that's what we should do.'

'I don't think anything can make me happy, not truly happy, not ever again, but I think I might find it easier if I didn't have to walk across the landing every day, see the place where...' Once again, she pictured Chloe's little feet sticking out of the end of her nightie. 'I don't want to see it any more, Tom, and I think a new start might be a good thing.'

'Maybe you're right.' Tom nodded as his tummy rumbled. 'Jeez, I wish I hadn't put all that scampi up my arse, I'm bloody starving!' And the two chuckled, as though life was normal, as though they had come home from the pub and Chloe was asleep upstairs and all was right in the world, like they had in the time before the nothingness.

'Cheese on toast and a glass of red?' Tom offered as he released her feet and stood from the sofa.

'Lovely.' She nodded. 'D'you want me to make it?'

He stared at her from the doorframe. 'Blimey, Grace, one step at a time.' He smiled at her and she smiled up at him. He turned to leave, but hesitated. 'You look beautiful,' he said, knitting his brows earnestly.

'Thank you.' She felt suddenly coy.

'I've missed you, Gracie. I've missed us.' He swallowed.

'Me too.'

'We can only do our very best, can't we?' he said.

'Yes.' She took a deep breath. 'That's all we can do, Tom. Our very best.' And she nodded. Lesson learnt.

Eighteen

Sepsis will kill approximately one hundred people today in the UK. That's one hundred families like yours and mine...

It was hard for Grace to believe that it had been six whole months since she'd last dialled the number and nervously paced the kitchen.

'Jason, hello!'

'Ah, Grace, it's really good to hear from you, and you sound a lot better – brighter, if you don't mind me saying.' As usual, he cut to the chase, blunt and to the point. Yet today she found this far from irritating, today she found it quite reassuring that he wasn't pussyfooting around.

'Small steps, Jason, but, yes, I do feel a lot better.'

'Good. That's really good news. We were all so worried about you. So, when are you coming back? I'm having to do twice the work here! Every time I get a doctor's note, for another month, another month, all I can think about is how much paperwork you're causing me! You are an admin vortex, woman!' he joked.

She pictured him with his feet up on the desk and the phone resting under his chin as he formed his fingers into a pyramid over his chest.

'Ah, well, that's what I wanted to talk to you about.'

'Uh-oh. That sounds suspiciously like the preamble to a resignation.'

'You're good.' She smiled.

'Obviously Grace, I've been half expecting it.'

'Have you already stolen my desk clock and business-card holder?' She laughed.

'Oh, Grace, I had them off you while you were still wandering up and down the stairs without your shoes!'

'God, Jason, that was a bad day. A really bad day.' She shook her head; even his humour couldn't ease the wave of distress and embarrassment that rippled through her.

'It really was. We were all in bits, no one knew what to do for the best, me included. When you left in the cab, we all just sat here in silence, shocked by how little we could do for you, how helpless we were to make things better.'

'Ah, well, that's the thing – no one can make it better.'

'I'm really glad to hear you've got some of your bounce back.'

'Thank you.' His warmth touched her. She found it hard to reconcile his tone with the bastard who had continually used fair means or foul to try and get one over on her. 'I'll drop you a line, make it formal.' She sighed, realising that this was it: she was walking away from the career she had carved out so carefully, made sacrifices for and clung to.

'I shall miss you, you know Grace. I've enjoyed learning from you over the years.' He coughed.

'Learning from *me*?' She chuckled.

'Absolutely. You're the best. You were always the best. I had to keep on my toes. I think you could do anything you put your mind to.'

'Thank you, Jason. Thank you for everything.' Grace ended the call and swallowed the lump in her throat.

As Grace and Tom pottered in the garden later, she told him what Jason had said. He listened intently, pausing from cutting back the hawthorn bush.

'He was probably a bit intimidated by you.'

'But I'm not scary!' Grace looked up from weeding the bed beneath the kitchen window.

'Well, you can be sometimes, especially when you get an idea that you can't and won't be deflected from.'

'Really? Like when?'

'Like... God, Grace, I have so many examples, I honestly don't know where to begin.' He shook his head.

She sat back on her haunches. 'That's not how I see myself at all.'

Tom threw the secateurs on the ground and pulled off the leather gauntlet with which he'd been handling the prickles. 'Okay, what about the extension on this house?'

Grace looked up at the red bricks that towered above them. 'What about it?'

'Do you remember the hours and hours of drawing up plans, going over ideas, looking at budgets and debating the detail until the early hours?'

'Of course, but luckily I was married to the architect, so I got all that consultancy for free.' She smiled.

'Yes, you did, but that's not the point. The point is that you didn't want to wait until we could afford the top floor as well, you wanted to rush it through so we could get the kitchen done first and then, if and when possible, go through a *second* extension in a few years' time, with all the mess, dirt, upheaval and expense doubled up. And I told you that was crazy, but you were adamant.'

She twitched her nose at him. 'So what's your point?'

'My point is, what's the first thing you said when it was finished?' He placed his hands on his hips.

'I can't remember.' She turned her attention to a rather stubborn dandelion root that was wedged in a crevice between the paving slabs on the path.

'You said, "I wish we'd waited and done the top floor at the same time. There's no way I want to go through all that mess and hassle again." And I had to bite my tongue not to say I told you so!'

She smiled as she dug the trowel into the sandy crack, conveniently deaf to his rambling.

'Or what about when you were pregnant and you would

only think of boys' names, totally convinced you were having a boy because someone had told you an old wives' tale about the way you were carrying. You refused to even think about having a girl and then when you had her…' Tom realised he was crying.

Grace quickly stood, threw the trowel onto the path, took her husband into her arms and held him tightly, matching him tear for tear.

'When I had her,' she continued for him, 'it was the most wonderful gift I had ever been given. I couldn't believe that she was mine, that she was ours! Half you and half me. She was without a doubt the best thing we ever did, the very best.'

'She was, Gracie. She was. And I loved her because she was so like you.'

'And I loved her because she was so like you.' Grace kissed his wet face as she held him close. The two stood on the path, letting tendrils of affection and understanding entwine them, fragile strands that in time would bind them together once again.

It was the very next day that the estate agent had turned up – promptly, at 11 a.m., as agreed. He knocked on the front door and Grace had been ready for him, having mentally prepared herself for the ordeal. He had shiny shoes, shiny hair and a shiny car and looked to be about fourteen. Grace didn't know whether to offer him coffee or squash.

She could sense a certain shyness about him that his established patter could not disguise; his nervous glances into corners and around doors made her feel jumpy in her own house. She tried her best to put him at his ease.

'So, really, Darren, we want it sold and wrapped up as quickly as possible. The price matters of course, but we don't want to drag it out for the sake of a few grand. We figure we'd rather have the equity sitting in a bank than tied up here while we haggle over money.'

Darren nodded, but Grace wasn't sure that he was listening; his mind appeared to be elsewhere. He then came out with it, quickly and with obvious relief. She correctly suspected that the words had been hovering on his tongue from the moment he'd arrived.

'I saw your daughter's funeral, Mrs Penderford.'

The admission threw her. She hadn't been expecting the subject to crop up. She mentally lost her balance and reached for the chair in front of her.

'You did?'

He nodded again, this time looking her in the eye. 'Not the actual service, but I saw the car drive past the office and I went out to stand alongside the route to pay my respects. We all did, actually.'

Grace listened. It was odd to hear about that day from the perspective of a stranger, especially as the whole thing had passed in such a blur; she could recall only patches of detail.

'Thank you for doing that, it was very kind; in fact, people's response generally has been very kind. It does make a difference, you know, so thank you.' She didn't know what else to say, or what he expected her to say.

He continued. 'It was one of the saddest and most significant days of my life.'

Grace smiled at him, not understanding. 'How do you mean, saddest and most significant?'

The boy studied his highly polished shoes, unsure about whether to go on. Eventually he found his voice.

'I couldn't get my head around the fact that someone with their whole life ahead of them could go, just like that. It seemed so... so unfair.' He grimaced at the inadequacy of the word and the inadequacy of his vocabulary.

'It is unfair,' she concurred. 'She died of sepsis – do you know what that is?'

He shook his head. 'I don't. I'm really sorry.'

'No don't be, that's not unusual, lots of people haven't heard of it. Look it up, Darren, when you get back to your office. Look it up and learn about the symptoms. People need to know what to look for. If we'd known... Well, just do that for me, will you?'

'I will and I'll tell my friends to do it too.'

Grace nodded, quite overcome by the lad's offer.

'Something weird happened to me on the day of the funeral, Mrs Penderford.'

'What was that?'

'It made me realise that life can end just like that, whether you're old or young, or even very young. And so I decided not to waste a single day, not one. And so far I haven't.' He grinned at her, clearly proud of his achievement.

They were both silent for a while. Eventually Grace smiled. 'So what do you do differently?'

He thought for a second. 'What do I do differently? Nothing really. I just feel different. I feel lucky and I appreciate every small thing. I don't take anything for granted and I'm being much nicer to my mum and dad. And if someone offers me the chance to do something, anything, then I always say yes. Because you don't know what's going to happen to you tomorrow, whether you'll get another chance. So that's it really – I say yes and I do more stuff.'

Grace smiled at him and fought her tears. 'You are so right, Darren. You never know what's going to happen to you tomorrow.'

Once he'd exorcised what he'd wanted to say, he relaxed and opened up. They drank a cup of much-needed tea and he regaled Grace with his plans to go to college and become a surveyor; he told her how he wanted to buy his own house eventually, and filled her in on all his other short- and long-term goals. She felt strangely privileged to be the recipient of this information, sensing that he didn't disclose it to many people. Business was dealt with just as he was about to leave, almost as an afterthought.

'Your house is lovely, Mrs Penderford, really lovely.

We'll have no trouble selling it at all. In fact, my colleague tipped the wink to a few couples who are in a good position, told them that we might be taking it onto the market, and we already have quite a bit of interest.'

It was Grace's turn to be barely listening; she was thinking instead about his words from earlier. You really never did know what was going to happen tomorrow.

'That's great. Thank you.' She smiled.

'Are you and your husband moving locally, Mrs Penderford?'

'I'm sorry?'

'I said, are you and your husband moving somewhere local?'

She stared at him as though the thought of moving locally, or indeed anywhere, had not occurred to her. And in truth it hadn't. For the first time she tried to consider the options, but kept drawing a mental blank. One thing was for sure, with this house gone, they would need to live somewhere.

Tom came into the kitchen. 'Hi there!' He shook Darren's hand. 'Good to meet you. How are we doing here?' he asked.

Grace looked up at her husband. 'We're doing great. Darren was just asking where we're moving to.' She bit her bottom lip.

Tom stared at her. 'That's a good point.' He placed his hands on his hips and looked skyward. The silence was acute. For some reason this made Grace chuckle.

'Tom?' she shouted through her giggles. 'Where are we moving to?'

Once she'd started, she couldn't stop; she was laughing so hard, she wheezed with tears. Tom placed his hand over his mouth and tried to stem his giggles. It seemed incredible that they'd forgotten to find a place to move to.

'I haven't got the foggiest idea!'

And for the first time in as long as either of them could remember, the two laughed without awkwardness, guilt or embarrassment. Grace banged her palm on the table and Tom leant against the kitchen cupboard.

Darren, crimson faced, looked from one to the other. He gathered up his folder and slipped from the room. The poor Penderfords had clearly lost the plot. He let himself out of the house and looked back through the kitchen window before jumping into his car. He watched them laughing, with tears running down their faces, before Mr Penderford grabbed his wife, pulled her from the table and kissed her hard on the mouth.

And now it was the day of the move, a clear, bright, beautiful English day. The house sat against a backdrop of blue sky, with a warm breeze ruffling the delicate blossom on the trees. It was a fine day to be leaving.

Grace stood in the driveway. She knew that soon she would be shutting the front door for the last time on what had been her family home for the last seven years. She had mixed feelings – sad to be leaving behind the rooms that held so many dear memories but excited to be making a new start. She sincerely hoped that the family who were about to move in would find peace and happiness within its walls.

Whenever she pictured Chloe, it would be within the confines of this house and so, for that reason alone, her association with it would always be wonderful. She closed her eyes for the briefest of seconds and could see her little girl's face pushed against the window in the conservatory, her little voice loud and clear, happy to see her mum arriving home. *'Mummy! Mummy! Chloe has made you a present!'*

Grace bit down on her bottom lip until it hurt, giving her something else to concentrate on until the vision of Chloe disappeared.

'How you doing, babe?' Tom walked over from the garage, where he'd been sweeping the floor and sorting out last-minute bits and pieces.

She sighed. 'I don't know. A mixture really. Excited, happy, sad, nervous.'

'Yep, me too.' Tom slipped his arms around his wife's waist. 'I thought Alice might like Chloe's wooden chair for Ted. I mean, he's a bit small for it now, but it won't be long.'

'Yes, that's a good idea.' She pictured her adorable new nephew and smiled. 'Chloe would like that.' She looked up at her husband.

'No she wouldn't!' they chorused together.

'One last look round?' Tom held her hand. She nodded.

The two of them wandered from room to room, letting their fingers trail over blinds and their eyes hover over surfaces and spaces where furniture had stood only the day before. They fell silent, walking gingerly into Chloe's room, which they had carefully packed up together, exchanging jovial memories and crying when the mood took them. Her precious bits and bobs, favourite clothes, comforter and books had all been safely wrapped and placed in boxes, waiting to be delivered to their new home, so that they could take them out and look at them from time to time.

Tom leant against the doorframe while Grace stood by the window.

'She was magic, wasn't she?' Grace smiled.

'Yes, she was.' Tom shook his head and smiled back. 'You're right, Grace, you know.' He paused. 'She's not here, in these bricks and this air; she's in us, isn't she?'

'And she always will be.'

'Yes, always.'

'And I think that I will see her again – I don't know where or how, but I have to believe that.'

'One day at a time...' He sighed.

'Yep. One day at a time.'

Tom gathered his wife into his chest. 'I love you, Gracie.'

'I love you too.' She closed her eyes, happy in his arms.

Epilogue

Somewhere in the world, someone dies of sepsis every three-and-a-half seconds; that's approximately one death every three-and-a-half heartbeats

The telephone was ringing in the hallway.

'Hello?' Grace wiped her free hand on her apron, trying not to get flour all over her dungarees as she grappled with the receiver, made slippery by her dough-streaked hands.

'Hey, you. Is this a good time to chat?'

She knew Alice would carry on chatting whether it was convenient for her or not, but she loved the bluff of her asking. 'It's always a good time to chat to you, darling. How are you?'

'I'm good, Gracie. Knackered but good! And you?'

'Sames.' Grace laughed. That was exactly how she felt and how her sister sounded: knackered but good. 'How are your lovely boys?' She had taken to referring to Patrick and Teddy as a unit.

'Oh, they're both driving me nuts in their own way, but they're both adorable. Did you get the new photos?'

'Yes, thank you. Mum brought them. He's really grown – can't believe it. And loving the Spiderman PJs!'

'Yep, he won't take them off, wanted to wear them to nursery the other day!' Alice chuckled at the memory.

'What did you do?' Grace asked.

'I let him wear them, of course!'

'Of course.' She smiled. Her nephew had his mum wrapped around his little finger. 'The photos were lovely. I think he looks a lot like Dad.' Grace swallowed the lump in her throat; it was still hard to mention her beloved father without that crushing ache of loss and longing, even one year after he'd passed away.

Alice was similarly affected. 'You're right, Gracie, he does look like Dad. How's Mum doing? Is she all right? I got her text, so I know she arrived okay.'

The sadness for Grace was not only that Mac was not around to witness this stage in her life, to share in her new-found peace and relish the beauty of their new place; he was also missing the opportunity to meet new members of the family, who she knew he would have loved. Her sorrow was also rooted in the fact that Mac had chosen to keep the severity of his illness a secret, denying her and Alice the chance to help him at the end or even to discuss the inevitable with him. There was so much she would have liked to have said to him, places she'd wanted to show him, had she known just how limited his time was, but primarily she wanted to thank him for all he'd done. His had been a steady hand on the tiller in the most turbulent of waters and she had loved him to the moon and back, as had Chloe.

Grace had interpreted his pallor and weariness as a combination of his cancer, but also his grief for Chloe, and she was right, up to a point. What she'd missed, however, was Mac's desire, in the face of his inevitable decline, to join his beloved granddaughter and not to put his darling girls through the rigours of his illness. He wanted to spare them in any way he could. Mac, quiet, dependable, unfathomable Mac... He had quietly faded in health and stature until that fateful morning when he'd been claimed. Further investigation by the girls revealed a letter dated six months previously that confirmed what Mac had already known, that the cancer had spread: incurable, inoperable, terminal. He had only confided in his Olive; his lover and his friend, unable to bear the heightened emotion and regrets that would inevitably follow had his daughters known. His last mutterings through failing breath that floated into his wife's ears, were uttered at dawn. 'Goodbye, my darling girl, I will be waiting for you.' This he spoke sincerely to the love of his life as she gripped his hand. He then closed his eyes as a smile broke across his face. The lines of pain relaxed and disappeared, as he slipped into another world and another time; only those that knew what to listen for heard the briefest of whispers into the dark as the words 'Hello, my little one!' escaped from his mouth.

Grace looked through the wide-open doorway at her mother, who sat in a wicker chair at the top of the garden with a large raffia hat protecting her from the sun. Her book was open on the garden table by her side, but with her reading glasses resting on top of it, it was obvious Olive wasn't reading. She was instead taking in the breathtaking beauty of the view, staring at the majestic Black Mountains in the distance, watching the water shift in the rushing river below, admiring the laughing canoeists as they paddled by. She looked upwards at the birds that dipped and soared overhead and were again drawn to the river, where fat brown trout hovered below the sun-dappled surface. Brown trout that tasted good when charred over an open flame in the darkness.

Grace continued to observe her mother's relaxed pose as she soaked up the sunshine. She considered Alice's question once again: how was their mum?

'She seems fine, Alice, or as fine as she is going to be. I'm looking after her, of course, and she loves being here. The sun is good for her and Huw makes a big fuss of her. But I don't know... It's difficult to phrase, but she's much... quieter. It's almost like she's lost her sparkle.'

'Oh, Gracie, she has. She only sparkled for him!'

'Yes, yes, of course she did.' They were both quiet for a second, acknowledging this to be the truth. Picturing the way Olive used to look at her husband with nothing but love.

'Do you want a word with her?'

'Yes, that would be great. Speak soon, Gracie. We love you!' Alice always ended on a high note.

'Love you all too.' Grace walked across the Welsh-slate floor, enjoying the cool feel beneath her bare feet on this hot, hot, summer's day. 'Mum? It's Alice on the phone! She wants to tell you all about Teddy – or Spiderman, as he's now known at nursery!'

Olive stood and rearranged her sea-blue sarong to preserve her dignity. 'Oh, how lovely! Thank you, darling.'

Grace admired her mother, who, in her late seventies, still wore her chunky bangles, and her customary beads around her neck, for a day alone in the garden; she was one classy lady.

'Hello, Alice! How's my boy?' Olive's voice was still commanding and mellifluous, despite her advancing years.

Grace sauntered out of The Old Cowshed and onto the vast front terrace, leaving her mum to chat to Alice and glean every possible detail about her grandson. She took in a huge lungful of air as she stood admiring the view from the top of the ridge and surveying the majestic garden, whose colours seemed even more vivid as the midday sun approached its maximum height.

She felt a pair of arms encircle her waist as a pair of lips kissed the nape of her neck. She placed her hands over his, feeling their wedding bands touching.

'I thought you were off quoting for a job?' She turned

towards her husband and put her arms around his neck in response. 'Because if you're at a loose end, I have a job for you.'

'Oh God, there's always a job for me! What is it this time?' He kissed her again.

'I was thinking we should maybe put a creak in the bedroom door.' She laughed.

'Now that's a genius idea. And for your information, we have just got back. Huw's gone to grab Gilly and I thought we might all have a spot of grub up here.' Tom kissed her on the mouth. 'What are we having for lunch?'

Grace laughed. 'You mean, what am *I* making for lunch?'

'No, no,' he protested. 'I can get us something, but I don't like to interfere. Plus I still can't work the Aga.'

'That old excuse is wearing a bit thin, Tom – the Aga is a doddle. I think you just like me waiting on you.' She smiled.

'I do a bit,' he admitted.

'I think I'll run up a salad and no pudding!' She stared at his tum. How she loved teasing her man, with his flat stomach and muscular frame.

He swung her around and put his hand on her distended tummy. 'You are in no position to tease me, Grace. Not when you are looking so fat today!'

She feigned shock. 'Did you hear that, Isabella? Your dad called me fat!' She addressed her bump and felt a kick.

It's okay, little one. Don't be scared, you're nearly here and I'm waiting for you.

'Don't listen to her, Isabella. I only said she was fat today, not fat every day,' he corrected.

'Same difference!' She batted at him with her dough-covered hand. 'I'm making cinnamon sugar buns for later.'

'Ooh, lovely.' Tom rubbed his hands together. 'My little domestic goddess.'

'Careful, or I'll be popping Lego bricks into yours.' She winked.

'Hey there!' Huw called from across the field as he and Gilly made their way hand in hand up to the terrace.

'Hey, guys.' Grace waved at their dear, dear friends and next-door neighbours. 'How did the job go?' she asked.

Huw pulled out a chair and sat back against the cushions, running his hand over his newly clean-shaven chin. 'Well, they liked Tom's designs and were impressed with my timescales for the build, so I reckon it's a goer.' He smiled.

'Sounds very posh, Grace. Huw was telling me on the way up,' Gilly piped up. 'I shall definitely want a peek when it's finished.'

'*If* we get the job,' Huw said.

'You will. You are brilliant. You can do anything.' Gilly bent over and kissed her man on the cheek; they were clearly deeply in love.

Grace smiled at the feint lipstick mark it left, 'ever fancied a man with a beard Gilly?' she asked.

Gilly shook her head, 'No, not really. I always think big beards are hiding something!' she laughed.

'Maybe they are.' Huw smiled, having removed his grief-laden mask just before they met.

Grace disappeared inside, returning some minutes later with a tray loaded with sourdough loaves, olives, a soft wheel of Welsh goats cheese and a waxed parcel of local ham.

'Ooh, this looks great. Shall I open a bottle of plonk?' Tom offered, rising from the table.

'Not for me, I'm teaching after lunch. I have a class of fourteen-year-olds waiting to be wowed by Thomas Hardy.' Gilly sighed. 'If I turn up sloshed, I don't think it will help matters.'

'Thomas Hardy, eh?' Tom said. 'That's a bit highbrow for me, but if you need any help with *The Gruffalo*, then I'm your man. It was Chloe's favourite. God, we had to read it over and over. She knew it by heart and if you dared miss a line or try and skip a bit, she'd tear a strip off you. I've put her original book in Isabella's room; I hope she'll love it too.'

'I'm sure she will.' Grace smiled.

Tom nipped inside to raid his wine fridge.

It had taken Grace by surprise to find herself pregnant. She wasn't consumed by joy and elation as she had been when she was expecting Chloe, but neither was she fearful. Her happiness lay somewhere in between. Chloe could never be replaced, but Grace was excited about the prospect of a new baby and raising a child in their beautiful new home in the magical Wye Valley. At the same time, she was circumspect, aware that there were no guarantees, ever. She knew far better than most parents how fate could deliver you a staggering blow, but she would not allow that knowledge to dictate how she parented her new little one. It would be all too easy to be overprotective, but it would be unfair to limit Isabella's experiences and horizons just because Grace knew what could or might happen.

She and Tom had decided the best they could do would be to provide an environment that would give Isabella the skills to deal with whatever life might throw at her. They would tell her all about her big sister, show her pictures and videos and make her laugh with tales of her antics. Chloe would be a big part of her sister's life, always, just as she was a part of theirs. Always.

Tom reappeared with a cold bottle of wine and four fat glasses. Sloshing the wine into two of them, he handed one to his buddy Huw. They clinked them together.

'This is the life.' Tom exhaled loudly, sitting back in the sunshine and throwing an olive into his mouth.

Huw placed his fingers between his lips and whistled. Monty came panting up the grass. 'Hey, Monts, good boy.' He patted his thigh and his faithful dog lay by his side in the cool shade of the terrace.

Grace stood up and stroked his head. 'I wondered where

you'd got to, mister.' Monty beat his tail on the deck, happy as ever to be fussed over by her. She wandered over to one of the raised planters on the terrace and plucked a stray blade of grass from among her prospering plants.

'They're looking good, Grace. You're obviously green-fingered,' Huw observed.

'I don't know about that, but I'm learning.' She pinched the leaves and raised her fingers to her nose. 'The smell is intoxicating.'

'That's why Leanne chose them; she loved the scent of plants as much as the way they looked. I remember her telling me, "Rosemary for courage, thyme for strength."'

'That's beautiful.' Gilly smiled. 'Do you think we should put some rosemary and thyme in my bouquet? Courage and strength – I can't think of anything better.' She grabbed Huw's hand.

'I think that would be lovely.' He kissed their entwined fingers.

'I shall pop it on my list.' Gilly smiled.

Grace turned to walk back to the table; that fresh sourdough bread was calling to her. 'I was thinking—' she started as she took her place.

'Ooh, dangerous!' Tom interrupted. Huw laughed.

'I was thinking about that boy, Darren, the estate agent who sold our house in Nettlecombe.'

'Why on earth were you thinking about him?' Tom asked.

'He'd never heard of sepsis, and he promised me he was going to look it up on the internet, and tell his friends about it too.'

'I didn't really know what it was either,' Gilly admitted as she cut the loaf. 'Huw had to explain it to me.'

'And I only knew because Grace told me. I'd heard of it, but I didn't know what it was, not really,' Huw confessed.

'That's what I've been thinking about.' Grace looked out over the valley. 'And I know it sounds bonkers, but I want to tell the world about Chloe's story. I want everyone to know about this horrible bloody disease that stole her away. I want them to know what to look for and what to say to the medics if they suspect it, and I want the medics to know how to treat it.'

Tom reached over and squeezed his wife's hand. 'I think that's a wonderful ambition, Gracie, but how are you going to tell the world?'

'Okay, well, don't laugh...' She placed a napkin over her lap. 'But it was something Huw said ages ago that got me thinking. He agreed that everyone has a book in them.'

Huw smiled, remembering that day. 'I did.'

'And so I was thinking, maybe I could write a book. I could tell people about Chloe, her story and what happened, to try and stop this happening to someone else, to try and get people talking about this bloody horrible, sneaky disease.'

'Do you *know* how to write a book?' Tom asked.

'No,' Grace admitted, 'but you know I love books and words, and my last boss told me I could do anything I put my mind to. He had faith in me. And Huw and Gilly can help me.'

'Of course, we will!'

'Yes. Absolutely!'

'What will you call it?' Tom sat forward, smiling at his wife with pride. This was her greatest strength: to have an idea and drive it though. He was confident she could make it happen, confident that she *could* indeed do anything.

Grace swivelled round, taking in the panorama of the river and the mountains. 'I don't know. I was thinking, something that isn't just a title plucked from the air, something that means something. Something that makes people think.'

All four sipped their drinks, stared at the view and listened to Monty's snoring.

Grace sat up straight. 'I've got it! How about *Three-and-a-Half Heartbeats*? Because,' she continued, quietly now, and with a sad, faraway look in her eyes, 'somewhere in the world, someone dies of sepsis approximately every three-and-a-half seconds – that's about every three-and-a-half heartbeats.' She put her hand to her chest and paused, counting the beats.

'I love it.' Tom nodded, staring at his brilliant wife. '*Three- and-a-Half Heartbeats*.'

The four carried on with their leisurely lunch. Listening

to Olive's shrieks of laughter in the hallway, until it was time for Gilly to get back to her class. Huw decided to take Monty for a spot of fishing after he'd dropped Gilly in town, and Grace and Tom cleared the table before making their way back inside The Old Cowshed.

Grace flopped down on the sofa with her feet on a cushion on her husband's lap. She picked up her pen and opened the first page of her spiral-bound notebook.

'Where shall I start?' she asked, tapping the pen on her teeth.

'I don't know.' Tom gave it some thought. 'I suppose just before Chloe was born?'

'Good idea.' Grace sat up tall and ran her hand over her baby bump before touching the pen to the page and beginning what she hoped would become a wonderful book, a book that would make a difference.

Grace Penderford had, for as long as she could remember, yearned for a child…

'I just wrote my first line!' She smiled.

'How does it feel?' Tom asked.

'It feels pretty good.' She nodded.

Tom smiled as his wife flexed her toes against his palm.

Sitting there with the man she loved gave her a glow of happiness. It was enough.

Grace paused and looked out at the majestic landscape of their Wye Valley home. She was unaware of being watched from behind the boundary hedge by a little girl in pink wellingtons and a matching raincoat, who gripped the hand of her grandpa; he, as ever, was resplendent in cricket jersey and striped tie, for once appropriate to the season.

The End. And the beginning.

A letter from the publisher

We hope you enjoyed this book. We are an independent publisher dedicated to discovering brilliant books, new authors and great storytelling. If you want to hear more, why not join our community of book-lovers at:

www.headofzeus.com

We'll keep you up-to-date with our latest books, author blogs, tempting offers, chances to win signed editions, events across the UK and much more.

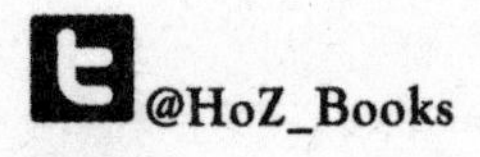

@HoZ_Books

HeadofZeus

@HeadofZeus

HEAD *of* ZEUS